IT TAKES TWO TO TUMBLE

It Takes Two to Tumble

to Tumble

A Seducing the Sedgwicks Novel

Cat Sebastian

AVONIMPULSE
An Imprint of HarperCollinsPublishers

Excerpt from *Unmasked by the Marquess* copyright © 2018 by Cat Sebastian.

Digital Edition DECEMBER 2017 ISBN: 978-0-06-282050-1

Print Edition ISBN: 978-0-06-282157-7

Cover design by Amy Halperin
Cover illustration by Fredericka Ribes
Cover photographs ©Period Images (figures); ©LeicaUntouched/Shutterstock (background, bottom)

FIRST EDITION

18 19 20 21 QGM 10 9 8 7 6 5 4

For everyone who had to find their home without a map.

ACKNOWLEDGMENTS

This book owes even more than usual to the insight and feedback of my editor, Elle Keck, and the help of everyone at Avon. My critique partner, Margrethe Martin, managed to make sense of an early draft despite my having changed the characters' names several times, sometimes mid-chapter. Many thanks to Laura Tatum, for sharing her experience with dyslexia. Deidre Knight, my agent, is endlessly supportive, and for that I'm truly grateful.

It Takes Two to Tumble

CHAPTER ONE

1817

England in June was greener than anything Phillip had ever seen, except perhaps the sort of mold that grew on badly potted marmalade after too long at sea. He had watched the land loom larger on the horizon as grimly as he'd greet an approaching squall. Now, with Portsmouth within a stone's throw and his ears filled with the familiar sounds of ropes straining and sails catching the wind as the crew brought the *Patroclus* into harbor, he fought a sudden, mad desire to have the ship turned around, to sail for new shores, places that were less soft and green and familiar. Places that weren't England. He had seen men go to the gallows with more dignity than he was going to his own damned home.

"We can tie you to the mast," Walsh said, coming up beside him along the rail, his hands stuffed into his pockets. "Like Odysseus, or whoever the fellow was."

"Get your hands out of your pockets and stand up straight," Phillip told the surgeon. "You're still on my ship."

There was no heat in Phillip's voice, but there didn't need to be. He was the captain and he was used to having his orders obeyed. Walsh straightened his back and rested his hands on the rail before him. "Besides, I'd quite willingly cling to the mast with my own two arms," Phillip admitted. "There's no siren song calling me away."

He felt a pang of guilt even speaking the words. He had known sailors who wept to leave their families, and here he was dreading the prospect of leaving his ship even for the two months it had to be in dry dock.

"I'm sure you'll be glad to see the children," Walsh said dubiously, as if hearing his thoughts. Walsh had read Ernestine's letter aloud himself, much to the entertainment of the wardroom, so he knew damned well what its contents had been. "They can't be that bad," he said in the same glib tone he used to assure sailors that a couple of stitches wouldn't hurt much at all.

Phillip hadn't thought they were, to be honest. In his mind's eye, his children were tidy, bright little creatures, standing neatly in the hall to greet their father during his rare visits home. Caroline had always kept the household running as smoothly as Phillip kept his ship.

But Caroline had been dead and buried these two years while Phillip and the crew of the *Patroclus* were on the opposite side of the globe. And his sister's most recent letter had left him deeply concerned about what he would actually find at Barton Hall. "Some of the lads aboard this ship aren't much older than Edward and James, so I know I'll be able to bring them around," he said, more to himself than to Walsh.

Walsh made a noncommittal sound. "One of my sisters has taken a fancy to visiting the lakes this summer, so I may pay a visit on you if you'll have me."

"God yes. Please." Phillip almost groaned in relief at the prospect of a familiar face at Barton Hall. Walsh had been the closest thing to a friend Phillip had aboard ship since McCarthy's death last year. Christ, McCarthy. The pain of his loss had been blunted a little by time, but Phillip couldn't think of him without feeling both his absence as the best lieutenant any naval captain could possibly wish for, and . . . well, best not to think of that. Phillip ought to visit the man's family. But what to say? There was a solid chance that Phillip would sit weeping in Mrs. McCarthy's parlor while the old lady brought him tea. It would be embarrassing for all of them. And it might raise questions. The sort of questions a man shouldn't have raised after his death. Probably best not to do the thing at all. "The place has plenty of beds," he told Walsh. "And my children probably won't actually murder you, regardless of what Ernestine thought."

Walsh laughed. "I'll write you."

"No," Phillip said too quickly. "Just come."

Later, after Phillip had been rowed ashore, after he had gone through the motions of thanking the crew and shaking hands with his officers, he threw a final glance over his shoulder at the *Patroclus* and took his first shaky steps on dry land.

"Did you hear the latest?" Mrs. Crawford asked as soon as Ben lowered himself into his usual chair. She handed him a cup of tea that he knew without tasting would be exactly as he liked it. She had probably added the sugar and the milk when she heard his footsteps on the path. There were no surprises for him or for anyone else in Kirkby Barton, and he wouldn't have it any other way. "Captain Dacre is expected back at Barton Hall in as little as two weeks," she said, shoveling a buttery crumpet onto his plate.

Ben paused, his teacup halfway to his mouth. He ought to be pleased. It was high time for the captain to return to England to serve as head of his family and—more to the point—deal with his hellion offspring. Ever since their mother had died, the children had been expelled from multiple schools and had driven off a series of aunts, tutors, and governesses. Ben rather admired the children's single-minded perseverance, if not their methods. Surely it was the best of news that their father was to return.

Ben hadn't ever met Captain Dacre, the man having apparently spent his entire life contriving to render himself as far from Kirkby Barton as geographically possible, while Ben seldom left the place. In fact, his only impression of Captain Dacre was from a rather sinister-looking portrait he had once seen up at Barton Hall. He was all dark eyes and dark hair and dark expression; frankly he seemed exhausting, hardly the sort of figure whose presence would add to the general good spirits of the townspeople. The mere thought of the brooding sea captain stalking the parish lanes seemed to threaten the hard-won comfort of Ben's life.

He glanced around the Crawfords' snug little parlor, as if searching for proof that his peace was built on real, substantial things that could not be disrupted by the arrival of one man. Mrs. Crawford had been a kind of mother to him after his own had died. Alice, his dearest friend, would become his wife before the summer was out. He was the vicar of St. Aelred's. Everything was peaceful, quiet, safe. Even the chair into which he had folded himself, despite being too small and too low for his limbs, had the comfort of long custom. It was all he had hoped for, everything he wanted. No man, however disconcerting his portrait, could compromise that.

"Not a moment too soon," he said equably, before taking a sip of his tea. "Something really does need to be done about those children. If Digby catches them in the bell tower again, I'm afraid he might thrash them." Really, the sexton ought to get a better lock for that blasted tower, but likely the Dacre monsters would manage to pick the new one too.

"I can hardly blame Mr. Digby," Alice said from the sofa where she was propped up on a flotilla of cushions. Every week there seemed to be less Alice and more cushion, and Ben briefly wondered how long until there wasn't any Alice at all. He got rid of that thought as quickly as possible. "Last week they trampled my violets," she continued, "and I would have thrashed them myself if I could have gotten up and done the job properly." Ben felt his heart stutter at the reminder that she could not get up, might never get up, and schooled his face not to betray his sorrow. "And if I weren't a thoroughly lovely person," she added with a wicked sideways smile at Ben, and suddenly everything was all right, because even if she couldn't walk, she was his Alice.

Ben let out a laugh that was mainly relief, and which he

turned into a cough when he saw Mrs. Crawford's indignant expression.

"Don't talk like that, Alice," Mrs. Crawford chided her daughter.

"About assaulting children or about my illness?" she asked sweetly. "Oh, never mind, Mama, I'll behave. Go leave me and Ben alone, won't you?"

"What's the word on Bath?" Ben asked as soon as Mrs. Crawford left them in the privacy they had suddenly merited when they became betrothed. Their marriage, which had always been taken for granted as a vague but certain future occurrence, became a matter of pressing concern with the onset of Alice's illness and Ben's bedside presence at all hours. Ben couldn't quite figure out how it had happened, given that Alice was delirious with fever and couldn't very well give her consent, but he was mightily relieved to have it all settled.

Alice pursed her lips. "Mama can't be made to understand that a long journey would be impossible. But the doctor says we have to go to Bath, which just means he's given up on me and wants Bath doctors to shoulder the blame for whatever happens." She spoke lightly, but Ben knew her well enough to pick out the strains of irritation and fear in her voice. "Really, Ben, how am I supposed to get in and out of a traveling carriage? How am I even supposed to keep myself from being jostled off the seat? And that's setting aside the fact that we haven't the money to travel anywhere, let alone as far as Bath."

Ben frowned. "Do you want me to talk to them? As a man of the cloth and all that?"

"That would only make it worse. They don't want you to think about how I'm more or less lame. That's one of the reasons they're so keen on whisking me away to Bath."

"I'd say the cat's rather out of the bag, my dear." Alice had fallen ill at Easter with a fever and sore throat, but when she recovered it was to find that she had hardly any feeling in her legs. Now it was midsummer and she had yet to walk more than a few steps. Everyone, Ben included, was starting to wonder if a full recovery was even possible.

Alice was looking at him with an affectionately quizzical expression. "Sometimes I forget that you think everyone's as straightforward as you are. My parents are afraid that if you stopped to consider the implications of having a bedridden wife, you wouldn't want to marry me."

Ben reared back. "Please tell me they didn't actually say that out loud."

Alice laughed. "I love that you think that's what matters."

"Do they think I'm too stupid to have noticed that you can't walk? Or do they think me such a fickle man?"

She smiled weakly. "Nobody who knows you could ever think those things," she said, not precisely answering his question.

"Well, I *am* going to marry you, so you'll all just have to get used to it. I'm going to read the banns myself this Sunday." And then they could marry inside a month.

"Is it already June?" She looked startled. He supposed it was hard to note the passage of time when every day was the same as the one that had preceded it. Sofas and cushions and well-meaning relations. "I thought I'd be better by now," she murmured. "Perhaps hold off on reading the banns for another few weeks, at least until I know whether I'm to be carted off to Bath." And then, in a brighter, brisker tone, she said, "I'm very tired, Ben. When you come tomorrow, will you bring me some seedcake? I can smell that your Mrs. Winston is baking and it's all I can think about."

He rose to his feet and dutifully kissed her hand. How hadn't he noticed how thin and pale it had gotten? Once in the hall, he leaned against the closed door.

"Ah, there you are, Sedgwick," said Alice's father, who had clearly been waiting for him to appear. "Wonder if I can see you alone for a moment?"

"Of course," Ben said, following Mr. Crawford into the study.

"Hate to trouble you," Mr. Crawford said as soon as the study door was shut behind them. He was the village solicitor, and he used this room to meet with clients as well as to escape family life. He was bluff and hearty, with red cheeks and sparse gray hair. "But it's about those children."

Ben didn't need to inquire which children. "I've spoken with Mr. Digby and we'll order a new lock."

"It's not only that, I'm afraid." He gestured for Ben to sit in another too-small chair and sat down himself behind the desk. "Since their aunt left, they've been in the charge of the few servants they haven't driven off. What they need is a young person to keep them in check."

"I was under the impression that their father is expected shortly."

"Captain Dacre's ship is due presently in Portsmouth,

but imagine how much mischief those children could get up to in the time it'll take for him to travel north." The older man shuddered. "It seems their efforts are intensifying," he said gravely, as if talking about an enemy army and not three motherless children.

"I could post another advertisement for a tutor," Ben offered doubtfully. "But I'm afraid that after what happened with the last one we've been blacklisted from all the respectable publications." Ben still remembered that poor fellow in his nightly prayers.

"Exactly," said Mr. Crawford, as if Ben and he were of one mind, when in reality Ben had no idea what to do with those children other than let them romp through the countryside like the misbegotten elf creatures they were. "So you'll go up to the hall and mind them for the time being?"

It took Ben a moment to realize that Mr. Crawford was serious. "My duties keep me here in the village," he said diplomatically. Every day he visited the poor and the housebound, trying to find small ways to improve their lot or at least their outlook. That was why he had gone into the church. Not to wrangle the naughty children of an absent gentleman.

"The hall is only a ten-minute walk from the village if anyone needs you. And you raised all those brothers of yours, more or less, so you'll know better than the rest of us what to do."

Ben was momentarily at a loss. The mention of his family threw him off balance, as it always did. And he couldn't tell if that "more or less" was meant to underscore Ben's mere partial success—the successful raising of three-quarters of his brothers and the shameful way he had failed the fourth. He passed a hand over his mouth. He was conscious that he was being presumed upon—in no way was child-minding one of his duties as vicar—but he also had a niggling sense that perhaps he ought to have done more for the wayward Dacre children than comforting their harassed tutors.

"You think I ought to stay at Barton Hall?" he asked slowly.

"Yes," Mr. Crawford said, clapping his hands together, "that's exactly the thing."

Sending Ben to Barton Hall might ingratiate Mr. Crawford to Captain Dacre. The Dacres did business with a firm of solicitors in Keswick; the Crawfords, who had always spent freely, could use the additional income from a wealthy client. That, he suspected, was Mr. Crawford's true objective. Indeed, a shifty expression flitted across the older man's face and Ben tamped down a surge of irritation. Ben deliberately relaxed his hands, which were trying their best to make fists. "Quite right," he agreed.

Ben took his leave and crossed the lane to the vicarage. Alice was sicker than he had realized and none too enthusiastic about getting married, it seemed. His future father-in-law didn't trust him. He was about to leave his cozy house for the mayhem of Barton Hall. And soon there would be a grim-faced stranger in his midst. By the time he had packed a bag and headed off to Barton Hall, he felt like the comfortable, safe life he had always dreamed of was somehow slipping out of reach.

CHAPTER TWO

After the fact, Phillip thought he might have handled the situation a bit more gracefully if the children hadn't been in a tree. But he was not at his best, having walked the distance from the coaching inn to the house, with each step growing more disoriented by the sheer familiarity of the terrain. Surely the place ought to have changed. But every rock and tree aligned precisely with memories Phillip hadn't even realized he still had.

Despite having sent a messenger ahead with the approximate time of his arrival, the children were not waiting in the hall to greet him. *Of course they wouldn't be*, he told himself. That had been Caroline's doing, and she was gone. Their failure to appear was just further proof of how badly Phillip's intervention was needed. He needed to get to work turning them into well-behaved, competent midshipmen. *Children*, he corrected himself. Yes, children.

The servant who opened the door told Phillip he'd find the children in the orchard with the vicar. Phillip found this surprising, as nothing in Ernestine's final letter had indicated religiosity as part of the children's reign of terror. But instead of discovering the children at work in prayer or singing hymns, he found them high up in a cherry tree.

The plain fact of the matter was that children did not belong in trees, at least not when they ought to be in the hall awaiting their father's return. Nor did vicars belong in trees at any time whatsoever. He might not have much experience with either, and thank God for it, but he knew trees were not the natural habitat of either class of person. He had expected to see his children for the first time in two years in a setting that was slightly less arboreal. Somewhere he could properly see them and they could properly see him and they could all say whatever the hell they were supposed to say in this situation without Caroline to manage things. Instead all he got was a glimpse of booted feet vanishing higher into the branches accompanied by the sound of stifled laughter.

The vicar spotted him first, and promptly swung down from the tree to land at Phillip's feet. At least, Phillip assumed it was the vicar, and not some stray stable hand who had taken to capering about the orchard. But didn't vicars wear uniforms of some sort? Special hats or black coats? The chaplain on the ship always had. This fellow was in his shirt-sleeves, and if that weren't bad enough, his sleeves were rolled up. The chaplain had never done that. The chaplain had been about sixty. And bald. This fellow had wheat-colored hair that needed a cut and freckles all over his face. He was nothing like the chaplain. Unacceptable.

"Oh damn," the vicar said. Phillip gritted his teeth.

Swearing was another thing the chaplain had never done. "I mean drat," the man said, his freckled face going pink. "Bother. You must be Mr. Dacre."

"Captain Dacre," Phillip said frostily. This fellow had to go. No discipline. No sense of decorum. No wonder the children ran amok if they spent time in this man's company. "You have the advantage of me," he said, not bothering to conceal his frown. He never did.

"Ben Sedgwick," the vicar said, smiling in a lopsided, bashful way. He stuck his hand out, and Phillip had no choice but to take it. The vicar's hand was warm and his grip was firm, and Phillip's gaze automatically drifted down to the man's exposed forearm, sun-burnished and dusted with light hair.

"Thank you, Mr. Sedgwick," Phillip said. "You may take yourself off." His effort to dismiss this careless young vicar was interrupted by a rustle of leaves and the thud of a child landing at his feet.

The child was tall, lanky, and excessively rumpled. "Edward," Phillip said, briefly startled by the changes a lapse of two years wrought in children. Phillip had last seen his older son as a coltish child of eleven. Now Phillip could discern two things—one, that he looked very much like Caroline, and two, that he was not best pleased to see his father. For an instant, Phillip could hardly blame him. Phillip had never much enjoyed seeing his own father either. When the navy had taken his own father away for years at a time, Phillip had rather thought they had all been the better for it.

He held out his hand and noticed the barest hesitation before his son took it. "You look so much like—"

"I know I look like Mama," Edward said coolly, dropping his father's hand. "I have a looking glass." His scowl was so intent that Phillip opened his mouth to scold the boy. "Mr. Sedgwick," Edward said, turning to the vicar, "I'm going to finish my history lesson." Without waiting for a response from Sedgwick or so much as a by-your-leave from Phillip himself, the child dashed off towards the house.

While Phillip had always striven to keep order on his ship in less brutal ways, some captains wouldn't have hesitated to have boys flogged for even less blatant insubordination. Phillip swallowed his anger and turned his attention to the tree, where he could see two pairs of dangling feet.

"Margaret," Phillip called up into the tree. "James."

"Oh, they won't come down," Sedgwick said cheerfully. "Not a chance."

"Excuse me?"

"I wouldn't even bother calling them. They'll stay up there until the sun sets or until the spirit moves them otherwise." He seemed utterly undisturbed by this. His eyes were actually sparkling, for God's sake.

"And you permit this?"

Sedgwick's brow furrowed. This was the first lapse in the blithe and idiotic good cheer he had displayed since Phillip's arrival. "Well, I don't know what you expect me to do about it. Rope them like a couple of stray sheep? They're safer up there than they are getting into whatever devilry they might seek out elsewhere. Really," he said, lowering his voice and leaning close in a way that made Phillip instinctively mirror the pose until he realized what he was doing and straightened up. Proximity was the last thing he needed with this man. "The tree's been a godsend. They haven't been capering about the rooftops even once since they discovered how climbable the cherry trees are."

Phillip blinked. "What I meant," he said slowly, "was that perhaps you would like to tell them to come down."

"Tell them?" the vicar repeated, as if Phillip had suggested a satanic ritual. "Won't do a blessed thing other than inspire them to more mischief, I'm afraid. No, no, leave them safely up there, and when they're hungry they'll come inside."

"Thank you for everything you've done," Phillip said in precisely the tone he'd use towards a sailor about to be assigned morning watch for the foreseeable future. "But now that I've returned I'll see to engaging a proper tutor."

The man had the nerve to look hurt. Really, what had he expected? If Phillip had wanted his children to run about like South Sea pirates, he could have stayed on his ship where he belonged, thank you very much. But instead he would hire a tutor for the boys and a governess for Margaret. And when they were ready, he'd send them off to school, where they belonged.

"About that," the vicar said slowly. "I'm not sure you'll find a tutor. They've run through a good half dozen and I fear that well has run quite dry."

"A half dozen!" Ernestine hadn't mentioned that in her last letter. Or at least he was fairly certain she hadn't. He knew there had been some trouble engaging suitable help, but quite possibly she had obscured the details. Well, it was a good thing he was here, then. He would see to it that his household was as it ought to be, that his children were on a safe course, and then he'd go back to sea. Two months. He had turned far more insalubrious characters into perfectly disciplined first-rate sailors in less time than that, hadn't he? He was used to commanding dozens of men in clockwork precision. Surely he could make a couple of children—his own children, at that—fall in line.

"Never mind that," he said. "I have everything in hand. Good day," he added when the vicar didn't seem inclined to take the hint and leave.

"Good luck," the vicar said, gathering his discarded outer garments and carelessly dropping his hat onto his head.

Phillip thought he heard the man laugh as he made his way towards the house.

Ben gave it fifteen minutes before Captain Dacre came begging for help. Half an hour at the outside.

Likely as not, the captain would be tied to a burning post before Ben had his valise packed. There was nothing like a stickler for discipline to incite an armed rebellion, and those children were already on the verge of insurrection. Had been for months.

No child wanted to be brought under bridle, especially not by a man who, as Ned had confided, seldom even bothered to write. But the Dacre children were especially committed to not being tamed, and Ben didn't see that it was his business to persuade them otherwise. During his two weeks at the hall, he had contrived to keep them safe and fed. He had amused them, mainly with the goal of limiting their sprees of destruction. And if he managed to get a few sums into their brains or teach them a couple of choice facts about the Peloponnesian War, then so much the better.

All told, the children seemed to be having a jolly enough time and hadn't let any cockerels loose in the kitchens or fallen into any wells, so Ben rather counted his efforts a success. Ben wasn't having a half-bad time of it himself. At some point during the few years since he had been installed as vicar of St. Aelred's, he had finally gotten it into his head that he was supposed to spend less time roaming about the countryside and more time inside his church. But he still preferred the duties that took him out of doors, visiting people and working with his hands. As far as he was concerned, he was serving his God by repairing fences and helping round up stray lambs.

Of course, minding the Dacres didn't leave him with much time for the rest of his duties. His last two sermons had been read directly from a dusty book he had found in the library at Barton Hall. But if the sermons had been a bit stilted and alarmingly popish, none of the two dozen sleepy congregants at St. Aelred's had seemed to mind or even notice.

Ben was stuffing the last of his shirts into his valise when he heard a tapping at the door. He turned to see Ned, his face set in a grim expression and his hand clutching a satchel.

"Going somewhere?" Ben asked easily.

"I'm going to the vicarage with you." Ned's lip was quivering. "I'm not staying here."

Ben paused as if considering this. "I'd love to have you.

But take a moment to imagine what the twins would get up to without you around. And besides, you might miss out on the sheep shearing if you're down in the village with me."

"It doesn't matter. I'm not staying if you leave."

Ned looked to be on the verge of tears and Ben knew there would be no recovering the boy's pride after that, so he strove for a light tone. "Lucky me," he said, hoisting his valise onto his shoulder. "It gets dashed lonely at the vicarage—I haven't any dogs or sheep or anything like you have here, just dust and books and old Mrs. Winston who comes to fix my supper. It'll be good to have someone to discuss serious topics with."

"You're funning," Ned said skeptically.

"Never in my life," Ben said with a wink. "Your father might have been looking forward to spending time with you, you know."

Ned snorted. "What does he care about any of us? He can go . . ." The child paused with his mouth open, as if debating how crudely to finish that sentiment. Ben raised a curious eyebrow. "Back to sea," Ned finished.

"Quite," Ben answered, leading the lad downstairs. "And so he shall. But this is his house, after all, and he is your father, and that has to count for something. So you might as well get to know him a bit."

"Did you get to know your father?" Ned asked with that sixth sense children have for drawing attention to the topic one least wished to discuss.

"I was rather closer to my mother," Ben said diplomatically.

"She died, though. Just like mine. You don't visit your father. Cook says he lives over at Fellside Grange, and that isn't even an hour's walk."

"Mrs. Morris ought to be a spy. How can I visit my father when I'm keeping the lot of you out of prison?"

"You're funning again."

"Not even slightly," Ben said dryly. "Come on, let's go downstairs and see if we can find things to pawn if we need to bail Jamie out of jail." This earned a laugh from Ned as they stepped off the bottom stair into the great hall.

They found Captain Dacre standing in the doorway of the library with his arms folded across his broad chest and the same exhaustingly furious expression he had in his portrait. Really, Ben had known as soon as he saw that portrait that the captain would cut up his peace. Why couldn't people just make an effort to get along? Wasn't life hard enough without going out of your way to cast stones into other people's paths? Why did some people have to be so disagreeable?

Why did some men have a way of looking even more dangerously handsome when they were angry than they did when they were pleasant? It made no sense. Ben liked jovial, mild-mannered sorts. He had no use for unpleasant people. *You could think of a couple interesting uses for the captain, though*, whispered the part of his brain that he always tried to ignore.

"What's the meaning of this?" the captain growled, interrupting the lewd turn of Ben's thoughts just in time. "It's no wonder the children have become rude and wild if this is the way you speak to them. I'll be writing to the bishop by the next post."

Ben had spent a decade trying to make the most of his short temper, stretching it out by seconds and fractions of seconds until he was, for all purposes, a patient man. But Captain Dacre was trying his already-worn patience dearly. He counted to ten before speaking. "You can write to the entire bench of bishops." Ben's post wasn't Captain Dacre's to dispose of. Ben's patron was off in London spending money he shouldn't and doing whatever else young aristocrats did in town, and worrying about provincial vicars certainly did not number among his amusements. "But if you're here, where are the twins? Come along, Ned. We'll likely have chickens to catch and magistrates to bribe before I go back to my own house."

He was about to congratulate himself on having defused the situation when he felt the grip of a strong hand on his arm. All his equanimity evaporated, and he felt that old familiar fury rising up in him. Fury, and something else. Something worse. It was all he could do not to clock the captain in the jaw, because that seemed like the best of all the possible bad ideas currently holding his mind ransom.

CHAPTER THREE

"Into the library," Phillip said through clenched teeth. "Now."

"Ned," the vicar said, his voice infuriatingly level, "track down the twins and let them know that there's a treat in the kitchen if they get back without committing any criminal mischief." Ned—and it annoyed Phillip that his son had acquired a nickname and he hadn't even known about it— hesitated a fraction of a second before nodding solemnly and heading outdoors. Only when they were alone did the vicar speak again. "You may let go of me," he said, his voice barely louder than a whisper. He spoke with the careful, quiet deliberation of a man who was keeping his temper in check.

So the vicar was angry. *Good*, Phillip thought. *Be angry. Let's have this out, whatever it is.* Because all Phillip knew was that he was angry—at the world, at himself—and he didn't want to think about why. He tried his damnedest to funnel all his swirling fury towards the vicar, because he seemed as apt a target as any. He gave the vicar's arm a tight, punitive, unnecessary squeeze, just to make sure he wasn't the only one ratcheting up to a fight.

"Into the library," Phillip repeated before releasing his grip. "Now." Once inside, Phillip shut the door loudly behind them.

"Let me speak plainly." The library curtains were drawn so Phillip couldn't see the vicar's face, couldn't tell whether its too-handsome features were disorganized by anger. "This is your house and they are your children, but they hardly know you."

Phillip's vision darkened with rage, and he was glad for the shadows, because the worst part of it was that at that very moment, he feared the vicar was all too correct. He was about the least competent parent imaginable, hardly a parent at all, but he was the only parent his children had left, and he would not allow them to become lazy, ill-mannered miscreants. "You have no right—"

"No, I don't. I don't care, though. I'm not leaving your children alone with a virtual stranger who doesn't seem kindly disposed to them."

Phillip sucked in a breath. "I have no intention of harming my children."

"Oh, I'm certain you don't. You'd likely call it discipline. But I'm not interested in semantics. I won't leave your children alone with someone who seems determined to make enemies of them. They've had precious few allies these past few years."

Phillip felt the blood rush to his face, and he wasn't sure

if it was anger or embarrassment or sheer bloody confusion. The vicar was right. He had no place here at Barton Hall and he never had. He was a damned good sailor, and he knew it, but he was useless on land. At sea there was work to do, and he relied on that constant work to blow away the cloud of darkness that sometimes descended on him. "Get out," he growled.

"First of all, you seem to be under the impression that I'm your servant, which I'm afraid I'm not, and if that's how you speak to your servants you'll soon find you don't have any."

"I'm aware that you're not my servant," Phillip said, clinging to the last shreds of his self-control. "But since you've seen fit to intervene in the managing of my children, the least you could have done was not bungle the thing."

Why would the man not just leave? Phillip felt helpless with frustration. If this had been his ship, he would have known what to do. Hell, if this had been his ship, it would never have happened, because on every ship he had ever served on, his crew had respected him. His crew did as they ought to, because to shirk duty or cut corners was to put a fellow sailor in harm's way. And Phillip didn't stand for that. His crew hadn't feared him. He wasn't a brute. He didn't need to be—that was the entire point of discipline and order; they were the grease that made the gears of the world turn smoothly and without pain. Even when there was nothing else, there was order, and you could count on that, at least.

He quickly ran through his options. If Sedgwick was determined to stay, then Phillip had no choice but to let him stay. Having a vicar thrown bodily from the house would set a ludicrous example for the children. "Fine. Suit yourself," Phillip said. "Stay for as long as you please."

Ben very nearly felt bad for Captain Dacre. He was all ready to start ordering the children about but they were nowhere to be found. Ned had no doubt told the twins that their father was an ogre, so they simply disappeared. The captain was left stalking up and down the front hall by himself.

After two weeks under this roof, Ben was used to the children's occasional disappearances. They knew this countryside well and weren't likely to come to harm in an hour's absence. Before too long had passed, Ben glimpsed Ned slip into the house, a fishing pole resting on his shoulder.

But when one hour turned into two and even the cook had seen neither hide nor hair of the twins, Ben began to worry. They were nearly nine, and if they had been born into a less well-heeled family, they might be sleeping in the hills with the sheep, nobody the least bit concerned about them. Still, Ben felt uneasy.

At the sound of a barking dog and a good deal of shouting, Ben sprang to his feet and looked out his bedchamber window. He could see two men and two much smaller figures, one of whom had to be Peggy because surely the entire neighborhood could hear her shouting like a fishwife. Ben ran downstairs and out the door.

"What's the meaning of this?" he demanded of the men.

"I caught these two poaching," said one of the men in a

broad local accent. "And they said they live here. Liars as well as thieves, I s'pose."

"They're Captain Dacre's children," Ben gritted out, leaving off the implied *you idiot*. "Not poachers. And you may let them go."

"Then what were they doing with this?" The man held up a snare.

"We were getting our dog out of it, you stupid lout!" cried Peggy, who evidently had none of Ben's reservations about calling a spade a spade. "And now Jack's had to walk this whole way on a bleeding leg. If he falls ill I'll take a knife to your leg and I'll like it, you shovel-faced horse's arse."

There was a moment of stunned quiet that was only interrupted by the injured dog's enthusiastic bark, as if agreeing with his mistress.

"You're saying this young, ah, lady is Captain Dacre's daughter," said the other man, who had thus far been silent. At the sound of this well-bred, sarcastic voice, very much out of place in this tableau, Ben looked more carefully at the man's face, and felt his heart sink.

"Mart—Sir Martin," Ben said. "I'm afraid I didn't recognize you." Ben hadn't seen Martin Easterbrook in five or six years, when Martin had been a boy of fifteen and Ben had been hardly twenty. That had been before Martin's father died, leaving no inheritance except encumbered properties and outrageous debts. Old Sir Humphrey had spent lavishly during his lifetime, including arranging the Sedgwick children's school fees and Ben's living. Ben might have felt bad for the fellow, if he hadn't spent the months since attaining his majority trying to make his tenants pay for his father's excesses. Indeed, the church poor fund was stretched to its limits due to his efforts to wring everything he could out of his estate.

"I ought to have known that you'd be mixed up in this," Easterbrook spat, with much more venom than Ben thought he had ever merited in his life. "Where there's rank thievery, you don't have to look far to find a Sedgwick."

Ben opened his mouth to ask what Easterbrook could possibly mean by that, but he was interrupted by a loud, clear voice.

"Take your hands off my children." The captain stood on the stairs that led up to the front door. "I don't know who you are or what you think you're doing, but you'll remove yourselves from my property and you will do it with alacrity."

Ben wasn't surprised that Easterbrook's henchman immediately complied with Dacre's command. When a man like Captain Dacre laced his voice with that touch of iron, it took a strong man to resist doing as he was told.

"I'll believe they weren't poaching this time," Easterbrook said. "But tell your brats to keep away from Lindley Priory."

The captain didn't answer, only lifting his eyebrows and making an impatient shooing gesture with one hand.

As the two men retreated down the drive, Ben knelt beside the twins. "Are you both all right?"

"Of course we are," Jamie answered. He cradled the injured dog in his arms as Peggy wound a handkerchief around the animal's leg. "But Jack ran off and we chased after him and when we found him he was caught in that awful trap." Jack, the result of a hound's liaison with a rat terrier, was small, fast, and lamentably fond of exploration. He and the twins were thick as thieves.

By then the door had filled with servants. "If he doesn't want traps set out all over his wood, he might want to stop starving his tenants out of house and home," grumbled one of them. Ben was inclined to agree.

"Let me look at that wound before you wrap it up," Ben said. He pulled back the corner of the handkerchief and saw a relatively clean cut on the dog's hind leg. "Go see Cook for some salve," he suggested. "Then put him to bed with you in the nursery." That, at least, would ensure that the children spent the night in their beds rather than heaven knew where. He watched the twins carry the dog into the house.

"As for the rest of you," the captain said in that clear, commanding tone that brooked no disobedience, "be gone."

Just those two words and the dooryard cleared out. It was utterly empty except for Ben and the captain. Ben stepped towards the house as if he could slip away from the captain's notice.

"Not you," the captain said in a clipped tone. "You stay."

Ben stayed. Even if he had wanted to, he didn't know how to resist.

"I take it this is your idea of how to manage children?" Dacre asked in about as chilly a voice as Ben had ever heard.

"They didn't do anything wrong," he said mildly. He had nearly let his temper get the better of him earlier, but now he was determined to do right by the Dacre children, which meant helping their father. "I'm afraid I can't say the same for Easterbrook."

"Be that as it may, if there are villains living next door, I do expect my children to stay far away from them." The captain's voice managed to achieve another layer of frost across the top. Ben held back a sigh. He wasn't the kind of person who inspired overt rudeness or provoked much in the way of anger; he was affable, good-natured, kind. Those qualities were very much his stock in trade. And he couldn't help but be a little hurt that the captain seemed intent to make an enemy of him.

But as he watched, the anger and stiffness drained from Captain Dacre's face, and Ben remembered that he was a man who had been away at war, lost a wife, and returned to a home that must seem alien. Earlier today, Ben had seen that Dacre was handsome, but Ben could ignore beauty. Now, lit only by the setting sun, Dacre was warm and human and a little bit sad. Ben wanted to reach out to him. Instead he clasped his hands behind his back so he wouldn't be tempted.

"There was a dormouse in my pocket," the captain said at length. "And salt in my sugar bowl. I don't know how they're managing it."

Ben felt something inside him sag with relief that they were now conversing like two ordinary people. He could manage conversation. He did not know how to manage the other thing, the heat in his stomach that straddled anger and something else. "Oh, that *is* naughty. The cook won't like that."

"I think she's in on it." Dacre sighed. "I went down to

the kitchen myself to give orders for the children not to be brought supper, and she said I could give all the orders I wanted but the devil takes care of his own."

Ben bit back a laugh. "I believe that what they're doing is called guerilla warfare. You'll never catch them at it. I'm afraid they're giving you the same treatment they gave their tutors. I'd definitely check my sheets before getting in bed, if I were you," he advised. "Oh, and shake out your linens before dressing. Spiders in the clothes press." Ben feared his playful tone was quite wasted on Dacre. "Look," he said seriously. "Everyone in the house and the village wants your children to keep out of mischief." On any given Sunday, Ben reckoned half the prayers offered up in St. Aelred's were for the Dacre children to stop wreaking havoc. "But if you make yourself even more disagreeable than your children, they'll pick the devil they know."

"Disagreeable!" Dacre turned to face Ben fully, his arms once again folded across his chest. "All I'm trying to do is make my children understand that they must behave for their tutors or schoolmasters. That's the bare minimum of what's required of me as their only parent."

"You do seem determined to be disagreeable," Ben said, resolutely mild.

"What would you have me do? Let them run wild?"

"Not precisely. Right now what they need is . . ." How to put it so he didn't sound like a sapskull? There were things he could easily say to women and the elderly but which made him feel self-conscious when talking to a man like Dacre. "Love. Affection." The words came out foreign and stupid, syllables no more meaningful than the bleating of sheep. "They've been alone for too long with nobody but one another and I think they've forgotten what it's like for someone else to have their best interests at heart. I agree with you that they've been shameless little miscreants, but—"

"There isn't any *but*, Mr. Sedgwick. Children need to learn discipline. It's the only way they can survive in the world. It's the only way anyone can survive, unless they have someone running before them, smoothing their paths." He paused, as if daring Ben to contradict him. "Believe me," he added in a lower, sadder tone. "I know."

A cloud must have drifted away from the setting sun, because suddenly Captain Dacre's eyes were lit by a shaft of sunlight. "Oh!" Ben said. "Your eyes are blue. I hadn't noticed earlier."

"Excuse me?" The captain was plainly disconcerted. Well, that was fine because so was Ben. He had never remarked on another man's eyes before in his life, nor had he planned to, and the fact that the observation slipped out of his mouth without his mind giving leave was somewhat troubling.

"They're black in your portrait," Ben said, as if academic attention to detail would somehow save the situation from awkwardness. But there was no escaping the fact: Captain Dacre's eyes were a pretty blue, and Ben rather wished they weren't.

He stammered out a barely civil good night, thinking he ought to make an exit before his thoughts proceeded further in a dangerous direction.

CHAPTER FOUR

The next day brought Ben a pair of letters. One had been hand delivered from Lindley Priory. It wasn't from Sir Martin Easterbrook himself; Ben had never merited direct communication with Easterbrook, but after last night he was probably lucky to have this missive from Easterbrook's man of business. The contents were simple: there was no money for a village school, no money to fix the church roof, no money for the widows' fund. Ben gathered that after yesterday's encounter, there might never again be money for any project of Ben's.

He sighed and threw the crumpled letter into the breakfast room grate.

"It's June," said a voice from the door. "There's no fire. If you're in the habit of receiving the sort of correspondence that requires burning, you'll have to do better than that."

Ben watched in dismay as the captain pulled out a seat at the breakfast table. He had been looking forward to a peaceful breakfast, the children being busy mucking out the stables under the watchful eye of the head groom. "I don't require my correspondence to be burnt," Ben protested. "I was upset with it. So I crumpled it up and threw it." He mimed a throwing gesture, and then felt his cheeks heat with embarrassment.

The captain blinked. "I see."

Ben could feel the man's chilly gaze on him. With fumbling fingers, he tore open the other letter, which was from Will, one of his younger brothers. He could barely manage to read it, knowing the captain was watching him intently.

Will had been lurking at the back of his mind these past two days. Years ago, for lack of any better prospects in the world, Will had joined the navy. He had been assigned to a ship with a brutal captain and had narrowly escaped a court martial. Ben didn't know the details; Will was exceedingly cagey about everything and Ben, out of a possibly misguided attempt to respect Will's privacy, hadn't read the official reports. Now Will scraped together a living in London somehow.

"Your correspondence stinks of gin," the captain pointed out. The infernal man didn't even have the decency to read a paper during breakfast. Instead he was watching Ben as if Ben were performing in a music hall.

Unfortunately the letter did indeed smell of gin, which could mean that Will was drinking heavily, or could mean that his bedmate was drinking heavily, or could simply mean that the innkeeper at the place where he left his letters had a moment of clumsiness. With Will, one never knew, and one would never find out.

"My correspondent is a testament to the corruptive influence of the navy," Ben said with as much dignity as he could muster.

The captain chewed a piece of toast. When he swallowed his throat worked in a horribly distracting way. "So now you're receiving corrupt correspondence. Busy morning, parson."

"No! I—" Ben shook his head, his face flaming. "Oh, never mind."

When Ben met the captain, he had thought of Will, had considered the violence of his captain and the way a sweet, absentminded boy had been turned into a jumpy, nervous man who kept his back to the wall and sent incoherent letters that stank of gin. Ben's instinct had been to do whatever it took to keep that fate from befalling any of the Dacre children.

But now he heard Captain Dacre's words about discipline and responsibility echoing in his ears. Because what had happened to Will wasn't entirely the fault of the navy. Some of the blame rightly belonged to their father, who hadn't raised them so much as turned them loose. The Sedgwick children had been allowed to run wild—or free, as Ben's father would have put it. All of them had been woefully ill-equipped for any of the usual professions, as Alton Sedgwick's mind was fit for loftier matters than arranging for his children's futures. That burden had fallen to his practical, eldest son, and Ben generally feared he had made a hash of the whole thing.

Thus, he had to concede that there might be some merit to Captain Dacre's insistence on discipline and order. The captain's methods were rubbish, but his goals weren't so bad, and if Ben could help him instill order in less muttonheaded ways, then he had to think it was his duty.

He was glad to find a thread of duty in the strange tangle his thoughts had knotted themselves into. It was nothing less than relief to find that and cling to it, a relief to know that no matter how unclear his feelings, at least he could resolve on the correct course of action.

That evening, after ensuring that the children were tucked into bed with the convalescent dog, Ben slipped out the garden door and made for the village. The sun had set, but with the full moon reflecting off the lake, Ben could make his way plainly to the Crawfords' house.

He found them all in the drawing room, arranged the way they always were: Mr. Crawford in the wing chair by the fire, Alice propped up on the sofa, and Mrs. Crawford between them so as to easily refill both their teacups. When Ben walked into the room, all three faces turned gladly towards him and he heard three sets of happy greetings.

From the first time he had set foot in the Crawfords' parlor, dirty and gangly, with uncombed hair and frayed shirt cuffs, he had made it his life's ambition to have a home as comfortable and safe and normal as theirs, and to do everything in his power to make sure his brothers had the same. A place where food appeared on the table at predictable intervals and regularly paid servants laid fires in the hearth. A home where he had his own bed and well-stocked cupboards.

It was, he thought, not too much to ask. The Crawfords seemed to agree.

"You're alive!" Alice called, her face bright with a smile.

"Cook made your favorite biscuits," Mrs. Crawford said, handing him a plate.

"Haven't heard a peep from those hellions since you went there," Mr. Crawford mumbled sleepily, his eyes barely open. "Job well done, my lad." With that easy praise, Ben swelled with pride. He had long since stopped resenting the man for insisting that he go to Barton Hall, but now any lingering unease from their last conversation was swept into a hidden corner of Ben's mind.

Ben pulled a chair in between Alice and her mother, drank good strong tea prepared precisely the way he liked it, and ate the lemon biscuits that were indeed his favorite. It was comfortable here. He belonged.

"We had word Mr. Farleigh is still doing poorly," Alice said, looking at Ben with concern.

Old Mr. Farleigh was doing poorly indeed, and was all too likely to continue to do even more poorly still, right up until the moment he died. He was old, he was sick, and, well, everyone died in the end. It was only a question of time, and Mr. Farleigh had rather less than Ben might have liked.

"I sat with him and Mrs. Farleigh for a bit this morning," Ben said. The Dacre children had fed scraps of stale bread to a gaggle of half-feral hens they had found in one of the Farleighs' disused outbuildings, and the sounds of laughter and squawking had been louder than the prayer Ben whispered.

He knew that he didn't need to tell Alice anything as

commonplace as the fact that he didn't want Mr. Farleigh to die. It was a small village, and people didn't tend to come or go except through birth and death; he had lived in this corner of the world for long enough that nearly everyone he buried was someone he knew, someone whose presence he would miss. He glanced at Alice and lifted one shoulder in a minute, helpless shrug. She raised a corner of her mouth in sympathy. That was all she had to do. This was friendship, and he was grateful for it.

At least, some small and vicious part of him whispered, it won't be Alice. God, he had thought it would be, for an endless succession of hours that spring. He had thought, *I will bury her; I will bury my best friend.*

The Crawfords were his second family, had been from the time Ben realized his own family was decidedly inadequate, and what was worse, not normal. The Crawfords had been fantastically normal: there was a sensible number of parents (two), a reasonable number of children (one), and, best of all, the desired number of those artistic hangers-on who seemed to colonize his father's home (zero). The Crawfords were solid and predictable and they had folded Ben into their family as if he belonged. Ben had craved regularity, and the Crawfords had regularity to spare.

It had been only natural and normal that he and Alice should marry. Of course they would. Alice was beautiful and kind; Ben was hardworking and had a modest living at St. Aelred's. It all made sense. Coming here tonight and seeing the friendly faces of people who loved him ought to feel warm and cozy after his hostile encounters with the captain. It ought to feel like stepping before a blazing fire after being out in the cold.

Why didn't it, then?

"What's that look for?" Alice asked him.

Ben realized he must have let some of his thoughts show on his face. "I think that after two weeks with the young Dacres, I hardly know how to conduct myself in civilized company. I'm waiting for turnips to be launched at me. Honestly, Alice, I'm a little hurt that you didn't greet me with a volley of French profanity and by setting something on fire."

"How churlish of me not to have thought of that," she said, her eyes sparkling. "Next time, send word and we'll come up with some suitable display of affection for you."

"Please do." He smiled back. She really was beautiful, both in the sense that anyone in their right mind would agree that she was lovely to look at, and in the sense that she was dear to him and therefore he found her countenance pleasing. He loved her, and he believed she loved him. It was right and good for them to marry; their union would be comfortable and easy. This was what marriage was for. But comfort and ease suddenly seemed like pale and flimsy things.

"That face again," Alice said, regarding him with concern.

Ben made an effort to be decent company. "It's lovely weather we're having." And then he wanted to slap himself, because since when did he have to resort to weather-related conversation with Alice?

"Is this where I mention that we're due for rain?" Alice shot back, an eyebrow gently raised. She knew him too well. "But I'll play along. Yes, Benedict, the weather is fine. I do wish I could experience it without a pane of glass between me and it, but it certainly looks well enough through the window." Even with the support of Ben's arm, she was only able to walk a few steps; that wouldn't bring her even to the garden door.

"I'll carry you outside," he said impetuously.

"No you will not," she protested. "We have a Bath chair due to arrive next week, and I'll be wheeled outside in tremendous dignity."

He was already on his feet. "Let me take you outside now, though."

She looked up at him steadily. "Suit yourself," she said, lifting her arms. "Haul me about wherever you like. Oh, up I go." She laughed as Ben lifted her, and her mother cast them both a look of indulgence shot through with weariness, and Ben was reminded of how much of a trial the past months had been for the older woman: her only child sick, crippled. It was surely a relief for Mr. and Mrs. Crawford to know that after they died, Alice would at least have a husband to care for her, if it came to that. She didn't have money or any family that could be relied on; Ben was all she had. He held tightly to her.

Alice felt insubstantial in his arms, as if she were entirely composed of muslin ruffles. Too light. He tried to keep the worry off his face, knowing she could read him perfectly.

He managed to open the French door that led out of the drawing room, then kicked it shut behind him after they stepped out onto the terrace.

"You can put me down on the bench," Alice said, so close her breath ruffled his hair.

"Must I?" he asked, squeezing her a bit tighter, then loosening his grip because he could feel the contours of her bones. He was seized by the idea that if he put her down she'd blow away.

"I'm afraid so." Her voice seemed graver than this conversation required. "How did you find Captain Dacre?" she asked after he had arranged her on the bench.

"He's cold and angry and seems dead set against kindness," Ben said, not mincing words, and then immediately feeling guilty for being so uncharitable. "He returns from two years at sea and instead of—I don't know—embracing his children or even greeting them or whatever it is fond papas do, he makes himself as disagreeable as possible."

"When my father came home from a trip he'd always bring me back something special. A new set of paints, or something else he could slip into his bag."

"Well, he was fond of you. Who can blame him?" Ben asked. He didn't want to talk about the captain. Not here.

"A doctor from London came last week while you were up at Barton Hall."

"Did he have anything helpful to say?"

"He thinks I'm malingering."

Ben sucked in a breath and held it until he could trust himself to speak calmly. "Did your parents believe him?"

"No, thank goodness. Or, even if they did, they'd never say as much, which is more or less the same thing." Ben disagreed there, but didn't want to point it out. "But I feel like I'm starting to believe him. What if I'm mad? He told Father that this is a form of hysteria he usually sees in older women who have already had children and now wish to get attention in other ways."

Ben would have liked to give this medical man some attention, preferably with his fists and quite possibly with his boots. "You haven't walked on your own in months. If you were shamming it, you'd have to be as mad as a March hare, and I think we'd all have noticed by now."

She was silent, the only sounds the hooting of an owl and the rustling of leaves. "He was so sure of himself."

"It's his job to be sure of himself. He can't charge five guineas to shrug his shoulders and walk away."

"I don't want to get married until I know for sure whether I'm going to recover."

"I don't care whether you can walk, Alice."

"But I do," she said vehemently. "I want to know what's in store for me before I make any promises. I want to know what my life will be like. I think I deserve that. My opinion on this matters, Benedict." She sounded almost angry on those last words.

Ben couldn't argue. He wasn't going to try to persuade her to marry him against her will. He took her hands. "Anything you want. However long you want. I'm not going anywhere. But in case you were in any doubt, I want to marry you, no matter what. There's nobody else I can imagine spending my life with."

He thought this was a good thing to say. It was the truth, and it was what he told himself whenever he thought about his marriage: there was nobody other than Alice he could imagine being with. But Alice tilted her head to the side and regarded him quizzically. "You know there are people who marry for other reasons."

He cocked an eyebrow at her. "You mean dynastic marriages? I never seem to have any money at all and you have three hundred pounds. I don't think we qualify."

She laughed, but her smile didn't last long. "No, I mean when the butcher's boy steps out with the baker's daughter. They have their own reasons."

His own smile faltered but he shored it up. "I daresay they do, and that it has something to do with sandwiches." His own parents had gotten married while drunk on lust; he was rather pleased with himself that he wasn't repeating their mistake. He preferred not to dwell on the fact that his own sobriety of thought owed more to his lack of interest in women than it did with any moral uprightness. That wasn't the point.

"Very droll," she said.

He kissed her hand, just a light brush of his lips over her cool skin, and tried not to notice Alice's slight frown.

Since it was already a terrible day and not much could make it worse, Phillip climbed the stairs to the schoolroom. He knew it would be empty but he wanted to see it, maybe to confirm that it was still precisely as bad as he remembered, no better and no worse. The schoolroom was tucked away in a dismal, north-facing corner of an upper story, grim even at noon but beyond dreary at night. When he pushed the door open, the hinges creaked angrily as if the door hadn't been opened recently. Indeed, it had the damp and dusty odor of a room long unused. The moonlight shifted, illuminating an unintelligible scrawl on the chalkboard and dredging up every stray particle of shame and confusion he had experienced as a child in this room.

For a brief moment he was glad the children were off making mischief in cherry trees or really anywhere else rather than this godforsaken tomb. But no, Phillip had his own particular reasons for which this room had been the setting of such misery. His children didn't share any of that. They belonged in the damned schoolroom and he was beyond annoyed that they weren't.

He went back down to the library and took out his frustration on the brandy bottle, so he was mildly drunk and execrably lonely when his gaze strayed to the pair of portraits on the wall by the hearth. Even in oil paints, Caroline was almost tangibly competent. Her competence was all over the house, from the neat arrangement of chairs against the wall to the way the servants tapped precisely twice on the door before entering.

Suddenly he resented Caroline for having died, which he realized was a ridiculous thing to do, but he did so anyway. He missed his boys in their matching short pants and his daughter with her neat plaits. And it was all Caroline's fault. Bloody scarlet fever.

Phillip wanted to beat his hands on the paneling of the wall. This was all wrong. This was not what he wanted. He was angry with Caroline for having died, he was angry with himself for not having returned sooner and not knowing what to do now that he was here, and he was angry with the bloody vicar for simply existing even though he knew none of this was the man's fault. God, he had never missed Caroline so much in his life. Or, which was worse, in her own life. He could add taking her for granted to his list of sins.

She had written to him, like any dutiful wife, and he had McCarthy read her letters aloud to him when they were alone in his cabin. He would dictate a reply for McCarthy to copy out. Christ, just thinking of it made him feel like he had somehow betrayed both of them at once.

He wanted to go back to his ship so he didn't have to think about any of this. He wanted to return to a time and a place far away when he could imagine his family safe and small on a tiny green island across the globe. Things were so much more manageable at a distance. But here, so close, he had to confront the fact that he didn't belong; his presence at Barton Hall would do none of them any good, he feared. He would never do anyone any good; these were the thoughts that assailed him in his blackest moods.

"Goddamn it, Caroline," he said, looking at her portrait. It had been commissioned on their betrothal, a lavish present from her wealthy father. She had been one and twenty when they married, which seemed frightfully young to look so palpably self-assured. "What the hell would you have me do now?"

Perhaps if he had been slightly less drunk he might have noticed that the door leading from the terrace had opened. As it was, he was bleary-eyed and didn't notice anything until he heard the sound of a throat being cleared.

Slowly, he turned his head and saw Sedgwick standing in the open doorway, one hand in his pocket and the other holding a lit cigarillo. Phillip could make out the burning tip, glowing red in the darkness.

Vicars definitely weren't supposed to smoke cigarillos. A pipe by the fireside, perhaps. But not a cigarillo and not out of doors. But vicars also weren't supposed to look at other gentlemen the way he had caught Sedgwick looking at him over the breakfast table, so perhaps Sedgwick was simply a terrible vicar. Phillip found that thought comforting. He thought he could coexist with a terrible vicar better than with a godly one who would judge his failings and see all the ways he fell short as a father, a husband, a man.

"Coming back from a midnight rendezvous?" How unvicarly. Phillip pulled out his watch to check it. It wasn't even half past ten yet, so perhaps Sedgwick had only been sweeping out the church or whatever vicars did in their spare time. Disappointing. Also, how could it be so early? He had been in Kirkby Barton for less than thirty-six hours and it felt like approximately three weeks. Time was passing in a hellishly slow manner here. On board a ship, time was crucial. It was tied up with location, and distance, and speed, and all the other things that were paramount at sea and irrelevant standing still on land. He wasn't moving, so perhaps the hands on the clock had just given up.

"I saw the light on in the library and thought I'd see if you needed anything," Sedgwick said.

Phillip was about to tell him how presumptuous this sentiment was, but got distracted by the sight of the vicar taking a last puff on his cigarillo before dropping it to the ground and extinguishing it with his boot, the sound of leather on stone somehow as loud as a whip crack.

Before Phillip could quite grasp what was happening, Sedgwick entered the room and came to stand before him. They were about the same height, and stood close enough for Phillip to discern the solemn expression on the vicar's face. Sedgwick put a hand solidly on Phillip's shoulder, and for a mad moment Phillip thought he was about to be kissed. The room, the whole world, was reeling crazily around except for that one point of contact where Sedgwick touched him, and there it burned.

Chapter Five

—————————————————————

Ben knew straightaway that it had been a mistake to stand so close to the captain, and an even worse mistake to touch him.

He was trying to do right by the man, trying to do his duty. Dacre was drunk, alone, and staring at his dead wife's portrait. It was quite clearly the right thing to go to him, to be with him, to offer whatever small solace he could. Any clergyman and indeed any decent human being would recognize this; Ben had to listen to his conscience rather than the voice that warned him not to get closer to temptation.

Because this man was temptation incarnate. If Ben had ever let himself imagine a man beside him during the furtive nighttime releases that he never thought of in the light of day, that man might have looked very much like the captain. Lean frame, wide mouth, eyes that seemed to know things Ben couldn't even dream of.

Feeling his face heat, Ben did his best to clear his mind of these unwelcome thoughts, to focus on duty and not on the heat emanating from Captain Dacre's body, the solidity of the muscles under Ben's hand.

"I apologize for having assumed the worst of you when you arrived," Ben managed. "Being here must dredge up all your grief."

The captain stepped backward, dislodging Ben's hand. "Grief!" he sputtered. "You don't know what you're talking about. And you can sod right off with your priestly rubbish, so spare it for someone who cares."

Ben automatically glanced at the portrait of the late Mrs. Dacre. He had only seen her a few times before her death. He had buried her, just as he would soon bury Mr. Farleigh and just as he had escaped burying Alice. "It's true that I've never had that kind of loss, but if you like I can—"

"I'm not grieving my wife, you fool." Captain Dacre sank into a chair. His words were slurred and Ben knew any confidence he was about to receive would be regretted when the captain sobered up. "I resent the hell out of her for dying, and it's utter . . ." He gestured futilely with his hands before dropping them to the arms of the chair. "It's utter shit that she won't get to see the children grow up. But I've finished grieving her."

There was something about the way he put the stress on the last word that gave Ben pause. "But you *are* grieving," he said.

For a moment Ben thought the captain wouldn't answer. "I lost my lieutenant fourteen months ago."

Ben didn't know whether it was the precise measure of

time or the magnitude of sorrow in the word *lost* that clued him in to exactly what Dacre was getting at. "I see," he said.

There was scorn in the captain's eyes. "I don't think you do, vicar."

Ben could have managed a platitude, something about friendship and loss. He could have extricated himself from this situation without giving up any of his own secrets. But that would be a betrayal of his own conscience; the right thing was to let the captain know that he wasn't alone, that his secrets were shared. This, he told himself, was why he searched out the brandy decanter and poured himself a glass. Nobody liked to drink alone, he reasoned. This was why he settled into the chair opposite the captain's. It was all to give the captain comfort and companionship, not because Ben desperately longed to talk to another man who shared his own . . . proclivities.

"I do know," Ben said after taking a sip of brandy. "I'm not unfamiliar with the way men can become close when living in proximity." Oh, that was so primly euphemistic, so desperately inadequate, as the captain's bleak laugh made clear. He tried again, measuring his words carefully. "When I was at school—"

The captain cut him off with an impatient wave of his hand. "Every schoolboy knows about having the convenient sort of friendship where you toss one another off and never speak of it in the light of day."

That was indeed so close to Ben's only experiences that he was momentarily speechless to hear it dismissed out of hand. He silently sipped his brandy and tried to look like a man who wasn't perilously out of his depth in this conversation.

"The worst of it is that maybe that's all it was to McCarthy. Perhaps for him, during a long sea voyage, beggars couldn't be choosers. But now he's dead and I'll never know." Dacre looked up at him with barely focused eyes, as if only now recalling that he was not alone. "I'm very drunk and I shouldn't be telling you this."

Ben couldn't argue with that. "If you'll pardon me for saying so, you already have."

Something like a smile whispered across Dacre's face. "Point taken."

"You're grieving your . . ." *Friend* was wrong. *Lover* seemed an invasion of privacy. But what else was there? "Your Lieutenant McCarthy," he finally said. "He was important to you." Ben knew how to have this conversation, this repetitive reassurance that grief can take its own time and shape. But that had been grief for parents, children, brothers, sisters, husbands, wives. Neat categories of valid relationships that everyone understood, phrases of belonging that could be etched concisely onto tombstones: beloved son, devoted wife. There were even rules for how to grieve people in each category, how many months to wear a black armband and whether one could dance. Captain Dacre didn't have any of that, and Ben felt his heart twist in his chest at what that must cost him.

"He was everything to me." The captain spoke with such seriousness, such earnestness, that Ben was taken aback. He tried not to imagine what it would be like to hear someone speak of himself in those terms.

"But you don't know if he returned the sentiment."

Dacre examined the contents of his glass. "It's worse than

that. I let him believe that it was the sort of schoolboy arrangement you mentioned earlier. And then he died." He took a slow sip of his brandy. "He died without ever hearing me give it a name."

"Does it matter?" Ben asked, addressing the question to Dacre, to himself, to God, to any other benevolent presence who might see fit to provide guidance. "Does it matter what it's called?" He genuinely didn't know, had indeed deliberately avoided thinking about what it might mean to find love and companionship and desire all in the same person, because to form that thought would mean to acknowledge a future he would never have.

"Goddamn it, yes!" Dacre nearly roared, and then fell silent. "Christ, Sedgwick," he said in a different, lighter tone. "I've never talked about that and never will again. Do me the favor of not mentioning this."

"Naturally," Ben said, ashamed to have been the recipient of regretted confidences.

By noon the following day, Phillip hadn't caught a glimpse of his children. They might spend the next two months hiding from him, and he would have wasted his entire leave. As little as he liked it, he was going to have to try a different strategy. And for that, he needed Sedgwick's help.

"Mr. Sedgwick will be in the barnyard, sir," a footman said when Phillip asked where the vicar might be. "Playing with the ducklings, like as not." An indulgent smile flickered across the servant's face.

Phillip blinked. He was about to enlist the help of a madman, it seemed. Well, if that was his only option, then so be it. He put on his sturdiest boots and walked to the part of the home farm that he recalled being used to raise poultry. Indeed, there was Sedgwick, kneeling on a patch of muddy earth and coaxing a pair of ducklings up his arm with a trail of seeds that led all the way to his shoulder.

"You'll spoil them," Phillip said nonsensically.

Sedgwick looked up, and he smiled as if he were happy to see Phillip, and it was the first time anyone had even pretended to be glad to lay eyes on him since he had returned. That smile was so honest and warm it was somehow shocking. Phillip nearly caught himself smiling back, the corners of his mouth twitching up involuntarily. He couldn't remember the last time he had smiled.

"I had no idea your philosophy of discipline extended to barnyard fowl," the vicar said. "Or that you knew anything about newly hatched ducklings."

"We had chickens on the ship," Phillip protested, before realizing how asinine it was to argue on those grounds, or any grounds, about so trifling a subject.

"I didn't realize I was dealing with an expert. Hop to it, ladies, you're being watched by a master. You'll make me look very stupid if you dawdle like that. Come on, Louisa, step lively, there is no way you don't want that tasty seed that's waiting for you on my elbow." He went on in this manner until both the ducklings were on his shoulder.

Phillip had to bite his lower lip to keep from laughing. It was absurd. Sedgwick raised his eyes and must have seen how close Phillip was to bursting out in laughter, because he grinned. Unless Phillip was mistaken, there was a touch of triumph in the vicar's smile, as if he had been desperate to wrench that reaction out of Phillip. Phillip couldn't remember the last time somebody had tried to amuse him. Impress, yes. Please, certainly. But amuse? Out of the question. Amusement was the sort of thing men wiped off their faces at Phillip's approach, not something they tried to cultivate in him.

Then one of the ducklings realized its path of seeds had come to a dead end, and got the inspired idea to see if additional treats awaited her at higher ground. With a squawk and an ungainly flap of the wings, she landed on the vicar's bare head.

"No, that's not at all the thing, miss. You'll make a spectacle of me, I'm afraid."

Phillip could hardly stand it. He wanted to swat the birds away so he and the vicar could have some semblance of a normal conversation. He couldn't be serious and stern with a man who had ducklings in his hair, or who talked to baby birds like they were guests at a tea party, or who seemed to dearly want Phillip to smile.

But at the same time he wanted to take a step forward and pet the birds, and maybe run his fingers through Sedgwick's hair, too, and see if it was as soft as the feathers. It was ridiculous.

He kept his feet planted firmly on the ground and resolved not to take a single step closer. "I came to ask for your help."

The vicar bit his lip. "You're fascinated by my skill with barnyard fowl and wish me to teach you my mysterious ways?"

Phillip strove for some sort of customary chilliness, just enough to see him through this nonsense. "Be serious for half a moment. I implore you."

"All right." The vicar scooped up the ducks and placed them gently on the ground. "Have at it." He spread his arms wide, inviting Phillip to hurl accusations or insults at him. But his eyebrow was arched ever so slightly, as if he and Phillip were in on the same joke, as if that were even a possibility.

With the force of a slap in the face, Phillip realized it would be terribly easy to develop a tendre for Sedgwick. He was all easy charm and raw good looks; after last night's conversation he had to know exactly where Phillip's interests lay, but he didn't seem repulsed or scandalized. Indeed, Phillip recalled something Sedgwick had stammered about his own experiences at school.

As Phillip continued to stare wordlessly, Sedgwick's smile dropped and he looked down at his feet, as if he knew exactly what Phillip was thinking. Phillip prepared himself for the inevitable distancing, the slight flicker of disgust. But then he lifted his eyes to Phillip and—oh hell, was he blushing? That just wasn't fair.

Phillip's prick had been all but asleep for fourteen months, and it chose this moment to remind Phillip of its continued existence, the stupid thing.

Well, it needed to settle down. Phillip was done with trying to get people into bed. He had learned his lesson after McCarthy died; all those nights of closeness had left him with feelings he could hardly name, had hardly even acknowledged to himself until after McCarthy was dead and at the bottom of a stormy sea. Their coupling had been convenient and discreet, which was all he usually sought in such arrangements. Hell, it was all he had ever hoped for. But then McCarthy was gone and Phillip, whose mind drifted so easily to sorrow and darkness, found himself not only regretting the loss of his lover but also regretting everything he hadn't said, everything he could never offer a lover anyway.

Phillip was done with convenient tumblings or any tumblings whatsoever. He wasn't equal to the emotions that came along with simple, honest fucking. Like bloody stowaways, and just as much of a hassle to deal with.

"I require your help with the children," he said frostily. "If you can get them to supper, we can come to an agreement afterward." He turned on his heel and walked swiftly back to the house, trying not to think of the look of disappointment on the vicar's face and what that might mean.

"Disgraceful," Mrs. Winston said, picking a feather out of Ben's hair. "A man of the cloth, wandering around out of doors bareheaded and acting like a simpleton. Ducklings, indeed. I brought you a tart." She added this last sentence as if it might present a solution to the problem.

"Thank you," Ben said, taking the dish from his housekeeper's hands and balancing it on a fence post, "but didn't I tell you that you might as well have a holiday while I was up here at the hall?" Her daughter was married to a brewer in

Keswick, and Ben quite clearly remembered suggesting that Mrs. Winston pay a visit while her services weren't required at the vicarage.

Mrs. Winston snorted. "As if I'd leave you and Franny Morris to see to the captain. She may know how to dress a joint, or she may not, but she doesn't know how things ought to be in a gentleman's house. And as for you . . ." She looked at Ben and shook her head in plain sorrow.

"Mrs. Morris is a very good cook." Mrs. Winston shot him an aggrieved glance. "Not as good as you," Ben hastily added.

"In any event, the hedgerow behind the church has more gooseberries than I know what to do with, so might as well put them to good use. Make sure that tart finds its way onto the captain's supper table. And I brought another one for your father." She balanced this dish on top of the other and wiped her hands on her apron.

"For my father?" Ben repeated stupidly. "Why?"

"Doesn't he eat pie?" she asked, a hand on her hip.

"Well, yes, but—"

"Then take it to him. Your knees are twenty years younger than mine, so you can stand the walk better than I can." Then, in a less annoyed tone, "Always did have a sweet tooth, your father."

Ben wanted to know how Mrs. Winston knew anything of Alton Sedgwick, who surely didn't number village housekeepers among his acquaintances. He preferred lunatic aristocrats and opium-addicted paupers but not much in the way of a happy medium. But before he could think of how to delicately frame the question, she produced a jar from her apron.

"Jam for the Farleighs. I suppose you'll be going up there too?"

"Naturally. Do you have any other errands you require of me before I attend to my duties?" he asked, feigning more irritation than he felt.

"Hmmph," she said, and stomped back towards the village.

Ben attempted to gather the two pie tins and the jar of jam into his arms and safely convey them into the house.

"I'll help," said a small voice. It was Jamie, and he seemed almost entirely composed of dirt.

"Do sweets summon you out of thin air, I wonder? Yes, take this dish, but you'll have to wait until supper to have any. Which, you'll notice, means you need to attend supper."

"Doesn't really," Jamie said. "I can steal some later on." He was honest, if nothing else.

"As a personal favor, please come to supper. If your father attempts to do anything drastic, I'll help as best I can, but we need to show him that we're all going on swimmingly and don't need to be ordered about."

Ben thought of Captain Dacre's demeanor in the barnyard that morning, a reluctant good humor so plainly at war with the urge to be cold and imperious. Dacre hadn't known what to do with himself, and Ben had seen it, and felt the power of it.

He had also felt Dacre's gaze on him, heavy with an intent that Ben might even have understood without the context of last night's confessions. He had felt the power of that too. He had felt the heat of that gaze on every inch of his skin, and he had been tempted to see what might have happened if he had stepped forward. But he hadn't, and he wouldn't, not with Dacre, not with anyone. He wasn't ashamed of the dark desires that plagued him when he couldn't sleep; Ben had never seen the point of shame and hair shirts. Maybe it was his unconventional upbringing, or maybe he had been lucky to meet men at university whose ideas of sin and salvation would have been thought blasphemous a generation earlier, but his susceptibility to men had always seemed a minor irritation, like a tendency to faint at the sight of blood, rather than anything concerning his soul. Nothing to worry overmuch about, especially if one avoided the situation in the first place. There wasn't going to be any avoiding Captain Dacre, though. They'd be thrown together for the remainder of his leave.

Ben could not afford a deviation from the path he had chosen; his future and his peace of mind required a home, a family, a sense of permanence and certainty that he craved with a bone-deep longing. There was no place for heated gazes or tempting thoughts in his future, and he was determined to be absolutely content with that.

CHAPTER SIX

Dinner went as well as could be expected, which was to say it was just this side of a nightmare.

With a bit of judicious bribery, Ben had gotten the children to the table. But once there, they had all three steadfastly refused to speak English. This was a strategy they had used with some success in tormenting former tutors. During the first few days of Ben's residence at the hall, the children spoke French with one another until it was clear that Ben wasn't going to force them to speak English. He understood enough French to feel confident that they weren't summoning devils or plotting treason, so he thought that if they wanted to practice the language together, it basically counted as a French lesson, and he couldn't complain. Of course he wasn't fool enough to let them know that he spoke any French. That would have utterly ruined their fun and likely inspired them to greater feats of mischief in their campaign to alienate him.

Their father was evidently not of the same mind.

Peggy was cheerfully and revoltingly describing the events

that transpired after she and Jamie gorged themselves on green apples, when Captain Dacre interrupted. "Speak English, Margaret," he said, making no effort to conceal his frustration. "And do confine your conversation to more genteel topics."

Ben suppressed a groan as the children exchanged wary looks. Really, Captain Dacre was dedicated to setting his children against him. Ben dug around in his coat pocket for a stub of pencil and a scrap of paper, and covertly scribbled a note to the captain under the table: *For heaven's sake, pretend not to speak French.* He folded it into a compact square and slid his hand along the table until his hand touched the captain's, tucking the note under the other man's palm.

He thought he did a fairly good job of ignoring the thrill that ran up his arm at the contact. Ben had no business feeling an attraction to this man.

He tried to push those thoughts to the side as he always did, something to acknowledge only when he could no longer avoid it. That, he was fairly sure, was what a man was supposed to do with any lustful inclinations, regardless of their object: ignore them in the way a sloppy housekeeper might ignore ashes in the grate, pretending they weren't there until their presence made it impossible to get anything else done. And then he indulged in a fit of barely satisfying pleasure before returning to his safe, predictable, orderly life.

At the slight touch of their hands, the captain went very still. Which was to say, even more stonily rigid than he had been before. But then, noticing the tightly folded square of paper beneath his hand, he did the stupidest thing imaginable. He tucked it into his breast pocket without even bothering to unfold it, let alone read it. Dolt. Ben gritted his teeth. It was a miracle England had defeated Napoleon if men with so little sense of strategy were in charge of the navy. That idiocy quelled Ben's improper thoughts, however.

"You look cross, Mr. Sedgwick," Jamie said.

"I am cross," Ben replied levelly. "I thought you might show some manners to your father. And we all know he cannot speak French any more than I can," he added pointedly, "so perhaps we could speak English together. Just as a novelty this one evening." He carved himself a piece of mutton. "Although I must say, it was very kind of you to present your father with a pet."

"A pet?" Peggy asked incredulously. Her hair, Ben noticed, was in plaits that had been quite neat a few days ago but were now positively disreputable. He had caught Captain Dacre staring at the twins in open dismay at their dishevelment. "We did no such—ow!" She glared at Jamie, who had evidently kicked her under the table.

"The dormouse, of course," Ben said mildly. "It was very clever of you to realize that your father was likely quite lonely after you absconded into the wild, leaving him alone and with nobody to talk to after two years at sea." The children all looked down at their plates. Out of the corner of his eye, Ben could see the captain's gaze steadily on him. He tried to ignore it but Captain Dacre wasn't the sort of man you could simply stop paying attention to.

The children sat sullenly. Ned poked at his mutton with the edge of his knife while Peggy loaded her spoon with mashed peas, positioned it like a catapult, and aimed it at her twin. Jamie saw this happen and looked ready to duck.

"There's a gooseberry custard tart on the sideboard, but something went terribly wrong when Mrs. Morris sliced it," Ben said to no one in particular. "She cut it into eight slices."

Out of the corner of his eye he saw Jamie watch him intently. Jamie knew this as the preamble to one of his favorite games. "That's fine by me," Jamie said. "Peg won't get any if she launches those peas at me, which leaves two slices each for the rest of us."

"Quite right, but she isn't going to launch peas or anything else." Out of the corner of his eye, he saw Peggy rest her spoon on her plate.

"One and three-fifths of a slice for each of us," Jamie said promptly.

"But what if I decide to allocate the pie according to weight? That seems only fair. I'd say I'm about twelve stone, and so is your father." The mere estimation of what the captain might have beneath his clothes by way of sinew and muscle was enough to make Ben's cheeks heat. "You and Peggy are maybe four stone apiece and Ned's about seven."

"That's about a tenth of the pie each for me and Peg."

"Ah, but I don't have tenths, I have eighths."

Jamie made an impatient sound. "Remove a quarter of an eighth and you'll have a tenth."

"Which is grossly unfair because I don't even care for gooseberry tart and I don't see why I ought to have twice as much—"

"Three times as much," Jamie corrected.

"—as you and Peg. So let's come up with a better model of distribution."

They went on like this for the remainder of the meal. Sums kept Jamie's mind busy, and a busy Jamie didn't set fire to things or get suspected of poaching by evil-minded neighboring landlords. Peggy, if her brother was content, was less inclined to divert attention with her own antics, so there was peace in the kingdom. And, frankly, Jamie was very clever at maths and Ben wanted to encourage the child's gift, especially since the boy was eight years old and could hardly read a word. Ben didn't know why he couldn't read, or if it was possible to teach him, only that it was a chip on the lad's shoulder and Ben couldn't blame him. So he did what he could to help Jamie use his mind in other ways.

If Ben had to guess, he'd think that the children had banded together to rid themselves of any adults who might make Jamie suffer for his illiteracy. Schoolmasters and tutors likely came down hard on him. Ned and Peggy had probably decided to protect their brother by driving off anyone who might discover he couldn't read.

Ben didn't want to let the captain know about Jamie's problem until he could be trusted; frankly, the captain seemed just the type to think punishing knowledge into a child a reasonable course of action.

After supper, he sent the children up to the nursery to eat their tart—in the end, they each agreed to get a third, which was extravagant, but it might put them into a deep enough sleep to last until morning.

That left him alone at the table with the captain. All of

a sudden it seemed like they were sitting too near to one another, even though neither of them had moved. Ben was close to people all the time. He prayed with the old and he sat with the sick. He dandled babies on his knee and embraced brides on their wedding days. He was no stranger to proximity.

What was new and unsettling was the way the captain was looking at him. There was something in the captain's expression, some measure of interest that Ben feared mirrored the expression in his own eyes. That was something he hadn't seen in a long while. Outside in the barnyard, the fresh air and tiny animals had washed the scene with ordinariness; he had halfway convinced himself that he hadn't seen anything like desire on the captain's face, or that if it was desire, it didn't matter. But now, alone in the candlelit dining room, there was no mistaking it for what it was, and there was no telling himself it didn't matter. The tiny spark that flared between them seemed, at this moment, to matter more than anything else in Ben's small universe.

He watched the captain open his mouth to speak, but then close it again, and instead swallow. He was handsome, Ben supposed, if you liked angry men, which Ben wouldn't have thought he did. Unfortunately, the captain's face relaxed a bit at that moment, some of his crossness smoothing away, and Ben had to acknowledge that he was rather desperately handsome. Ben hastily looked away and took a drink of his brandy.

"It's getting late," Ben said, flustered. "I probably ought to get some sleep."

"Wait." The captain took a sip of his brandy and regarded

Ben over the edge of his glass. Those eyes, which were supposed to be black, were undeniably, unforgivably blue, and Ben felt a surge of inane, betrayed anger at the portraitist. "Don't go yet."

For a moment Ben was at a loss. He didn't know if it was the low timbre of Captain Dacre's voice or the heat of his gaze, or if maybe he had managed to get drunk on a few sips of wine, but if the captain had leaned over and touched him, kissed him, done whatever he liked to him, Ben would have hardly known how or even why to protest. He felt rooted to the spot.

And he didn't want to move. He didn't want to come up with another feeble excuse to get out of the dining room. He wanted to stay here and find out what happened after another hour and another few glasses of wine. He knew it would be putting paid to his hopes and dreams, because it was one thing to quietly and privately desire men and quite another to act on it, or so he told himself. He could lust after all the men in the north of England and he could still have the safe and comfortable life he longed for. This was what he told himself in the quiet hours of the night when doubts assailed him.

Sitting there, wishing there was some way to will Captain Dacre to act on the interest that was so plain in his eyes, the truth struck him. This was something he wanted, and it was something he'd never have if he married, and neither would Alice; he'd be selling himself and Alice a bad bargain by going through with their marriage.

He wanted to turn back the hands of the clock to a time before he had realized that.

"Why do you look like that?" Phillip demanded. The vicar's face had turned grave. Gravity didn't sit well on his cheerful features. His mouth belonged in a smile. And if that wasn't a harebrained notion, Phillip didn't know what was.

"Oh, woolgathering," Sedgwick said, looking almost normal again except for a slight furrow between his brows.

Suddenly Phillip wished he hadn't insisted that the vicar stay at the table. He had been quite attractive outside in the barnyard, but here, two feet away, lit by candles and dressed in spotless evening clothes, he was something else entirely. And that little performance with the children might have been amusing or even impressive if they had been anyone else's children who required such bizarre management.

He had felt like a guest in a foreign land, a country where children came to dinner with seams unraveled and hair that hadn't seen a comb in many moons, children who resolutely did not acknowledge their father. Beneath the grime and raggedy too-small clothes, Phillip could see only ghosts of the children he had known.

Sedgwick must have guessed some of that, because he frowned and slid his hand closer to Phillip's as if thinking to offer comfort. Then he snatched it back, whether because he didn't think Phillip worthy of comfort or didn't want to risk touching him, Phillip could not tell.

"What was the meaning of that business earlier?" he growled, trying to bring them back to comfortable antipathy.

"Oh, did you want a slice of tart?" Sedgwick asked, an amused sparkle in his warm brown eyes. "And I gave it all away. Bad form."

Phillip bit back a renegade smile. Damn the man for trying to make him laugh and nearly succeeding. Phillip didn't have defenses that could withstand this sort of assault. "No, blast you. What the hell kind of circus did I just witness? This house is like some kind of lunatic asylum." He noticed that the vicar did not disagree. "And now I—you—*we* have to come up with a better arrangement. There must be some sort of tutor who can manage them properly and give them the education they require."

Sedgwick took a sip of his brandy. "Your children seem quite determined not to have a tutor, or a governess, or to remain enrolled in any decent school. If there were any other option, I wouldn't be here."

Phillip grumbled his assent. "But why?"

Sedgwick shrugged and looked into his brandy glass. Phillip had the distinct impression that the vicar was holding back vital information, but he suspected this man couldn't be strong-armed or badgered into doing anything he didn't want to.

"What do you suggest I do?" Phillip asked.

"I think your first priority needs to be just getting to know them."

"But—"

"I know, discipline. I might even agree," he said, leaning back in his chair, still holding his glass in his hand. "But they'll take orders more willingly from someone they trust."

Phillip had to concede the wisdom of that approach. That was how he had always run his ships. "They don't trust me." He hadn't trusted his own father, come to think.

The vicar regarded him sadly. "They aren't acting like they do."

Phillip poured himself another glass of brandy and shoved the bottle towards his guest. It would have been better if he could have stayed away. He didn't belong here; he had nothing to offer. These were the constant whisperings of his mind during its darkest times, and he had lived long enough to recognize this voice, but not long enough to disbelieve it.

"Ned's bright and responsible," the vicar said in a reassuring tone. "You've nothing to worry about there. Peggy is about twice as clever as any person needs to be, and she knows it. As for Jamie, you can see for yourself how intelligent he is. Get to know them, spend some time doing what they like doing, and then by the end of the summer they'll trust that whatever arrangements you make for them are for the best."

Phillip did not like waiting. He preferred action. But either the calm tones of the vicar had lulled him into agreeableness, or that second glass of brandy had rendered him totally insensible, because he found himself nodding. "All right. We'll do it your way. And with you here." There Sedgwick's face went again into that unsmiling wrongness. "God help me, I'm not that bad," he said, affronted. "You know, my officers actually like me. I can give you their addresses for references, if you like." It was only half a joke, but Sedgwick laughed—a sad echo of his usual laugh, but Phillip felt inordinately pleased with himself for having made it happen. "So it's settled," he said. "You'll stay on as the children's tutor. As for salary, I was thinking—"

"No," Sedgwick interrupted. "Definitely not."

"You're doing the work already," Phillip protested. "You might as well be paid for it. It's hardly unusual for a clergyman to earn an extra income by tutoring young people." Vicars in need of extra income sometimes helped gentlemen prepare for university. That wasn't what Sedgwick was doing here, and they both knew it.

"If you want to slip a few extra shillings into the poor box, I won't complain," said Sedgwick. "Some families in the parish are having an unusually bad time of it."

Phillip noticed that the vicar didn't mention by name the reason for this unusual distress. After less than two days here, Phillip had already heard of rents being raised, tenants evicted, pastures closed off by the same Sir Martin Easterbrook who had suspected two of his children of poaching. Phillip did not find that he was inclined to look favorably on his neighboring landowner.

"I don't need extra money," Sedgwick continued. "They do." He took another long drink of his brandy.

Phillip wanted to protest, but he could hardly force money on someone who was unwilling to take it. "Fine," he said. "You can stay here, or you can stay at your own house, or whatever arrangement suits you, I suppose. But I do need to make one point clear. I am not a violent man. I don't do that sort of thing. Not to children and not to anyone else. I give you my word, and I assure you that—I'm dead serious now—if you asked any man who has served on any of my ships, they'd say the same thing."

Sedgwick ran his finger around the rim of his glass, as if not sure what to say or whether to say anything, and Phillip suddenly, wantonly, wanted those broad fingers on his mouth. Sedgwick cleared his throat. "My brother served on the *Fotheringay.*"

Phillip drew in a sharp breath of air. "Under Captain Dinsdale?"

"Yes."

Phillip grasped for something to say. "He was a monster." This wasn't an understatement. There were harsh captains, there were cruel captains, but Dinsdale was in a class of his own. "He's dead now. Died last year. Typhoid."

"I know," the vicar said in a tone of grim satisfaction.

"Is your brother . . ." Phillip hardly knew how to finish the question. Alive? Well? Tormented by the memories of what happened on board that ship?

"He lives in London," Sedgwick said, which answered only one of Phillip's concerns. "Anyway, you understand . . ."

Phillip passed a hand over his mouth. "If that bastard is your family's only experience with naval officers, then I damned well can't blame you for thinking me likely to cause trouble." He ought to leave it there, but he didn't want Sedgwick to think him a villain. It mattered, somehow, that this man with his frank smiles and his blatant efforts to make Phillip smile in return not think him anything like Dinsdale.

"But, Sedgwick, I do hope you can see the difference between a man like that and a man like me." He was openly pleading now, so badly did he want this man not to think the worst of him.

Something in the strain in his voice must have been apparent to Sedgwick, because he raised his eyes to look directly at Phillip. "A man like you," Sedgwick repeated. From any other man Phillip would have recognized the words and the intent look as a plain invitation.

But this was the vicar. Phillip hadn't planned on lusting after the vicar. The vicar, of all people. There could hardly be anyone less suitable. But all that bashful, freckled righteousness was too good to resist. Phillip decided to take a chance. He slid his hand over to where Sedgwick's rested on the table. It was no more of a touch than when Sedgwick had slid him that note earlier—that blasted note, which Phillip hadn't the slightest idea what to do with. Sedgwick's hand was warm and solid, as tan with the sun as Phillip's own.

Sedgwick lifted his eyebrows questioningly.

Phillip lifted one of his in return, and moved his hand to cover Sedgwick's. They were alone, and it was only hands, innocent to any observer, he told himself. Sedgwick's hand felt strong under his, a little rough with work. He laced his fingers into Sedgwick's and was startled to find that it felt right, as if he had always wanted to hold hands with a madcap vicar at his dining table, and only realized it now.

Maybe Sedgwick's thoughts were along similar lines, because Phillip could feel the man's pulse quicken. Then, suddenly, the vicar let out a huff of laughter, as if it were only mildly amusing that the two of them were sitting here acknowledging an attraction, actually touching one another.

Then Sedgwick pulled his hand away and cleared his throat. "I ought to go finish up tomorrow's sermon. I suppose I'll see you in church?"

Well. That rather dampened Phillip's ardor. Nothing like talk of sermons to ruin a moment. "Doubtful," Phillip said, and he knew he sounded annoyed. The truth was that he didn't trust the church any more than Sedgwick trusted the navy. He didn't want any part of an institution that shamed and vilified what Sedgwick had alluded to as *men like him.* And he was rather surprised, disappointed even, that Sedgwick did. "Good night," he said curtly.

"Quite all right," Sedgwick said, as if it did not matter to him in the least whether people went to church or had relations with other men. And maybe it didn't. Phillip was out of his depth.

Ben took the stairs up to his bedchamber two at a time, shut the door behind him, and turned the key in the lock because there was no doubt in his mind about what he was about to do. He flung his coat onto the bed and had his breeches unfastened before he had stopped walking.

He groaned when he wrapped his hand around himself. The past few days had been torture, trying not to stare openly at Dacre while he did things like . . . smile . . . and talk. And every now and then he got this imperious look in his eye and he was clearly on the verge of ordering people about, but then he quelled it and did something decent instead. Even if he hadn't been the handsomest man Ben had ever laid eyes on, Ben would still be here in an attic room with his hand tightly around his prick, tossing himself off like he hadn't done this in ages, when in reality he had done it yesterday. *Yesterday.* He was acting *depraved.*

He wasn't even going to pretend this wasn't about Dacre. He didn't even stop himself from thinking about the man, the taut muscles of his arms and the habit he had of biting back a smile as if smiles cost extra and he was saving up for an especially big one. Every stroke of his hand, he imagined it was actually Dacre's, spreading moisture along the length of his aching prick.

And then he remembered the press of Dacre's long fingers against his own, the heat of his palm and the strength of his touch. He brought his own hand to his mouth to wet it, and from there, it was easy to imagine himself licking Dacre's fingers, drawing them into his mouth, watching Dacre's eyes flare in desire. And then, since this was wanking logic and nothing had to make sense or even be physically possible, it was Dacre's cock in Ben's mouth and his hand on Ben's cock.

Ben braced his free hand against the bedpost and stroked himself faster now, not even bothering to hold back the images that flashed before his eyes. Hands, lips, sweat, wanting, being wanted—and then he was spending in his hand.

He cleaned himself up and tried to steady his thoughts. Usually he regarded this a basic biological necessity, like eating or sleeping, and he didn't refine too much on the passages in the Scripture that suggested masturbation might be sinful or shameful. He tended to think that when the Bible condemned something practically everyone did, whether it be tossing oneself off or eating pork, there was likely some nuance that had been lost either to history or to translation. And then he didn't think about it anymore. He wouldn't do the people of Kirkby Barton any good by thinking about bacon or wanking, so he didn't think about either and had to imagine neither did God.

This time, though, it hadn't felt like a basic biological need but like an indulgence. This was the first time he had focused his desires on one person rather than the act of getting himself off efficiently.

He realized to his horror that he felt like he had done something wrong by thinking about Captain Dacre. Was it that he thought the captain would mind? Hardly. Was it because he thought Alice would mind? That, he felt, was closer to the mark. He couldn't know whether Alice would mind him wanking off to thoughts of a man because that wasn't something that they could ever possibly discuss. And that, itself, was a problem.

But there was more, lurking at the edges of his consciousness, if only he could be brave enough to look. He made himself examine his thoughts. He would never feel the enthusiasm for the marriage bed that he felt for tonight's solitary relief. He had always known that, to some extent, but now that he had fixed a name and a face to his desire, what he had to offer Alice seemed inadequate in comparison.

Men such as he married for many reasons. They wanted families; they wanted companionship; they needed a shield against suspicious minds. And Ben didn't fault them. Couldn't fault them. But now, for the first time he thought that his conscience might not let him go through with it.

And if he couldn't marry, then he'd need to jilt Alice. Sick, disabled Alice, who might not have any other chance to marry and certainly didn't have any other means of providing for herself. The solution would be to talk about it, to see if they could find their way to a meaningful agreement on what their marriage would be like, but this wasn't something he could talk about. To admit to his desire for men would be to risk his position and his life.

He went over to the window, thinking that maybe the view from this height would give him some perspective, but it was all darkness below, and above was nothing but stars and a waning moon.

CHAPTER SEVEN

Phillip, waking at dawn on Sunday morning, was the last person in the household to rise. The children did not number sloth or idleness among their vices, it would seem. He found the twins mucking out the stables while Ned talked with a man Phillip dimly remembered as the land steward. The vicar, his coat once again gone missing, was nominally supervising the twins but any fool could see that he was actually feeding apple cores to one of the foals. The foal, predictably, was following him around as if he had the elixir of life.

Phillip crossed the sun-dappled stable yard. As he approached he realized the twins were not working silently, but rather reciting something. For an astonished moment he thought it had to be a prayer, but then realized it was a history lesson.

"James, Charles, Charles, James, WilliamandMary—" these last monarchs were said in a single rush "—Anne, and then three Georges."

"You've rather glossed over the interregnum, but you're in

good company there. Also I'm afraid there were a couple of wars in there we ought to at least be able to name, but I can't for the life of me remember the name of the one that wasn't against the French."

"The War of the Spanish Succession," Jamie suggested.

"No, that one was all about the French," Peggy said.

"Perhaps Peggy wouldn't mind looking it up for me later. I'd be mortified if one of my parishioners asked me and I didn't have an answer. I'd look daft. Can't have a daft vicar."

The twins giggled, but then Jamie caught sight of Phillip, nudged his sister, and the two of them dropped their rakes and vanished into the stables. He heard rustling and creaking and supposed they were hiding in the loft. Ned, looking over at the commotion, saw his father and immediately stiffened.

"Hullo!" Sedgwick called, waving his hand and smiling like an idiot, like someone who was genuinely glad to see him. Liar. Phillip knew it was all for the children's benefit, that Sedgwick was behaving with exaggerated friendliness so the children might follow his lead. This only made Phillip resent the man more. The vicar seemed to have his own personal ray of sunshine following him about, casting light in his path and drawing people to him, while Phillip was ever under a storm cloud.

"Good morning," he said tightly.

"Good day, Captain Dacre. Did you come to assist with our history lesson?" the vicar asked with a smile that let Phillip see a mouthful of teeth.

Phillip very nearly responded that as far as history lessons went, this was perhaps the least adequate he had ever conceived of. A list of monarchs—an incomplete list of monarchs, no less—without any dates or events. Even Phillip had managed to learn more than that at school, not that he could remember any of it now. Not that he'd want to. For a moment he questioned the wisdom of expecting his young children to master facts he had forgotten two decades since, but then thought better of it. Children were supposed to learn these things, and it wasn't for Phillip—or the vicar, damn him—to decide single-handedly what children were and weren't supposed to do.

Phillip couldn't believe he was going to put his trust in a man who had straw in his hair, a foal nuzzling his pocket, and no knowledge of the—ha!

"It's the Great Northern War," Phillip said in triumph. "The one that didn't involve France during the period you were discussing."

"Oh, there's a good half dozen," Sedgwick said airily. "All those dos involving the Dutch and the Portuguese, to start with. Peg will look it up and by dinner she'll know the belligerents and the casus belli for all of them. And then she'll tell the rest of us and we'll all be the wiser. She's a wizard with that sort of thing."

Phillip now felt very stupid, first for not knowing all the Dutch wars and second for not having grasped that the vicar had manipulated the twins into doing the research on their own. "Ah," was all he said. "And what of Ned?"

"Who do you think told me about all those Dutch wars in the first place?" the vicar said cheerfully. He had too many freckles, and he was only going to get more if he stood out here bareheaded. "Also, he's been working with Mr. Smythe on estate matters. Mr. Smythe has a passion for drains and is cultivating in Ned a proper appreciation for them as well."

This was, in substance, unobjectionable. Phillip was rummaging through his brain in search of some objection, and came up empty-handed. "I thought you'd be at church this morning," he said instead. "It's Sunday."

"It's hardly eight o'clock. But I ought to go clean up, I suppose," he said, glancing sheepishly down at his clothes. "Can't be trailing hay into the church, can I? If you're looking for a way to amuse the children, promise to read them *Robinson Crusoe* at teatime."

Fat chance of that. "You're going?" Phillip asked, frowning. "You don't take them with you?"

"You can manage it on your own," Sedgwick said, his cheerfulness undimmed. And then he walked into the house. *Whistling.*

By the time the clock struck noon, Ben had hung up his cassock and put on a sturdy pair of boots to walk the distance to Fellside Grange.

He made the journey as seldom as possible. He had a litany of excuses—he didn't like to borrow a horse to go over such uneven ground, his duties kept him near the parish, he hated to intrude on his father without warning—but the truth was that he much preferred life on this side of the lake.

His parishioners might hear tales of his father's doings,

but nobody repeated a word to him. After all, there was nothing he could do. He had spent most of his life trying to get his father to act reasonably—respectability and responsibility were beyond hope, but the man could have aspired to reason—and failed at every turn.

It was a hot day, and Ben shed his coat before he had gotten a quarter of the way around the lake. The path was steep in places, rocky in others, and familiar throughout. It was much easier to reach the grange from the other side, from Keswick or wherever his father's many admirers disembarked from the stagecoaches they had taken to visit the old man. So very many admirers. And creditors, acolytes, partners in failed business ventures, spurned lovers, illegitimate children, legitimate children, and prospective lovers.

The grange had seldom been empty.

He paused halfway up the crag, in a place where a few convenient boulders made a place to look down at the lake and eat the sandwich Mrs. Winston had wrapped for him. He had always felt that at this elevation everything looked manageable. His father had written a dozen or so poems about the wild beauty of the lakes and mountains, but for Ben, all the wildness was confined indoors. Out here, high above the village, Ben could very well believe that all he had to do was walk the distance from the grange to the orderly white buildings of Kirkby Barton and find safety.

Which wasn't to say that his father's house was precisely unsafe. Everyone was perfectly kind. He might have had to forage in the woods for mushrooms to eat and the roof might have perpetually leaked in the attic room he shared with his brothers, but nobody wanted to harm him, at least. The general sentiment among Alton Sedgwick's disciples was that the Sedgwick children were beautiful and picturesque, much like the sheep that dotted the hills. Ben and his brothers had a handful of mortifying poems written about them, not that anyone had seen fit to ask for their permission.

Alton Sedgwick hadn't had much to do with his children beyond siring them and sometimes conscripting one of his friends to serve as occasional tutor. But none of Ben's resentment had to do with that. What fueled Ben's bitterness was how little his father had prepared them to live in any way other than his own mode of living—scrounging, scraping, borrowing, occasionally cheating. If any of the Sedgwick boys wanted a more commonplace life, it had been up to them to figure it out on their own.

He finished his sandwich, drained his flask of cider, and continued up the hill until the path curved and he saw Fellside Grange, with its ivy-covered gray stone and the mullioned windows that were scattered across the front with no apparent rhyme or reason. He hesitated there, wanting to enjoy the last few moments of the house still seeming benign, wanting to preserve his sanity for that extra half minute.

His father answered the door himself, and then seemed surprised to find a person standing on his doorstep, as if he had forgotten how doors and knocking worked.

"Father," Ben said.

"Good God, is that you, Benedict?"

Ben wanted to protest that he didn't visit so very seldom—

he had been here twice since Easter, he was quite certain. Instead he stepped into the house and pasted on the smile he used when the sexton was being difficult. "My housekeeper made you a tart." He produced the dish from his satchel and placed it on top of a stack of books, which seemed the only available flat surface. "So I thought I'd pay a visit."

"I'm glad you did," Ben's father said. "I'm quite alone." He hated being alone; after all, he had written an entire sonnet on the theme of solitude. "Norton and his—ah—lady friend have gone traipsing through the hills and I haven't seen them since last night."

Ben widened his eyes in alarm. "Do you need help assembling a search party, Father?"

"A what? No, no, they're sleeping beneath the stars, my boy. And stop calling me Father. You know I can't stand it." Ben did know, which might have partly been why he reverted to using the title. "Now sit down and we'll see if we can find something to feed you with."

"You look well," Ben said when they were settled in the book room, eating a random assortment of fruits. Alton Sedgwick was only fifty, and he didn't even look that old despite the bushy gray beard he had allowed to grow. Ben supposed that blithe indifference to everyone's well-being other than one's own let a man sleep well at night. He tried to sweep aside that uncharitable thought. It wasn't that his father didn't care, he told himself, but that he had his own notion of what was worth caring about. His own frustrating, impossible, largely fictitious notion of what mattered.

"Are you still marrying that girl?" his father asked.

"Alice Crawford. Yes. Later this summer."

His father narrowed his eyes. "Then there's still time for me to tell you what I think."

"You've already done so." Ben sighed. "Please spare yourself the trouble." *And spare me the embarrassment*, he wanted to add, but that wouldn't have mattered. Alton Sedgwick was beyond such mundane concerns as embarrassment. He was also beyond concerns like imprisonment, defrocking and pillorying. "Please tell me the servants are out," Ben said quickly, before his father could start in.

"Servants?" he asked, as if the concept hadn't occurred to him. "The woman isn't here today. She comes in when she comes in." He gestured in a direction Ben supposed was the direction from whence "the woman" came when the spirit moved her to do so. He wondered if she was motivated by wages, more esoteric forms of remuneration, or sheer pity for a dotty old man. "You cannot shackle yourself for life to a person you don't love."

"I do love Miss Crawford," Ben said evenly. Truthfully.

"You're being deliberately obtuse. If you wish to hear a lecture on the different varieties of love, I can hold forth—"

"That won't be necessary."

"I didn't think so. You cannot marry someone you don't wish to take to bed."

Ben winced at this frank speech. "You'll forgive me if I don't wish to take advice on this topic from a man who believed he could live as man and wife with more than one woman at a time," he said primly, and then immediately regretted it.

Alton Sedgwick waved his hand dismissively. "That arrangement suited me and your mother and dear Annette perfectly fine." He was right, of course; Ben wished he could have cast his father as a seducer and betrayer of innocent women, but the three of them had been as happy as larks with their arrangement. "Better than your marriage will suit either you or Miss Crawford."

"You can't know that."

"Does she understand this to be a marriage of convenience? Or does she think she's marrying a man who might have a use for her in his bed?"

"I didn't come all this way to be lectured by my father about what I do or don't do in my bed. I don't know why you're so certain my marrying Miss Crawford would be any different from any other marriage."

"Because you and I both know what I caught you doing in the hayloft with Robbie Briggs."

Ben sighed. The hayloft incident had been a source of extreme mortification, mainly because his father had taken it as an opportunity to tell sixteen-year-old Ben about the Greeks. Ben had wanted to sink into the earth, not have his private matters become the subject of his father's vague musings. He supposed his father's reaction had been better than what he might have expected from a more conventional parent, but it had been embarrassing in its own way. "For all you know I sneak into haylofts with women all the time," he said, trying to lighten the conversation.

"Do you?" his father said with a skeptically raised eyebrow.

"Of course not. I'm a clergyman."

"That's a subject for another day." Alton Sedgwick did not have much use for the Church of England.

"I got a letter from Hartley," Ben said, trying to change the subject. "He says the heat in London is becoming unbearable and he might visit us this month." Hartley was the brother nearest to Ben in age. His godfather, Sir Humphrey Easterbrook, had left him a bequest that amounted to what Ben understood to be a modest competence. Ben winced at the realization that Hartley's inheritance, however small, must be more fuel for Martin's grudge against the Sedgwicks.

"What about Will?"

Ben's fingers tightened around his mug of cider. "It's rather hard to say. His letters . . . meander. But I've had letters from Percival and Francis." Ben's youngest brothers were both training to become solicitors, no thanks to their father.

His father furrowed his brow, as if trying to recall who Percival and Francis were and why they mattered. Ben resisted the urge to draw a family tree.

"At any rate, most of your children are doing well."

"Debatable," his father said, frowning. "I still don't like this marriage."

"Happily, it isn't up to you." Ben didn't need his father's approval, and in fact was fairly certain that this father's disapproval in itself constituted a reason to go forward with any plan.

The sun was lower in the sky but still shining brightly as Ben made his way down the hill. He bypassed the village and headed directly to Barton Hall, and at no point during the trip down did the landscape arrange itself into something that looked manageable and orderly.

CHAPTER EIGHT

Phillip had experienced summers on all seven seas and in cities circling the globe, and very few at Barton Hall, so he was surprised that the combination of scents in the air registered in his mind as precisely what summer ought to smell like. There were roses, of course, but also other flowers the names of which he'd never bothered to learn, knowing he'd only leave before the next time they bloomed. A soft breeze blew in across the lake after wafting over fields of clover. Somewhere in there were less pretty smells—sheep and manure and sweat—but they only threw the rest of it into relief.

The sun had dipped behind the hills and the children were in the nursery, where Ned was reading aloud from a book of adventure stories that would quite possibly inspire tomorrow's mayhem. Phillip paused silently in the doorway, hesitant to make a noise, lest his presence disrupt the peace of the moment.

Sedgwick hadn't returned from wherever he went after

church. Phillip imagined him surrounded by convivial faces, sipping tea and eating biscuits, sharing tales of the ornery sea captain and the children who barely tolerated their own father. Phillip desperately hoped Walsh turned up soon. It would be a relief to share space with someone who actually liked him rather than grudgingly endured his company. The ship surgeon's presence would be a welcome reminder that Phillip belonged somewhere, that he was needed and wanted somewhere.

But one by one the children noticed him. Ned gave him the quick nod of one man to another, which Phillip solemnly returned; Peggy cracked a fraction of a smile; and Jamie waved cheerfully. These tiny scraps of acceptance felt more valuable than any prize money Phillip had ever won over the course of the war. He felt almost triumphant when they all returned to listening to the story without rejecting his presence.

Slipping from the doorway, he decided to walk to the lake. The day was still warm despite the approaching dusk, and Phillip shed his coat as soon as he reached one of the graveled paths that led towards the water. As he wended his way further down the path, he heard lapping water, a sound that might have been comfortingly similar to the sea, if not for the accompanying calls of birds he ought to be able to identify but never would.

At some point he became aware of a sound that didn't quite belong—a sort of exaggerated rustling. It could have been a cat in one of the trees lining the lakeshore, but only if it were a very large cat indeed. Then he heard what sounded like a muffled oath, and he stopped walking.

There, balanced on a branch that reached over the water, was the vicar. He had a knife between his teeth as he tugged on a rope looped over a higher branch, testing to see whether it would support his weight. Even from the ground Phillip could tell that the knot was a poor one.

"That won't do," Phillip called.

The vicar startled, dropped his knife, and nearly lost his footing. "Oh, terribly sorry about that," Sedgwick said, recovering his balance by gripping the trunk. "You probably weren't expecting to get stabbed."

"Not by you, at least," Phillip said, bending to retrieve the knife. He reached up and passed it to the vicar. "I can't say I'd be surprised to get knifed by Jamie."

"Not Jamie. Possibly Peg, but even she seems to have declared an armistice. I keep telling you, they're cheerful little souls as long as nobody makes them study."

He had obviously been right about this, so Phillip didn't argue. "What are you doing up there?"

"The children have been jumping from a branch into the lake, which, while daring, isn't as safe as I might like. I thought I'd tie a rope for them to jump from, to take them out a bit further from the lakeshore, where the water is deeper and clearer of weeds."

Phillip bit back the urge to say that the safest and most appropriate solution was for the children not to jump into the lake at all. But that wasn't an option, it seemed. And Phillip dimly remembered having jumped his own fair share of times into this very lake, although that seemed so distant in the past as to have happened to a different person. Had he actually enjoyed jumping into the lake? He must have, but that kind of joy seemed so remote, so inaccessible to his present-day self that he couldn't quite believe it. He regarded the branch. It appeared sturdy and strong. "Then what you want is a bowline knot." The vicar's knot was a slapdash affair. This was the first time in a week that Phillip had felt even slightly competent. "Here, let me up." He tossed his coat onto the grass at the base of the tree and swung himself up onto the lowest branch.

"You don't need to—" the vicar started to protest.

"It's the least—oh, damn." Phillip lost his footing, but Sedgwick caught his hand and steadied him.

Now they were face-to-face at the trunk of the tree, sharing the same branch, rather closer than Phillip had counted on when he had thought to clamber up. "A bowline knot," Phillip said, because he had to say something, and knots were as safe a topic as any, "is the most secure way of making a loop at the end of a rope, and it's easy to untie even after it's carried a load, in case the children want to move it."

"Show me how," Sedgwick said, and if there were any words in the English language guaranteed to buy an old sailor's patience, asking how to make a knot might just do the trick.

Phillip demonstrated. "See, over and under. Right over left." It was getting darker, and he doubted Sedgwick could properly see his fingers or the rope, but he seemed to be paying attention. "The only problem with this sort of knot is that it sometimes works itself loose when it isn't bearing a load, but it'll be fine if you check it before every use. Even the children could, if you showed them."

"Or you could show them," Sedgwick said. "They might like your company out here. They use the boathouse as a secret lair. Peggy's been pestering me about rowing across the lake, but I told her I wasn't fool enough to have them row me to the center of the lake only to throw the oars in and leave us all stranded."

"But maybe I would be?" he asked, smiling despite himself.

"Well, you're the nautical chap. I'll sit in the shade, saying a prayer to—oh, rats, who's the fellow who looks after mariners?" He bit his lip in a way Phillip found far too interesting. "St. Elmo!"

Phillip raised his eyebrows. "It's been a long time since I've seen the inside of a church, but I feel certain that's not how we're supposed to do things in England."

A smile played on the vicar's lips. "Don't tell anyone," he said confidingly.

"Your secrets are safe with me," Phillip responded, only realizing after he had spoken that the words had come out more seriously than he had intended. Secrets, indeed.

"You can go first," Sedgwick said.

"Pardon?"

"To try the rope."

Absolutely not. "The water will be freezing."

"And . . . ?" Sedgwick was already untying his cravat, a giddy light in his eyes.

"And I don't fancy a cold plunge."

"Then stand back while I have a go." He shucked his boots and threw them to the ground. He stood on the branch in nothing but his breeches, shirt, and braces. "Ready?"

Good God, he was really going to do this. "It's getting dark. You'll drown."

Sedgwick laughed. "I've been swimming in this lake night and day my entire life." And with that he took hold of the rope and was flying over the lake. He hit the water with a splash that reached Phillip's trousers, and even through the fabric Phillip could tell the water was icy. As he waited for Sedgwick to surface, Phillip found that he was holding his breath.

When Sedgwick finally appeared, he was smiling brightly. "The water's lovely," he said, a bald lie.

"Is it?" Phillip asked. "Then you ought to enjoy a good long swim."

"I'd feel stingy hogging all the lake to myself. Miserly. Very wrong. It's a mortal sin, I'm nearly certain. You really ought to come in and keep me from vice."

Phillip tried to keep his face stern. "I'll pray to one of your saints."

"No, you won't. I think you're an atheist. And, what's a good deal more concerning to me at this moment, a coward who's afraid of some cold water."

"I thought you said the water was lovely."

"And so it is." Sedgwick's teeth were chattering. "In a bracing way. Now come in."

If there was a way to resist this man, he hadn't found it.

Phillip unwound his cravat. He threw it and his waistcoat to the ground, hoping they didn't get too muddy to put back on later. Then he pulled his shirt over his head.

"I didn't realize it was to be that sort of swim," Sedgwick said, and the overt flirtatiousness of it nearly knocked Phillip into the water.

"I don't fancy a walk back to the house in a freezing, wet shirt," Phillip said, striving for a normal tone of voice, whatever that even was in this situation. "You'll envy me my dry clothes, just you wait."

And then, chasing an old forgotten joy and the flicker of hope that he might feel such a thing again, he dove in.

The water was freezing. Ben thought he must have gone mad to have even considered jumping in. He hadn't any intention of getting in the water, but he couldn't spend another moment on that branch flirting with Dacre. And there was no question that they were flirting. Ben might be inexperienced but he wasn't a fool. Jumping into the lake seemed his best and most dignified mode of escape, but the only thing he could do to lessen the horror of the cold was to lure Dacre in too.

Dacre surfaced beside him, dark hair slicked back from his forehead. They could both stand at this depth, but just barely. "Fuck shit bollocks," he ground out. "Bugger."

"A bit chilly?" Ben strove for a level of insouciance that wasn't possible when your teeth were rattling in your head.

"F-fuck yourself."

Ben laughed. He was too cold for proper arousal, otherwise he might take undue notice of the breadth of the captain's shoulders, the spare musculature of his upper arms and chest. And he didn't want to let his gaze linger on things he might not be able to stop himself from remembering when he was warm and dry and alone.

"Oh, that's a pity," Dacre said, and for a second Ben thought the man knew Ben's private imaginings. But his gaze was on Ben's shoulder, and Ben had the notion that he was being ogled through the water. "I was afraid that would happen."

"What?" He looked down at his chest, thinking he'd see a leech or some other underwater horror.

Dacre slid two fingers under the strap of Ben's braces and lifted the sodden fabric slightly away from Ben's body. "Too bad, really." He tugged slightly, and Ben drifted closer, his body nearly weightless under the water.

"What do you mean?" Ben whispered. He didn't know whether he hoped or feared this really was about leeches and not something entirely different.

"This," Dacre said, and brought his free hand up to Ben's shoulder, plunging Ben underwater. The last thing Ben saw before ducking beneath the frigid water was the captain's face lit with a wicked smile.

But it was better to be under the water, away from the night air that seemed to chill him even more than the water, away from tempting sights and smiles. So he stayed underwater and swam as far as he could before coming up for air. By then he was not precisely warm, but slightly less freezing.

Dacre was swimming towards him with a neat hand-over-hand stroke. "Warmer if you keep moving," he said, treading water by Ben's side.

"Bastard," Ben said without heat. He was too cold to be serious. He did the only thing a man could possibly do, which was to take hold of the captain's hard, slippery shoulders and dunk him beneath the water in return. Dacre surfaced laughing and shivering, taking his plunge as his due, as a necessary part of whatever code of retribution he had triggered by dunking Ben.

By then the sun had fully set, and their only light was a crescent moon that hung low in the sky. But the night was clear and the moon reflected off the lake, so they could see enough for safety.

Or at least they wouldn't drown. Other kinds of safety, Ben couldn't vouch for. If he spent another minute in proximity to Dacre's bare torso, he might start stroking it.

Worse, he felt like Dacre wouldn't mind.

Worse still, he felt like they'd both have a jolly time, and go happily to bed where Dacre could show Ben what he'd been missing out on during these years of celibacy, and then they could both be properly resentful and awkward in the morning. No thank you.

And then Ben would be the sort of fellow who was engaged to marry one person and went to bed with somebody else. And that would never be right. But looking over at the captain, he couldn't help but think that touching this man, seeing what happened, might carry its own kind of rightness. This wanting felt like such a part of Ben's soul that it had to mean something, had to carry with it its own kind of moral gravity.

Damn it. The icy water must have frozen his conscience. He could almost hear a line from the poem that had made his father's name, something about turning your face to beauty like a flower to the sun, and that being the only righteousness the world could ever know. Never had Ben been able to figure out what good a sentiment like that could do anyone on a day-to-day-basis. But when he saw Captain Dacre, when he watched the moonlight glint off his bare shoulders and the water drip from his dark hair, when he felt within his own chest something stir that had been asleep so very long, he thought he might know what his father had meant.

The fact that he was finally understanding his father's poetry was not, he thought, a good sign. He sighed and ran a cold-stiffened hand through his hair. The trouble always was that there was nobody to talk to about his peculiar predicament. He didn't know how to live as a man who desired other men, and he didn't have anyone to look towards for guidance.

"You look like you stepped on something suspicious." Dacre's voice pulled him out of his reverie. "Wait, did you?"

Ben felt his mouth twitch upward in the beginnings of a wry smile. "If I told you I was thinking of the Bible, would you believe me?"

A slight hesitation. "I daresay you ought to think about it sometimes. It's your job."

Ben laughed despite himself. "You say it like it's the most unsavory part of my job. As if I'm the rag collector. 'Oh, I do suppose you ought to sort through that dirty business some-times. It's your job, after all.'"

"Well, I don't think it's the *most* sordid part of your duties."

Ben smiled. He knew all the arguments against religion, had learned them at his father's knee, in fact. But he didn't want to go into that now. "I'll race you back to the shore," he said, and took off without waiting for the captain's go ahead.

Dacre won anyway, and soon they were dripping and shivering on the grass.

Ben immediately peeled off his shirt, regretting that he didn't have a dry shirt to put on. "You were right about the shirt." He made for the boathouse, thinking he could at least find one of the blankets the children had stowed there.

"I have a lot of experience jumping into cold water," the captain said, following him towards the shelter. "Usually you want to be as naked as possible, but . . ."

"But?"

"I felt like it would be a good idea to keep on as much clothing as possible tonight." He fell silent, and the moment stretched out dangerously. "We'd better have a couple layers of fabric between us at all times, vicar." On the last word, the door to the boathouse snapped shut, and Ben was very aware of how there was very little of anything between them now. They stood inches apart, bare chested in the gloom and seclu-sion of the boathouse.

Ben felt his chest tighten. Dacre's admission of desire was uncharted territory for him, and he didn't know how to re-spond. He settled for irony, and knew it to be a cheap substitute for sincerity. "You fear my roving hands," he intoned. "My reputation as a libertine precedes me."

The captain's huff of laughter was barely audible, mingled as it was with the soft sounds of night birds and rippling water. "Not precisely. How on earth did a man like you wind up a vicar?" The way he spoke the words wasn't quite a question. He didn't expect Ben to supply a reasonable answer; he asked the question because he didn't think there was a reasonable answer, and Ben wasn't in the right frame of mind to justify his choices.

"Do you know, you're the second person I've spoken to today who said much the same thing."

"Good God, if you have conversations like this more than once a day, I'm surprised you don't have a reputation as a libertine."

Now Ben laughed in earnest, and it did something to ease the tension that was building in his chest. "Not precisely like this."

"Good," the captain said, and it was a rumble. When he stepped closer, Ben didn't move away, because by that point he felt well beyond any need to pretend that he didn't want Captain Dacre within touching distance. They were so close Ben could hear the water dripping from Dacre's hair, could hear the other man's breathing, and any reason Ben might have had to step away seemed very distant and abstract.

It was dark in the boathouse, too dark to communicate by glances or gestures. That left only speaking or frank touches, and Ben didn't think he was capable of the former. He had always been better with his actions than with his words anyway. So he took his hand and stroked his fingertips down Dacre's forearm, learning the sinews and hairs by touch. He heard a sharp indrawn breath, then Dacre's hands were on him, tugging his hips close.

When their lips met they both went still, and Ben had the fleeting impression that Dacre was more startled than Ben was himself. Ben wasn't startled at all, come to think. Dacre's mouth felt right on his, as if Ben had been waiting all his life to taste the stern line of this man's lips, as if this was what Ben's mouth was for and he was only now realizing it. He slid his hands from the captain's shoulders to the lean muscles of his upper arms, pressed his own bare chest against the other man's, gave an experimental lick along the seam of the captain's mouth, and it all felt right. He was waiting, he realized, for this to feel wrong, for it to feel shameful or traitorous, but it only felt good, and safe, and honest.

Dacre made a noise at the back of this throat, a sound of capitulation that was somewhere between a moan and a groan, and then he was kissing Ben in earnest. One of his hands was at the back of Ben's head, holding him steady for Dacre's devouring kisses.

"Oh, damn it," the captain said against the sensitive skin of his neck. "Sedgwick. Are you—"

Ben cut him off by taking his mouth in another kiss. Dacre steered him so Ben's back was against the rough wood wall of the boathouse, one of Dacre's arms braced on the wall beside him. There was nothing but the wall behind him, Dacre a solid mass in front of him, and the desire growing deep within his belly.

"Won't do," Dacre breathed. "Splinters." And then they were on the floor, side by side, trousers discarded and a blanket beneath them.

It was all so much easier than Ben could have imagined. Dacre's hands exploring, waiting a moment for Ben to object, then grasping, stroking. Ben might have thought he'd find it strange, maybe overwhelming, to be touched so intimately by another person. It was neither of those things, and that itself was surprising. Dacre's hands felt like they belonged on Ben's body, and when Ben thought to return the favor, fumbling with the backward logic of another person's body, his hands felt perfectly right there as well. His fingers wrapped around Dacre's shaft as his face nestled into Dacre's shoulder, a carpenter's joints fitting together perfectly, as if this had always been the plan for their bodies.

They were quiet except for necessary whispers. *Yes. Shh. Please. I have you.* Ben tipped over the edge into bliss and felt Dacre follow, and all he could think was that it had all been so easy, so right, and that it would have been a good deal simpler if that hadn't been the case.

Chapter Nine

The morning post brought a letter in Phillip's sister's acrobatically spiraling hand. Usually, at the cost of a headache and a good deal of patience, Phillip could make out enough of a letter to pretend to understand its contents. Ernestine's penmanship, however, refused to stay still. The letters jumped around the page and twirled out of his brain before he could corral them into anything resembling words. By the time he gave up, he had worn the paper soft around the edges.

Thinking to employ one of his usual tricks to enlist help, he set off in search of the land steward or an upper servant. This would conveniently take him into the bowels of the house where he would be unlikely to run into Sedgwick. He hadn't been able to slot the previous evening's events into the category of convenient pleasure. Their kisses had been too hungry, their caresses too gratuitous, their shared pleasure too pregnant with feeling for Phillip to be able to carry on in the way he generally did—which was to ignore that anything had happened in the first place.

Somewhere along the way, his thoughts muddled by memories of the previous night, he must have missed a turn, because he found himself in the kitchens, where the cook, her cheeks red with exertion and emotion, seemed to be taking out her frustrations on a piece of dough.

"Never heard of putting wine in a suet pudding, no matter what they do in London or anywhere else," she muttered. "My mum worked five years in the kitchens at the Priory and never saw nobody put wine in any suet pudding." She punctuated each sentence with a slap of the dough onto the worktable. She was plump and rosy, her cap and apron equally clean and white and starchy. Phillip realized he was being confronted with a variety of human he hadn't encountered in years: an Englishwoman in her kitchen. He had summoned the cook the day of his arrival to order that the children be sent to bed without supper, but he hadn't yet been to the kitchens.

Phillip cleared his throat and the woman jumped backward, nearly dropping her abused ball of dough.

"Ooh," she said, dragging the sound out to several syllables of vexation. "It's like working in a madhouse, people coming in at all hours, stealing your pies and telling you how to make your puddings."

"I do beg your pardon," Phillip said, feeling genuinely remorseful. He knew better than to interrupt servants at their work. "I'm—"

"If you're after a taste of the damson tart, yonder pie-thieving hellion—" she gestured with a floury hand towards the garden "—has already run off with it." Phillip gathered that "yonder hellion" was meant to refer to Jamie. Her imperious air made sense: this was her domain, and she ruled it with an authority as absolute as his over the *Patroclus*. He knew a rush of fellow feeling for this young woman whose sensibilities about puddings had been challenged. "And what I say is that if plain suet pudding was good enough for Sir Humphrey, and he a baronet, then it's good enough for you."

"Quite," Phillip replied in what he hoped was a conciliatory tone. "Mrs. Morris, is it? Were you Sir Humphrey's cook?"

She looked at him as if he were dim. "He's been dead these three years, and if you think I look old enough to have been his cook, then it's only because the last two months working here have tried my soul, they have." She was, Phillip realized, scarcely more than a girl. Twenty at the utmost. He wondered if the "Mrs." was simply there by custom or if there could possibly be a Mr. Morris on the premises. "My da owns the Blue Boar in Keswick, don't he. And my mum was Lady Easterbrook's cook before she married my da. If you want puddings finer than what was good enough for Lady Easterbrook and what's served at the Blue Boar, you can hire a grand London cook, and she'll quit after two days once she realizes she's cooking for a pack of bedlamites."

"That won't be necessary," Phillip said hastily.

"And that old witch Mrs. Winston can keep her ideas about suet pudding—"

"Quite," Phillip agreed, trying to forestall any further complaints on this topic. "Last night's mutton was most competently prepared," he said.

She stared at him. "That supposed to be a compliment? All right, then. Thank you. I suppose." Then, in a more agreeable tone, "You can tell Mr. Sedgwick I'm making those lemon biscuits he fancies. Mr. Sedgwick, for all he's a vicar, knows how to keep the twins out of mischief. Or at least too much mischief. Stands to reason, since he's one of that old lunatic's children."

Phillip shook his head in confusion. "I don't follow."

"His father is the poet fellow who lives on the other side of Buttermere. Something Grange."

Phillip had spent so little time at Barton Hall that it took him a while to figure out the girl's meaning. "Good God. Alton Sedgwick is the vicar's father? Didn't he have two—" He cut himself off, realizing he couldn't finish that sentence around a woman.

The girl had no such scruples. "Two wives!" she said in obvious delight. "He was actually married to Sedgwick's mother, I think, but there was a French lady too. Mrs. Winston says he's a very respected poet, for all his peculiarities," she said, in the tone of a person who doesn't care overmuch for poets, respected or otherwise. "Mrs. Winston also says he's settled into a quiet sort of life these days and hasn't gotten into anything too shocking lately." She deftly turned the dough into a bowl and covered it with a towel before setting it near the hearth. "And the vicar is a good man," she said, pointing her finger at Phillip as if he had suggested otherwise. "Never heard a whisper against him. He's going to marry Miss Crawford before the end of the summer, and she's as respectable a young lady as you'll find within twenty leagues of Kirkby Barton."

"Miss Crawford," Phillip repeated. "I hadn't realized he was to marry." But of course he was. Vicars tended to arrive on the scene already married, in Phillip's limited experience. He shouldn't be surprised. Perhaps Sedgwick liked men and women equally—it happened, he knew. Even McCarthy had been known to bed women when they were in port.

"She was a niece, or maybe a cousin, of old Sir Humphrey. He was friends with the vicar's father and took a shine to Mr. Sedgwick when he was a lad. Mrs. Winston says Sir Humphrey saw which way the wind blew and fixed Mr. Sedgwick up with his post at St. Aelred's to make sure that his niece would marry a man with a decent income."

"Ah," Phillip said, his voice strained. "An advantageous match."

"I suppose," the cook said with a shrug, as if she didn't deign to comment on the merits of the vicar's marriage. "If you ask me, none of the Easterbrooks are the sort to give away anything without a fair price, but it's not my place to judge, or that's what Mrs. Winston says. Whichever way it happened, Mr. Sedgwick has St. Aelred's and Miss Crawford has Mr. Sedgwick, and now you know as much as I do."

Phillip tried to take all this in. "While I'm here," he said casually, "would you mind reading me this letter?" He had noticed a book open on the worktable, likely a cookery book, so he knew the girl could read at least a little. "My spectacles have gone missing and I don't want to waste a day going into Carlisle to be fitted for a new pair when the old ones might yet turn up." He was talking too much. Better to hand the paper over to the cook, so that's what he did.

The girl took Ernestine's fine paper in her plump, floury hands and read the letter aloud with only the slightest hesitancy over some of the more florid language. The letter was, as Phillip expected, largely irrelevant—a stream of apologies for having fled Barton Hall in advance of his arrival, mingled with a stream of invectives against the children's wicked ways. He might as well have tossed it into the fire unread, but of course he couldn't have known that.

Phillip felt old familiar tendrils of shame curl around his insides at the sight of this girl, a common servant, the daughter of an innkeeper and a cook, mastering a skill he hadn't and couldn't and never would. On his ship, he knew how to arrange things so he'd never be called upon to read—he dictated, delegated, and when all else failed, simply ordered someone to read for him. Here, he felt like he'd be exposed at any moment as a fraud, not a real gentleman, not worthy of this house.

Those wisps of shame, flimsy and easily brushed aside on board a ship, took hold of him inside this house, the place where his father had made it all too clear that Phillip, illiterate and uneducable, was about as unworthy an heir as could be imagined. At sea, there was the comforting reminder that the Royal Navy did not promote fools or idiots to the rank of captain; the mere fact of his position was a reminder that he was competent, and there was always a task he could complete in order to reaffirm his value. Here, he had nothing to stop him slipping into a relentless eddy of drear and doubt.

He had a moment of landlocked panic, as if walls of earth

and stone were closing in on him, and he desperately wanted to get back to sea.

Ben was stupidly surprised that the world was precisely the same as he had left it. The previous night, for all it threatened to set him on a course that was new and unknown, hadn't changed the world outside his window.

He hadn't thought something that felt so gentle and right could change everything. Twelve hours earlier he had been able to at least pretend that he was still clinging to all his old hopes and dreams. Twelve hours ago he at least thought himself an honest man.

Now, though. Now he was ruined.

Now he knew what it was to truly want something, to truly want someone, and he had to figure out how to live with that knowledge.

But until then, there was work to do, and he thanked God for it.

The lambs needed shearing, and Ned was determined to learn as much about the process as he could. Strictly speaking, Ben didn't need to be there, but the twins wanted to watch and Ben, for all he had spent his life in proximity to sheep, never got tired of watching the lambs. Alice always told him he had the aesthetic sensibilities of an infant: he liked summer, and baby animals, and fruit tarts. He rather thought there was nothing not to like there, but he didn't doubt that Alice's tastes were more refined.

The thought of Alice pierced through the pleasantness of

the morning with an icy sharpness. It wasn't guilt that he felt, but the uneasy certainty that he needed to speak with Alice. Either he needed to tell her that they couldn't marry, or he needed to find a way to confess to her the truth of what their marriage would be. Because now he knew what it wouldn't be—it wouldn't be breathless, desperate, heated touches. It wouldn't be the mad rush to get hands inside clothes, to get lips onto skin.

Jamie came and sat on the fence beside him, and picked up a conversation they had ended some hours earlier. Ben hadn't the faintest idea what the boy was going on about, but it had to do with numbers and it was unintelligible. Unintelligible, but consistently so, which made Ben think his failure to understand was a lack of comprehension on his part, rather than a lack of sense on Jamie's.

This was the only flaw in his scheme to persuade Captain Dacre to have the children educated at home. Jamie really couldn't go to school—not where he'd be ostracized and shamed for not being able to read. But an ordinary tutor might not be able to teach him more mathematics than what the boy already knew. Ben vaguely remembered a mathematically inclined scholar who had been a frequent visitor of his father's at Fellside Grange. He had spoken of a blind mathematician. If the blind could learn and excel at mathematics, then it stood to reason so could Jamie.

Perhaps his father's friend would know of a tutor who could work within Jamie's abilities. But Ben shrank from the idea of deliberately bringing one of his father's set into his current orbit. They tended to arrive on the scene with grand ideas, expensive habits, and no sense of who was to pay the butcher or what to do when the roof sprang a leak. One winter they had gotten snowed in—Alton Sedgwick, his five sons, and Sir Humphrey Easterbrook. His father and Easterbrook had spent the duration of the storm planning some kind of utopian community in the Argentine; before the snow melted, Easterbrook had pledged a sum of money to the founding of this delusional paradise. Ben, who spent that same time quietly panicking about dwindling rations and hungry brothers, had hardly been able to contain his wrath at men who thought they could plan an entire village but could not lay in supplies to weather a storm. However, it had been Easterbrook who paid Ben's fees at university, and Easterbrook who appointed Ben as vicar of St. Aelred's, so Ben tended to bite his tongue on the subject of men who spent too freely and without sense. In truth, a part of him suspected that a man with more sense might have balked at the notion of one of Alton Sedgwick's sons being a clergyman.

Ben himself ought to have recognized it as a mad idea. But he had dreamt of being a clergyman the way other boys might have dreamt of being cavalry officers. He had grown up in genteel chaos and wanted nothing more than a chance to bring peace and order to the world around him. Peace, Ben knew, was a series of small things, each insignificant but together making landmarks for a life: his parishioners knew that when they were sick, he would visit, that when they were needy, he would find a way to help. Marriages and funerals, morning prayer and evening prayer, all a recognition that they were here for a greater reason. This, too, was peace, and he believed he served God and his flock by bringing it about.

He dragged his thoughts to the present: woolly lambs needing shearing, a boy who needed a teacher, three children and a father who needed a little help trusting one another. He could restore order in these small ways.

"You look like you ate a green apple."

Ben spun to see his father standing in the dappled light of the Barton Hall barnyard. "What are you doing here?" This was hardly cordial, but Alton Sedgwick seldom left Fellside Grange. Today he wore a large straw hat that might have been borrowed from a local plowman, or might have been imported at great cost from someplace like Constantinople. With Alton Sedgwick, it was never easy to say.

"I needed to meet whoever was responsible for the gooseberry tart."

"Mrs. Winston? She's my housekeeper, so I daresay you'll find her at the vicarage."

"Your housekeeper," he repeated, as if this were an unfamiliar concept. Which, to be fair, it might have been, given Alton Sedgwick's meager experience with the management of normal households. "There were currants in the hedgerow behind the grange, so I gathered some for your Mrs. Winston." He indicated a basket that dangled from his arm. There was also a bottle of wine in the crook of his elbow. Mrs. Winston's gooseberry custard tart must have made an impression for Alton Sedgwick to have come this distance and bearing gifts, no less.

With that, Ben's father absently tapped the brim of his hat and carried on down the hill.

"Wait!" Ben called. "I need to ask for the direction of that mathematician friend of yours."

It was his duty to help the Dacres. And something more than duty, something like fondness combined with responsibility and multiplied by some arcane mathematical process that only Jamie would understand. And if asking for his father's help was what Ben needed to do to help the Dacres, then that's what he'd do, however little he liked it.

CHAPTER TEN

Sedgwick was an absolute rotter. He didn't even have the decency to make himself scarce after that episode in the boathouse. For two days—forty-eight bloody hours, damn it—he dogged Phillip like a shadow, like a rash, like a bloody plague. Every time Phillip opened his eyes, there was the vicar, all freckles and smiles, as if they hadn't had their hands inside one another's clothes, as if they hadn't kissed one another like their lives depended on it. It had taken all Phillip's training and self-command to summon up the necessary chilliness. The worst part was that occasionally he'd catch Sedgwick looking at him as if he were thinking of what they had done together, like he couldn't even do them both the courtesy of pretending it hadn't happened.

"How would you like to visit some tenants?" Phillip asked the twins. Sedgwick was blessedly absent and Ned was off helping with a lamb who had gotten caught in brambles. "You can bring that dog," he added to Peggy. "And perhaps we can persuade Ned to read us *Robinson Crusoe* when we get back," he said to Jamie. He was learning what currency he could use to curry favor with them and it seemed to be working.

The children agreed, and they set off in the direction of the tenant farmers the steward had suggested Phillip visit. They were an elderly couple who were no longer able to work their land as well as they once had. The steward suggested they lease part of the land to the farmer whose land adjoined theirs, but the couple hadn't made a decision. Phillip intended to let them know that they'd have the use of his solicitor to look over any paperwork that would be required in the lease.

"We forgot the jam," Peggy said when they were about halfway there.

"Jam?" Phillip asked.

"Whenever we visit people with Mr. Sedgwick, we take baskets of jam and cheese," Jamie explained.

Too late, Phillip remembered that this was indeed proper protocol. "Will you go back and get it? With my thanks to Mrs. Morris, of course," he added, thinking of the rather fearsome cook, "and meet me at the Farleighs' farm?" It wasn't far, and he wasn't sure if this was a reasonable task for a pair of eight-year-olds. He didn't know what young people were expected to do when they weren't on board a ship. But this farm was along a single lane from Barton Hall, and according to Sedgwick, the children had spent months roaming freely around the countryside, so he decided to use his judgment and send them on the errand.

"Yes!" the twins cried at once.

"You'll need to keep the dog," Peggy added. "He always tries to eat the basket. And I don't think his leg is good enough yet to make the trip twice."

Phillip agreed and they set off in their separate directions.

When he reached the farm, Phillip tied the dog to a fence post. The dog didn't look too happy about it. "It's only for a few minutes," Phillip explained. "And then the twins will be back and I'm sure they'll have something good for you to eat."

"That you, Captain Dacre?" came a voice from the door. He turned to see Mrs. Farleigh, the wife of the farmer he had come to speak to. She was gaunt and slightly stooped; as far as Phillip remembered, she had always been old but now she was ancient. "I heard you were back." She didn't look entirely pleased to see him. Her hands were fisted in her apron.

The dooryard contained none of the usual bustle Phillip was accustomed to seeing at even the smallest farmsteads. A few chickens wandered by an overgrown vegetable garden. The gate had rot off a small pen, perhaps explaining why there was no longer any pig in residence.

After delivering a civil greeting, Phillip said, "I came to speak with Mr. Farleigh about drawing up papers for the lease of your land."

She didn't move out of the doorway, and Phillip thought he saw her forehead wrinkle beneath her large white cap. "He's in bed, and there's no chance of his getting out of it, not in this state. But I'll tell him you called." She took a step backward into the house.

This, Phillip understood, was a dismissal. "What I have

to say is very much to his advantage," he called. He saw the paint peeling from the door, the torn seam of the woman's sleeve, and knew they could use any extra money that could be scraped together. And if what the steward had said was correct and Mr. Farleigh wasn't likely to live much longer, it was imperative that they get matters settled as soon as possible. "If I could talk to him for just a few moments. I promise not to overtax him."

"Tax, indeed. Oh, you don't know the half of it." With these cryptic words, she stepped aside with obvious reluctance and gestured inside the house as if to say that Phillip could have his way if he insisted.

"I assure you," he repeated, "this agreement would be very much to your benefit."

Her rheumy eyes looked skeptically at him. "I don't suppose I have any reason to believe you mean to bleed us dry," she said, "but that's what seems to be happening lately."

Ah, so that's what this was about. "I have no intention of treating my tenants as Easterbrook does his," Phillip said. "You have the leasehold of this property for another ten years, according to the land steward. So even if I were inclined to raise your rent, which I am not, I couldn't."

The old woman's mouth twisted into a grimace. "My brother had another five years left on his leasehold, and that's what he told Sir Martin's land agent when he came to demand a rent increase. Sent the land agent away with a flea in his ear. Next he knows, his grandson is brought before the magistrate for poaching."

Phillip's eyebrows shot up at this mention of poaching. "Surely that's a coincidence," he protested.

"Oh, come now. You know better than that." She shook her head. "Sit here by the fire until the vicar comes out, then you can go in."

"The vicar?" Phillip asked stupidly.

"Aye, Mr. Sedgwick is here to do whatever he does with invalids. Pray, I suppose. Mr. Farleigh is always in a cheerful state when the vicar leaves. So sit by the fire and make yourself comfortable, I suppose."

She went into the kitchen and shut the door loudly behind her. Phillip had no interest in sitting by the fire. It was a warm day and the parlor was stuffy and close. But he sat anyway, because he'd be damned if he'd disobey a woman as old as Mrs. Farleigh. As he sat back against a chair that smelled of must and long-dead lavender, he heard Sedgwick's voice. He knew he shouldn't lean closer to hear, but he did so anyway.

Sedgwick's voice was low, and Phillip couldn't quite make out what he was saying. But the rhythm of the man's speech suggested a prayer. Or, was he singing? A hymn, then, perhaps. It was an unwelcome reminder that the man he had touched and kissed was part of an institution that disapproved of everything they had done and everything Phillip most wanted to do.

Then Phillip heard a phrase that didn't make sense in either a prayer or a hymn. Something about a blacksmith and his forge? What the devil was Sedgwick up to in there? He leaned even closer, so his ear was all but pressed against the rough wood of the door. Now he could make out individual words.

"Six times did his iron by vigorous heating grow soft in her forge in a minute or so . . ."

It was a bawdy drinking song. He clapped a hand over his mouth to stop the shocked laughter that threatened to burble out.

"And as often was hardened, still beating and beating, but each time it softened it hardened more slow."

Phillip managed to get outside before he was overcome by laughter. Then, leaning against the crumbling stone of the woodshed, he laughed until his sides hurt and he thought he might be sick. The dog pulled at his rope and whimpered, plainly thinking something was deeply wrong with this human. He bent forward, bracing his hands on his thighs, and tried to catch his breath. He hadn't laughed in so long, he felt out of practice.

"Dare I even ask what's gotten into you out here?" It was Sedgwick, of course, hands in his pockets and an amused expression on his face.

"Well you might. Did my ears deceive me or were you truly serenading that poor old man with a song in highly questionable taste?"

"Oh dear." He looked decidedly sheepish. "Nobody was meant to hear that."

"I should damned well think not." Phillip straightened up. "'A Lusty Young Smith,' good God." He started a fresh peal of laughter and had to wipe tears from his eyes. "'He's always in such a cheerful state when the vicar leaves,'" he managed, quoting the old man's wife. "I can see why."

Sedgwick frowned. "Poor old Mr. Farleigh hasn't much time left, I'm afraid, and if bawdy songs amuse him, then who am I to be disobliging?"

"I thought you were praying," Phillip sputtered.

Sedgwick was silent for a beat. "Mr. Farleigh doesn't go in much for that sort of thing. He says he prays in his own way and doesn't need my assistance. But he likes being reminded of his youth. The last of his friends died years ago, and he hasn't anyone to reminisce with. I don't feel the songs do anyone harm. Now, if you'll excuse me, I have a few other people to visit this morning." He turned away.

Realizing that Sedgwick was serious, and that he had interpreted Phillip's laughter as scorn, Phillip tried to compose himself. "I didn't mean to mock you." He took a step nearer and put a restraining hand on Sedgwick's sleeve. "You were kind, Sedgwick. I'm sure you did the old man good."

"I try to do what's right." Sedgwick looked pained. It was such an uncharacteristic expression for the man that Phillip was momentarily taken aback. He instinctively brought his hand up to touch the vicar's face. Sedgwick's eyes went wide, but he didn't pull away. His lips parted a little and Phillip felt his own heart speed up. They were alone in a corner of the neglected farmyard, invisible to any passersby, but Phillip glanced hastily over his shoulder anyway.

"You're so good," Phillip murmured. "So good." He pushed a lock of hair off Sedgwick's forehead, wanting to see his entire face, needing to watch for any signs of hesitation or distaste. Nothing. Sedgwick's face was open, willing. Wanting. Phillip threaded his fingers through Sedgwick's hair, bringing his hand to cup the back of his head. They were only a few inches apart, and almost the same height, and all it would have taken was a single fraction of a step forward and they would be kissing. Not even a step, just a sway, a mere leaning in the right direction. Phillip felt like it was taking more effort to *not* bend towards Sedgwick than it would take to simply give in.

With his hand still threaded in Sedgwick's hair, Phillip leaned forward, let his lips brush against Sedgwick's. Just that, nothing more. He felt a puff of air come from the other man's mouth, the faintest sigh, and then Sedgwick's body was against his own, and Phillip felt something terribly like relief.

As Dacre's lips brushed across his own, a ripple of awareness spread down Ben's body. He didn't know how a mere whisper of a touch could send him spiraling into a world where he cared about nothing but the need to have this man in his arms. Instinctively, he touched Dacre's cheek, feeling the rasp of stubble against his fingertips, and heard a groan come from the other man. Then Dacre's arms were wrapped around him, his mouth heavy and hot on his own.

Their time in the boathouse had been about pleasure, satisfaction. In broad daylight and with no possibility of release, their kisses were slower and softer and infinitely more dangerous. Ben could have stayed like that forever, could let his life collapse into a shape the precise dimension of his body and Dacre's pressed together. His world was Dacre's jaw beneath his fingertips, Dacre's steadying hand on his own waist. Everything else could slip away—St. Aelred's, Alice, all of it. He'd happily wave goodbye to duty, to order, to everything he had ever wanted, because this was more, and better, and true.

The starkness of this realization made him pull away and stare at Dacre in dismay. He could not allow this to happen. He couldn't plunge into disorder; he couldn't let the chaos of his youth find him in the idyllic peace of his village, surmounting his duty to a dying parishioner.

Some of his horror must have shown on his face, because Dacre dropped his hands to his sides and stepped away.

"Forgive me," the captain muttered, plainly misunderstanding the cause of Ben's anguish. "I thought you . . . I didn't—"

"No," Ben said quickly, trying to explain that the kiss hadn't been unwanted, but merely catastrophic. He reached a hand out to touch Dacre's arm before realizing that additional contact was the last thing they needed. He hastily snatched his hand back and saw the hurt flash in Dacre's eye. "No, dash it. That isn't—"

They were interrupted by a cacophony of sounds. The dog was barking and Mrs. Farleigh was shouting and Jamie and Peg were racing down the lane.

Ben had never been so glad to see the Dacre children as

he was at that moment. What he needed was time. Time to figure out how to make sense of this world he now found himself in, how to do what was right and good.

It took about three-quarters of an hour for Ben and the twins to unload the hamper into Mrs. Farleigh's kitchen while Dacre spoke with Mr. Farleigh, and then another several minutes to collect the dog, who had gotten off his rope and was attempting to menace a pair of bored-looking chickens.

That ought to have been enough time for Ben to get his thoughts in order, to weed out any stray impulses and mad desires that didn't belong in the life he wanted. But that was just the trouble—the more he thought, the clearer it was that he didn't want a life that didn't include soft kisses and steady hands, whispered praise and shared touches.

CHAPTER ELEVEN

Phillip was stationed at his monstrous fraud of a desk. It was the size of a dinghy and it was beyond Phillip's imaginings why anybody needed such acreage on which to write their letters. He was determined to puzzle through his correspondence, but so far had only managed a single paragraph of a letter from the naval yard detailing the progress that was being made with the *Patroclus*. The clerk's handwriting was a marvel of restraint, and Phillip could understand enough to grasp that the repairs were continuing on schedule, more or less. But his head was pounding, and there was nobody about to trick into reading the rest of his correspondence, so when he looked up and saw Sedgwick in the doorway, his annoyance was tempered by relief at having an excuse to stop reading. He stacked all the papers neatly and dropped them into a drawer.

"How can I help you, Sedgwick?" Phillip asked frostily. *Go away*, he wanted to plead. The way Sedgwick had looked at him after that ill-advised kiss had been like a bucket of icy water in Phillip's face. He had felt guilty, sordid, unworthy. And now the man was back to torture him some more? It really was most unfair.

Sedgwick ought to be safely tucked in his bed, or saying his prayers, or visiting the drawing room of the lady he intended to marry. He was going to go off and have a nice, pleasant, safe life. That was all well and good, even if the idea of Sedgwick living at the vicarage with a faceless wife and a passel of towheaded children made him feel vaguely ill. A dalliance with Phillip would likely plunge the man into some kind of moral panic. Phillip didn't want to be the subject of anyone's penance or regrets. He would never again enter into an arrangement where convenience outweighed honesty, and he didn't know precisely where he stood. His heart wasn't cut out for it.

Sedgwick had his hands stuffed in his pockets and he was shifting foot to foot. "Well," he said, "I came to talk about Jamie."

"What about him?" It came out harsher than Phillip had intended. "Is he all right?" The lad had seemed fine at dinner—Sedgwick had led him through the usual mealtime mathematic acrobatics while Phillip tried not to look at Sedgwick.

"Oh, quite. I wanted to speak with you about hiring a tutor." He pulled a folded square of paper from his coat pocket. "I wrote to an acquaintance of mine." He was holding the paper between two fingers as if he weren't quite sure what to do with it. "Well, really a friend of my father's. He's a mathematician in Edinburgh. I thought Jamie might enjoy seeing what can be done with his talent but it isn't my strong suit, you see. And I hoped this friend of my father's could point us in the direction of a suitable tutor."

Phillip frowned. "Won't he learn that in school?" Wasn't that the point? Phillip was spending time with the children so they would ultimately trust his decision to send them to school. School was undoubtedly the best place for them in his absence. That way they could be with other children and, well, learn the things children needed to learn in order to belong in the world.

"Jamie's abilities are a bit . . . varied from those of other children his age. Perhaps school would be . . . tedious for him." Sedgwick was lying. Phillip didn't know about what, and he couldn't imagine why, but the man didn't have a face made for deceit. He hoped the vicar didn't make a habit of playing cards, because he'd be fleeced by anyone with the slightest bit of cunning. "I didn't want to send the letter without your permission." He stepped forward and placed the paper on Phillip's desk.

Phillip shook his head in frustration and leaned back, as if to distance himself from the paper. "Just do as you see fit."

"Oh." Sedgwick looked deflated. "Well, then." He made no move to leave. "I thought you might take an interest. But I see that I misjudged."

Phillip sighed. "You have the wrong end of the stick. I trust your judgment, that's all. If you think Jamie needs a mathematics tutor, then I agree."

"Oh." The vicar looked taken aback, but not displeased.

"You look as if you expected an argument. I keep telling you that I'm not a monster."

"I'm well aware that you're not a monster." Sedgwick's eyes opened wide and his cheeks darkened. For a moment Phillip saw a flash of temper in the young vicar's face, something he had caught a glimpse of that first day when Phillip had grabbed his arm in the hall. "If you think that I'd do . . . what we did . . . with someone I thought a monster, you're grossly mistaken."

"Go to bed, Sedgwick. I can't figure out what you're still doing here."

"Can't you?" Sedgwick said, his voice low with anger. Phillip's cock pricked up in a way it surely ought not to have.

"This may amaze you, Sedgwick, but I can't be bothered to imagine the secret workings of your brain. All I know is that you've been following me about like a stray dog for two days, and then when I—today at the farm, you looked at me like I had slapped you."

"Well, I'll spare you the hassle, then." Sedgwick shut the door, and Phillip's mouth went dry. "I'm here—like a stray dog, very flattering, I thank you—because I enjoy your company, you infuriating man. I like you, and I thought we were becoming friends, and—"

"The sort of friends who grope one another in boathouses and behind woodsheds? The sort of friends who imagine one another while bringing themselves off? Because I most definitely did that this afternoon." Twice, in fact. And once the night before.

Sedgwick's cheeks went even redder, and his lips parted

slightly. Phillip forced himself not to look away even though his breeches were growing tighter at the thought of what he'd like to do to those lips.

"I did that, too, you know, but that's neither here nor there—"

It took Phillip's brain a moment to catch up with his cock. "You thought of me while tossing yourself off?"

"Yes, but I can't see—"

"Is that a typical mark of friendship for you? The boathouses and the wanking and so forth? Because I'll have you know it isn't for me, Sedgwick."

"Don't be absurd." The vicar's mouth was caught between a scowl and a smile and Phillip desperately wanted to kiss it. "But just because I want to touch you doesn't mean I need to." He sounded gratifyingly uncertain about that.

"That's absolutely right it doesn't," Phillip growled. "I haven't the slightest interest in going to bed with someone who's going to have to do penance for it afterward. Rather ruins the moment."

"Penance," Sedgwick repeated slowly, as if he had never heard of the term. "You thought . . ." He shook his head, and when he spoke again it was in a deliberately light tone. "We don't much go in for penance in the Church of England. I have a whole pamphlet you can read on the topic." There was a twinkle in his eye, damn him. He was about to laugh, of all things.

"You can keep your blasted pamphlets. What I mean is—"

"I know what you meant. And don't worry about penance. That's . . . not a concern."

"Isn't it, though? If not actual penance, then guilt. Shame. I won't have any part of your sin, Sedgwick."

"You can leave it to me to decide what I think a sin is. Everybody's a damned theologian on this topic. I'm so tired of it. If we can all quietly agree that eating pork and shaving aren't sinful, I don't see why we can't extend that same grace to men like us."

Phillip had never seen Sedgwick this angry. His body was taut with emotion and his cheeks were flushed. Phillip had the distinct impression that if Sedgwick hadn't been carefully controlling himself, Phillip would already have a black eye.

Phillip's cock was already hard. His cock had terrible, terrible judgment, but that was nothing new. He got to his feet, almost without thinking about what he was doing.

"Don't bring me into it," Phillip said, perversely trying to egg Sedgwick on, trying to see what lay on the other side of this hot anger. "I'm not ashamed of who I am or who I want to touch. And I don't believe in sin."

Sedgwick waved his hand in frustrated dismissal. "I tell you, there's no shame between us." He gestured between their two bodies. "Nor any sin."

"Oh?" Phillip was playing with fire, and he knew it. "Then what is there?" He made the same gesture. It was a barefaced challenge, a shameless dare, and they both knew it. Sedgwick's eyes glinted with acknowledgment. He could no more ignore the challenge than he could have avoided jumping in the lake a few nights ago.

Sedgwick shook his head, as if in disbelief at what he was about to do, and then his mouth crooked up in the barest hint of a smile.

He turned the key in the lock and stepped forward.

They were standing so close Ben could almost feel the heat rolling off Dacre's body. He ought to leave, or at least come up with any excuse to put some distance between them. But he knew he wasn't going to. He had known since walking into this room what was likely to happen, and he knew he wasn't going to try to stop it.

He had spent days trying to ignore the awareness that flared between him and Dacre whenever they were in the same room. He had walked the circumference of the lake, half in prayer and half in a knotted web of thoughts. And he had decided that it was wrong to ignore what he was feeling. He couldn't ignore it any more than he could ignore his faith in God. It felt like denying a core part of himself. He believed that it would be here, with Dacre, with a chance to be honest about who he was and what he wanted, that he'd figure out what his next steps must be.

He took a deep, steadying breath. Dacre still had the challenging look in his eye from when he had asked—dared—Ben to say what lay between them.

"You know better than I do. You tell me," Ben said, with more courage than he felt. "Tell me what there is between us." That *tell me* felt like jumping into a lake that wasn't filled with mere cold water but with sea monsters and thorns and perils he couldn't even name. It wasn't a question. It was an invitation.

And Dacre knew it. His eyes opened fractionally wider, as if he had been expecting something else but was caught unawares. "Where to start," he murmured, his eyes hot on Ben's face.

"What I mean is . . ." Ben took a deep breath and searched for the words he needed. "I know about what you called 'convenient friendships.' I don't want that." He had thrown himself into this lake of dangerous desire, body and soul, and he didn't want to be the only one there.

Dacre stood perfectly still, his hand arrested halfway to Ben's arm. "No?" The word came out on a breath.

"No," Ben said firmly, and felt Dacre's hand settle solidly on his arm. "If I just wanted to bring myself off and then feel unsatisfied afterward, I could do that on my own. Tell me what it would be like if we had something else." *Something more*, he wanted to say. "I want everything." He rested his own hand on Dacre's hip, feeling the warm flesh beneath the linen of his shirt and the wool of his breeches.

Dacre groaned. "God help me, Sedgwick. When you say things like that . . ."

"When we're together it feels right. I want to go down that path and see what's there."

"With me?" It was a hoarse whisper.

"Together."

Dacre looked at him thoughtfully, as if giving his words the fullest consideration. "It's private here. We'll be safe." Ben knew that. He had locked the door himself, and he knew the servants never bothered their prickly master. "God, Sedgwick, I want to touch you."

Ben swallowed. "You've touched me already."

"I'd touch you more. Everywhere. If you let me."

"Yes," Ben breathed.

"I'd start with your hair," Dacre said. "I'd get it out of your eyes so you could watch me. I'd want you watching my every move." As he spoke, he threaded his fingers in Ben's hair, pushing it off his face and then brushing a too-gentle kiss to Ben's parted lips. He steered Ben backward, so the backs of his legs hit the desk. Ben took the hint and sat, pulling Dacre forward to stand between his parted legs.

He felt Dacre startle under his touch, but only for the merest moment. Then he wrapped his arms around Ben, like he was welcoming him, accepting him, holding him close. Their lips slid over one another's, soft and searching.

There was no hesitation. Ben knew what he wanted and he knew Dacre wanted it too. He kissed the captain with perfect conviction that this was good and true and right.

When he felt Dacre's tongue touch his lips, Ben opened up to let him in. At the first stroke of Dacre's tongue on his own, Ben felt desire unfurl in his belly, hot as a brand. Deep within him, a fuse had been lit, ready to ignite something fierce and bright and wonderful. "Yes," he murmured.

Dacre moved his mouth across Ben's cheek to the underside of his jaw, to the soft place right above his collar. Ben felt the rasp of Dacre's stubble against his own, then gentle, wet suction. He let out an inarticulate noise. Nothing in his life had prepared him for the idea that his neck was a particularly erotic place, but he guessed there were a lot of things his life hadn't prepared him for. He lifted his chin to give Dacre room to work. Dacre's mouth trailed lower, and Ben tried to shove his cravat out of the way, but found his hands weren't steady.

"Get rid of it," he pleaded, his voice gravelly and desperate.

"Sedgwick," Dacre said, pulling back. He threaded his fingers in Ben's hair, pushing it off his forehead, as if he needed an unimpeded view of Ben's face.

"I need to hear you say my name," Ben said. "My Christian name." He needed to know—he didn't know what. That they were friends? Friendship seemed a minimum condition for what they were doing, and Ben required it.

But when Dacre spoke it was with what sounded like relief. "Benedict," he said, and Ben felt the way he had when those strong arms had closed around him. And then his mouth was again on Ben's, more urgent this time.

Ben tried to press closer, and wound up sliding back and pulling Dacre on top of him. He groaned in pleasure at the weight of the other man on top of him, the promise of friction if he tilted his hips up, the other man's hardness jutting against his belly.

Ben slid his hands up the captain's back, feeling in vain for flesh. "Capt—Phillip?"

"Mmm?" he murmured into Ben's neck.

"Show me. Everything."

Chapter Twelve

Hearing his name on Sedgwick's lips did something peculiar to Phillip. It made his heart feel like it was about to crack into pieces, and it made Phillip think that would somehow be a wonderful thing to happen. He could have spent all night and well into tomorrow like this, Sedgwick in his arms, kissing as if they had all the time in the world.

Instead he pushed Sedgwick back onto the desk. Finally, something the desk was good for. He propped himself up on an elbow and looked down at Sedgwick beneath him. "That all right?" he asked. The way they had landed settled their chests flush against one another. Phillip was as hard as an iron rod, and at the sensation of the other man's answering hardness, Phillip nearly groaned.

Sedgwick buried his face in Phillip's neck and ground his hips against him. "Yes." He kissed Phillip's jaw in much the same way Phillip had done. Phillip nearly mewled. Lord, it had been a long time since he had had an encounter like this, touching and kissing and exploring, rather than an efficient meeting of bodies.

Perhaps the other night in the boathouse had been more, but Phillip hadn't wanted to admit it then. It had felt safer to cling desperately to the fiction that this was casual, normal, fine. But then he thought of McCarthy, who had gone to the bottom of the sea without knowing how Phillip felt, and without Phillip knowing if his feelings were returned. He never wanted that again. Sedgwick wasn't letting Phillip hold on to a single convenient pretense; he was giving no quarter. Phillip was at once grateful and terrified, and the sight of Sedgwick open and willing and utterly honest beneath him was almost more than he could take.

Phillip was old enough and sufficiently accustomed to the relief afforded by his own hand to at least pretend something like restraint. He didn't want to scare the man off. He didn't want to go too far. He didn't want—and this was the crux of it—he didn't want to do this, whatever *this* turned out to be, and then discover that it was yet another meaningless encounter, yet another night to be dismissed and brushed aside. "Are you certain you want—"

"Pay me the compliment of trusting that I mean what I say." If he hadn't been grinding his cock into Phillip's, he might have sounded very stern indeed, and Phillip thought he might even like that. "And that I know what I want. This is what I want. You're what I want. Now." His voice was low and gravelly, more urgent and commanding than his usual easy tones. Phillip somehow got even harder at the sound.

With that, he began tugging Phillip's shirt off. Soon they

were both bare to the waist, and Phillip was damned grateful for the lamp that sat on his desk. Because here was Sedgwick, half-naked and in his arms, and Phillip would have lit the curtains on fire if that was what he needed to do to get a good look.

"You have freckles on your chest," Phillip said. He also had a dusting of sandy hair there, and down his belly leading to his breeches. Phillip skimmed a hand over one pale, flat nipple and saw the shudder pass through the vicar's body. Good. Phillip closed his mouth over the other nipple and Sedgwick bucked beneath him, his hands tangled in Phillip's hair. Phillip licked lower, feeling hard muscles and coarse hair beneath his lips. He tasted of salt and smelled like summer, like the warm lake, and trees in leaf, and *home*.

He had never used his mouth on another man. God, he had wanted to. He had let other men do it to him but had always held back, feeling like it would expose some fragile and secret part of himself to admit that he wanted another man's cock in his mouth, that he wanted a man beneath him, inside him, panting and needy and hard, and to know that he had done that.

But with Sedgwick he felt almost safe, as if there would be no shame in any way they came together, no embarrassment in their pleasure. He slid lower, so his lips were level with the waistband of the other man's breeches, where his cock was straining against the fabric. He pressed his face against the hardness and heard Sedgwick's groan.

And then strong hands were on him, pulling him up, bringing him down for a kiss that was clumsy and frantic and perfect. Phillip held himself up on one forearm so he could unfasten his breeches. "I've got to take it out," he muttered, as if he needed to explain or apologize, but then Sedgwick's hands were there, too, opening his own breeches, and his mouth was on the muscles of Phillip's upper arm, kissing softly.

At the first touch of their erections together, Phillip swore and Sedgwick gasped. Phillip bent his head down to see—he needed to see this—and watched his fingers close around the silky hardness of the other man's cock, thick and already wet. Sedgwick let out an inarticulate sound of pleasure and need.

"You like this," Phillip said, gliding his hand along the other man's erection. That much was obvious, but he wanted to hear it. He wanted to know exactly how much Sedgwick wanted this, wanted him.

"So much," Sedgwick breathed, thrusting helplessly into Phillip's fist.

"I want you in my mouth," Phillip whispered. "I want to suck you." He had never said those words, never thought he would. "Will you let me?"

A shudder of a breath. "Yes, yes, please."

Phillip got to his knees, occasionally pressing haphazard kisses along his way. He tugged Sedgwick's breeches a bit lower to give him better access. For a moment he sat on his heels and admired Sedgwick's body, golden and strong, his erection arcing towards his belly. Then he leaned closer, wrapping his fingers around its base and bringing it to his lips before licking the head with the flat of his tongue.

Sedgwick's hips bucked towards him. Phillip could see him half leaning on the desk, his head bent down to watch.

"Steady," Phillip murmured. "I haven't done this before." He hadn't meant to admit that, but this was Sedgwick, this was Benedict, this was a man who played with ducklings and sang lewd songs to the elderly, and Phillip didn't need to worry about dignity, or whatever it was that usually hampered his desire. He knew in his heart he could tell him everything, anything, and it would be fine. He was safe. His heart was safe, or as safe as it ever would be.

At the feel of Phillip's lips closing around his cock head, Ben had to stuff his fist halfway into his mouth to muffle any noises he might make. With his other hand he gripped the edge of the desk, never taking his eyes off Phillip.

Phillip lifted his head away, and Ben nearly cried out at the loss of sensation. "Are you planning to watch me?" he asked, his voice husky.

"Yes?" He had to watch. There was no other option. "Please?"

Phillip huffed out a laugh and swiped his tongue across the underside of Ben's shaft.

Ben put his fist back against his mouth and stifled a moan as Phillip slid his mouth down lower, carefully, almost tentatively. He said he had never done this before, which surprised Ben, but then again it wasn't as if Ben had ever done this either.

And now Phillip was working Ben's cock with his fist

and his mouth, his eyes half-closed. It was all Ben could do to keep still, to not thrust up into the wet warmth of Phillip's mouth. He looked so intent, his brow slightly furrowed in concentration as he took Ben's cock deeper. But he also looked like he was enjoying himself, and when he raised his eyes to Ben's, all Ben could see in them was pleasure. Ben imagined what it might be like if it were he kneeling on the floor with Phillip's cock in his own mouth and he felt his climax beginning to bear down on him.

"I—soon, Phillip."

Phillip didn't pull away, but he shifted, and Ben realized he was stroking himself. Oh, hell. He really was enjoying this, then. He moaned around Ben's cock, and that was what finally sent pleasure crashing through Ben's body.

At the last second, Phillip lifted his head and Ben spilled onto his own belly, his entire universe dissolving into sparks of pleasure.

For a moment they stared at one another, Phillip produced a handkerchief, and Ben had the horrified notion that they were going to get dressed and walk away as if nothing had happened. He didn't think he could bear it, not after this. So he grabbed Phillip's arm and pulled him up.

He reached his hand between them, feeling for Phillip's erection. "Let me touch you," he pleaded.

"You don't—"

"*Please.*" His mouth met Phillip's as his hand closed around Phillip's hardness, and he stroked him the way he would stroke himself, and when it grew even harder he knew it was his doing, his hand and his body that had made it happen. He dropped to his knees without a second thought, and licked the bead of moisture that had gathered at the tip of Phillip's erection. Phillip mumbled something incoherent that sounded like Ben's name and dragged Ben up for a kiss. Ben kept stroking Phillip's shaft with his fist, rubbing his thumb along the head, as Phillip kissed him hungrily, almost desperately. Soon Phillip was swearing a warning, one hand twisted in Ben's hair and the other braced on the desk behind Ben's back. Then Ben felt Phillip's body go taut and still, followed by the warmth of his release.

"Ben," Phillip said, his hand still combing through Ben's hair, his expression bewildered and ravaged. "Benedict."

Ben didn't know how long they stood there, Phillip's head buried in Ben's neck, their heartbeats finally returning to normal and their breathing becoming less ragged. Ben stroked his hand up and down Phillip's back, as if soothing him, as he would soothe a crying child or an injured animal, because something about the way Phillip was almost clinging to him told him that he needed whatever small comfort Ben could give him.

"Thank you," Ben said, long after the lamp on the desk had burned out, leaving them with only the scant light from the banked fire and the waning moon. He kissed Phillip's forehead. He wanted to ask whether Phillip was all right, but didn't know how to do it in a way that this prickly, proud man didn't interpret as interfering or condescending.

Phillip raised his head. "Still no penance?" His voice was gruff.

Ben smiled, and hoped Phillip could see it. "Not a chance.

Not for this. Never for—" He had nearly said love, but that was rather putting too fine a point on the thing. "Never for friendship or affection." And since that sounded both mawkish and inadequate, he added, "Or for whatever this is."

Phillip let out a breath that might have almost been a laugh, or might have been a sigh of relief. "Good."

Chapter Thirteen

It was with a headache and an ill temper that Phillip walked to Lindley Priory the following day. He had spent the afternoon closeted with his land steward, listening to tales of that blasted Easterbrook's poor treatment of his tenants. Strictly speaking, Easterbrook could do whatever he pleased on his own land within the limits of a law that strongly favored landowners, but in practice Phillip's tenants were stretched thin by having to provide food, money, and sometimes even shelter for family who were or had been Easterbrook's tenants. Phillip felt badly equipped to manage this problem, and resented Easterbrook for having brought matters to a point where Phillip couldn't ignore them. He heartily wished Easterbrook to the ends of the earth.

Lindley Priory was much older and grander than Barton Hall, but the gardens were overgrown and there was no sign of the army of servants that would be required to maintain a place like this. A surly footman opened the door, and after some confusion, showed him into a dusty, sparsely furnished parlor. It suddenly struck him that he'd be glad to return to Barton Hall. Barton Hall was as properly run as his ship, and he felt a pang of belated appreciation for Caroline, that even two years after her death the household still operated like clockwork. At some point in the past week he had gone from loathing the place to being almost comfortable there. It wasn't the dark home of his childhood, but rather a place where his own children were happy. And there was Sedgwick, radiating joy and making Phillip almost believe that he could perhaps deserve some happiness of his own. Almost.

His thoughts were interrupted by the sound of a door. Sir Martin Easterbrook stood there, plainly annoyed. In the light of day, Phillip could see how young the man was. He was closer to Ned's age than to Phillip's.

"How can I help you, Dacre?" Easterbrook snapped impatiently, and any sympathy Phillip had been feeling for the young man entirely evaporated.

"I came to offer you the use of my land agent. If you're in need of ready money, Smythe can help you figure out better ways to get some than strong-arming your tenants."

The young man sneered. "I have my own land agent."

"Yes, the fellow who thought my children had been poaching on your land. Pardon me, but I doubt the man's judgment."

"I can't afford to pay him proper wages, so he takes a percentage of the rents he brings in."

"You can't afford to pay him?" Phillip repeated. But he looked around the room more closely, and noticed that it was devoid of any art, vases, or decent furniture. Anything that could be sold already had been.

"It's only natural that he's a bit zealous, but I'm certain his actions are within the letter of the law." There was a shadow of doubt in Easterbrook's face, though, and Phillip had to wonder if the younger man was in well over his head. Managing an estate, Phillip was learning, was fraught with complication. If Ned had been left the running of Barton Hall's land, and he hadn't had the guidance of a man as fair and practical as Smythe, might he have behaved as badly as Easterbrook? Phillip doubted it, but he could see how Easterbrook had gotten into this mess. "My father died with a great deal of debt," Easterbrook went on, "and as I'm saddled with this place, I need to figure out some way to make it pay for itself."

"Sell it off. Sell the Priory, the land, all of it."

"It's entailed," Easterbrook said with obvious bitterness.

"Marry, then." That's what Phillip had done when his own father died penniless.

Easterbrook's face crumpled, and for a moment, Phillip thought the younger man might break down in tears. But then he straightened his spine and resumed his earlier surliness. "Thank you for your advice, Captain Dacre, but I have an estate to run." His voice dripped with sarcasm.

"Talk to the vicar," Phillip said in a flash of inspiration. "He could surely figure out a way to help you that didn't quite punish your tenants so much."

"I'm well acquainted with Ben Sedgwick. I'm entirely too acquainted with all the Sedgwicks, in fact, and if I have to see any of them again I don't think I could resist slapping the smiles off their faces."

"I beg your pardon?"

"For the Sedgwicks to be happy and comfortable while I'm sitting here without a penny to my name is just a bit much, Dacre."

"What on earth do the Sedgwicks have to do with your predicament?" He was trying to remember precisely what the cook had told him about the late Sir Humphrey. If Sir Humphrey hadn't given the living of St. Aelred's to Ben, it could have been sold off; this was a common enough practice. It seemed far-fetched that Easterbrook's resentment stemmed from what had to be a trifling sum of money, however.

"You don't know." Easterbrook sat back in his chair and regarded Phillip with something like amusement. "You really don't. Well, my father spent every last farthing on that family."

"Why?" Phillip asked, baffled.

Easterbrook's mouth curved into an angry smile. "I'm not going to tell you. Ask your precious vicar."

As he left Lindley Priory and headed home, Phillip wondered whether Ben knew how bitterly Easterbrook resented him and his family. He doubted it, recalling Ben's confusion that night when Peggy and Jamie had been caught on Easterbrook's land.

Ned and Jamie waylaid Phillip on his path back to Barton Hall. "We're having a picnic by the lake," the younger boy shouted. And indeed, they were carrying a picnic hamper between them. "Peggy and Mr. Sedgwick are already there."

Phillip was in no condition for company, but the sight of his children laughing and struggling with the basket made him smile. And wasn't that something. When he arrived a week ago, he would have been annoyed with how loud, dirty, and undisciplined they were. He would have grumbled that they ought to have been studying, that they ought to have been eating a proper meal rather than whatever cakes they had pilfered when the poor put-upon cook had her back turned. But now he took the basket and gestured for them to lead the way, his heart already a bit lighter for having seen them happy, and for knowing he was about to see Ben.

They found their little party disposed on a blanket in a clearing by the lake. Peg was braiding flowers into the dog's hair while Ben leaned back on his elbows, his long legs crossed at the ankles before him. His coat was slung on a low branch of the nearest tree, and his sleeves were rolled up. He hadn't yet noticed Phillip's approach.

Phillip felt the doom of impending awkwardness. What the hell could even be said after last night? He had let Ben see a part of him he hadn't ever wanted to acknowledge to himself, let alone show to anyone else. Now he felt raw and vulnerable and somehow embarrassed; the old familiar cloud began to descend upon him. He was better off on his own, far away, where he couldn't disappoint anyone. He didn't belong here after all; he belonged on the *Patroclus*, where he was in control, at a safe distance from anything that might pierce his defenses or expose him as lacking.

But then Ben turned his head, and when he saw Phillip, his face broke unhesitatingly into a smile. Phillip smiled back despite himself. How could he not? He couldn't even muster up any icy reserve. This man was the antidote to chilliness. He was a counterweight to Phillip's natural inclination to aloofness.

Phillip set the basket down and then sat on the blanket at a discreet distance from Ben, near enough so that they could talk without being overheard, but not so near that they could touch. He didn't trust himself at closer range.

Jamie distributed the contents of the hamper. Cakes, cakes, and more cakes, as Phillip had expected, but no matter. If Mrs. Morris enjoyed making cakes and tiny little tarts and lemon biscuits, and the children enjoyed eating them, then everyone won. He watched as Ben's eyes lit up at the sight of the biscuits.

"What did you do today?" Phillip asked, and was regaled with tales of sheep shearing and medieval queens and square roots. He wasn't sure how the topics came together, or if they even did, only that three happy, smiling faces were turned towards him, telling him their stories as if they wanted him to know.

They were treating him as if he did belong here, not on a ship a thousand miles away, but on a picnic blanket, basking in the sunshine. As if he belonged to these children and they to him, as if he were at all worthy of that. And somehow, this country vicar belonged there, too, with them.

After the cakes had been reduced to rubble, the children ran off to wade in the lake. Phillip knew he ought to acknowledge how happy and healthy the children were, not to mention how they had even come around to not openly detesting the sight of him. He ought to thank Sedgwick for giving him his family. But he couldn't find the words. And even if he could have, he wouldn't have been brave enough to speak them.

"I had a fine afternoon cleaning up the mess your Sir Martin Easterbrook made," Phillip said, trying to put some distance between them with an unpleasant topic. "He's closed off more grazing land." He didn't need to explain to Sedgwick, who had been raised here, that this communal grazing land was all that made it possible for some of the more modest tenants to scrape together a living. "And then he evicts the tenants who can't pay their rents. So now my tenants expect the same treatment from me, which makes it damned hard to do business with them."

"I doubt that Martin Easterbrook, whatever his faults may be, is single-handedly responsible for the tradition of mistrusting landlords."

"Goodness. You're a radical."

"Hardly. But I was raised by radicals, so some of it might have rubbed off."

"I called on him and he was an ungrateful little wretch."

Benedict frowned. "He swam in this lake with my brothers and me. And now he's . . ." He shook his head, obviously not wanting to say precisely what Martin Easterbrook was.

"He doesn't seem overfond of your family," Phillip said, striving for tact. "Says he can't bear to see you happy when he's miserable. And he seems to resent some expenditures your father made on behalf of you and your brothers."

"He must mean my living or my brothers' school fees, although the latter can't have amounted to much. One of my brothers was mentioned in Sir Humphrey's will, but I don't believe it amounted to much."

Phillip thought of the tiny church in the village and the rather tumbledown vicarage beside it; he took in the well-worn soles of Ben's boots and the frayed edges of his cuffs. Giving the living of St. Aelred's to Ben rather than selling it hadn't been what impoverished the Easterbrooks. And the venom in young Easterbrook's voice suggested more than resentment over a few hundred pounds a year. *You really don't know,* the man had said. And now Phillip wondered if Ben even knew what lay at the heart of his neighbor's antipathy. Whatever the source of Easterbrook's rancor toward the Sedgwicks, Phillip knew Ben wouldn't be pleased to learn of it. Phillip realized he would have given a good deal to protect Ben from what seemed an inevitable disappointment.

"You know," Phillip said. "There's a time-honored method of dealing with encumbered estates. When my father left me with debts to pay, I found a wealthy wife. I daresay Easterbrook could do the same. He has a title and an estate."

He watched as Ben sucked in a breath and let it out slowly before he responded. "Is that the only reason you married? Money?"

"No, of course not. Caroline wanted a home and children of her own, and the fact that I would generally be away from home was, ah, perhaps a factor she weighed in my advantage when considering potential suitors." She had quite explicitly said that she did not require a husband on the premises, and

Phillip, remembering what life had been like for his mother during his father's tenure at Barton Hall, felt that he quite understood. "I was fond of her. She was, I believe, fond of me, and marriage was the answer to both our problems. At the time I thought it not a bad bargain for either of us."

Another minute passed in silence, and Phillip thought Ben might let the subject drop. "Did she know?" he asked, his voice pitched low.

The sound of the children splashing in the water fell away at this reminder of their shared predicament. He felt a sense of responsibility to help Ben navigate these muddy waters. "No, I don't believe she did. I hardly think she would have known that there was anything to be known, if you follow me. It's hardly a topic that a lady can expect to hear about in the ordinary course of things. And I couldn't have told her without exposing myself to ruin." That wasn't true, though. Caroline would have kept his secret. She was too practical to do otherwise.

The real reason Phillip had never spoken of it to his wife, the woman who had been his ally and friend, was that he had been afraid she would think less of him if she knew his desires. And that perhaps she would think less of their marriage, their family, their friendship. He never wanted to risk finding out, so he had kept it a secret. Now Phillip wondered if he had spent his entire life keeping hidden the parts of himself that he feared would invite scorn. But the situation hadn't been fair for either of them, and he felt a sudden swell of anger at the injustice of a world that left a man like him with so few options.

He turned to Ben, thinking of saying something to the younger man, some word of advice, but he realized he didn't have anything useful to say. He couldn't tell him not to marry this girl, not to live a lie, because what else was there? He had nothing to say, nothing to offer. And that felt terribly familiar.

Ben wanted to punch somebody. It had been a good number of years since he had actually needed to hit anyone, and he dearly wished he had a convenient target now—some fool who was unwise enough to bother one of his brothers or mock his mother and who desperately needed a corrective sock in the jaw—because his right hand was clenching into a fist on its own.

But now he was furious and he didn't even have the satisfaction of knowing who he was furious with, unless it was himself. He was angry at life, and wasn't that a stupid thing. He was angry that there was no way for him to have what he wanted, what he needed, what surely was any man's dream—a home, a family, a place of his own in the world—without a wife, and he didn't know how to have a wife without deceiving or misleading her on a matter that she must find of the utmost importance.

And it wasn't only that. It wasn't fair to himself. Until meeting Dacre, his attraction to men had been vague. He had known that he was drawn to men in a general way, as a category of people, but the objects of his desire had thus far been faceless, safe in their abstraction. Until he had felt

Dacre's hands on him, he hadn't quite grasped what it meant to be with a person you desired.

Now he wanted this man's hands on him, this man's skin on his own, his mouth on his mouth. Only Dacre would do. Ben had to figure out what to do with himself now that he had this very inconvenient piece of knowledge. Because he couldn't have Dacre or any other man if he married Alice. But he couldn't marry Alice if he planned to go to bed with anyone else. And without marriage and children and a place in the world, he didn't know what to do with himself. He'd feel incomplete, cheated of his own future.

Punching somebody was out of the question, so he hurled a stone into the lake. He didn't even try to skip it; he just plonked it into the water to cause the biggest possible splash. Then he did it a couple more times. It was utterly unsatisfying, but it must have looked more thrilling than it was, because the next thing he knew Jamie had materialized from whatever tree he had been climbing and started hurling rocks into the water beside Ben. And then the dog, who really was not a very bright creature but was possessed of good intentions, thought he was meant to run after whatever Jamie had thrown. In due course they had a very wet, very confused dog.

Ben found himself laughing despite himself as the children tried to soothe the animal.

"You can hit me if it'll make you feel better," Dacre said, coming up behind him to watch the children.

Ben huffed out a laugh. "Am I that easy to read?"

"Sometimes. But I was angry myself, and I guessed."

That they shared this reason to be angry did nothing to

make Ben feel better, but solidarity was worth something. It had to be, because it was one of the few things Ben had left.

Dacre cleared his throat. "You said you don't go in much for penance, and I believe you, but I'm afraid that I do. Not in a spiritual sense," he added hastily. But he stepped closer to Ben, still watching the lake. "I'll always regret the secrecy. I'll always regret that I couldn't be more to Caroline. She deserved better. But I don't know what else I could have done."

"Did you ever think that maybe *you* deserved better?" The words were out before Ben could really think of what he meant. "That you deserved the kind of life you believe you deprived your wife of?"

"We both know that's impossible."

"No," Ben said, his fists clenched at his sides. "We don't." This was too close to the central problem of Ben's life for him to talk about calmly, so he made what he hoped was an apologetic gesture and turned away to watch the children.

Dacre didn't walk away. Ben had thought he'd surely take any opportunity to leave, but he stayed beside Ben. Several minutes passed before either of them spoke. "Earlier, when they were talking to me," Dacre said, his voice gruff, "it felt . . . normal. I think they were pleased with me. Thank you."

"You did the work," Ben said softly. "You showed them they could trust you, and now they do. They're fonder of you than I would have thought, if I'm honest," he added impishly.

Dacre stomped his boot in the shallow water to splash Ben, and Ben laughed. "What's that supposed to mean? I inspire fondness in all sorts of people."

Ben looked away and shoved his hands in his pockets. "I can attest to the truth of that."

When he looked back at Dacre, he found the man blushing.

In truth, Ben was pleased to see that once they realized that their father was not going to ship them off to school or consign them to the nearest tutor, the Dacre children accepted his presence, and later his participation, in their activities. The children had lost their mother and would soon be without their father for another extended sea voyage. It seemed to Ben that what this family needed most was time together, time to remind the children that they weren't orphans, alone in the world.

The sun began to dip below the hills, and the children splashed barefoot in the shallow water while the dog ran back and forth. Ben perched in a branch of a tree, and Dacre seemed to be having a bit of a sleep against the trunk.

Despite his misgivings about his future, Ben had no doubt about the present. He was content with the Dacres and he knew he had achieved something good. He had restored something important to the entire family. This was why he had endured his father's scorn and his brothers' confusion by going into the church. When people needed help, they went to a clergyman. And he wanted to be that person who people turned to for help. Somebody had to fill in the gaps—make sure the elderly had company, the sick solace, the poor food. He had spent his childhood doing that for his family and he knew he wanted to spend the rest of the life doing more of the same.

His thoughts were interrupted by the sound of hoofbeats and carriage wheels, and he turned to see a gig approaching. That was strange, because they were on Dacre's land and Phillip hadn't mentioned expecting anybody. He dropped down from the tree and stepped towards the conveyance.

There he saw the last two people on earth he had wanted to see.

Phillip looked up at the sound of carriage wheels to see a strange gig approaching. It was being driven by a man who was dressed at the absolute height of fashion, and by his side was a very pretty young lady whom Phillip did not recognize.

"Hullo!" cried the lady, pulling off her hat to wave it towards the lake. "Is that you looking like an urchin over there, Benedict?" She had hair a few shades darker than Ben's, more dark gold than flax.

"A sad lack of dignity," murmured her companion. He had maneuvered the conveyance close enough so that Phillip could see and hear them quite clearly despite being concealed by the shade of the tree he leaned against. "Look, he's about to come greet us, as if he's decent. My eyes, Alice."

"I didn't expect to see you so soon," Ben said to the gentleman, shrugging into his coat. "Your letter made it sound like you'd come in August."

"Well, London got a bit too hot to hold me," the gentleman said.

Phillip could see Ben frown at this. "And Alice, I'm so glad to see you out of doors."

"It's Hartley's doing. He came to the house looking for you, and only found me instead. And then he insisted on putting me into his new gig—"

"What was the use of buying the thing if not to escort the prettiest woman in Cumberland?"

"And I haven't even fallen out!" she added triumphantly.

"I should dashed well think not," the gentleman said. "Would be most unbecoming, and if you expect me to drive around with a woman who's covered in dust, you can guess again, Alice."

"And a provincial woman in an unfashionable frock," the lady added with a rueful shake of her head.

Phillip only understood enough to gather that the three of them were on terms of intimacy. He felt vaguely jealous of their easy camaraderie, and even more jealous when he realized that the lady must be the Alice Crawford Ben intended to marry. He stepped farther away from the little group, wishing he could disappear.

"Captain Dacre," Ben called, not at all like he was doing a duty but as if he were genuinely eager to have Phillip's company. "Miss Crawford, this is Captain Dacre. And Captain Dacre, this is my brother Hartley."

Phillip bowed to each of them in turn. Now that he looked at this Mr. Hartley Sedgwick, he could see a faint family resemblance. Hartley was built on altogether more delicate lines than his brother, but the similarities were there. Phillip had the stray notion that Hartley took great care to prevent his skin from freckling the way his older brother's did.

He was spared the necessity of attempting conversation

by the twins' loud whoops of laughter as they went careening into the lake. They were both fully dressed, so that was at least something to be thankful for. The dog evidently thought this a great emergency and barked at the top of his lungs.

"I had quite forgotten the bucolic charm of the country," Mr. Hartley Sedgwick said dryly.

"Take him home and get him some smelling salts," Ben said to Miss Crawford. "And a cool cloth to put over his eyes." Then, as if realizing what he was saying, "Wait, Hartley, where are you staying? You can put up at the vicarage, but you'll have to let Mrs. Winston know."

"Never worry, brother. I took a room at the George and Dragon."

"You must come to dinner during your stay," Phillip said impulsively. "Both of you." All three were staring at him with round eyes, and he realized the words had come out more as a command than an invitation. He tried to adopt a less authoritarian tone. "Your brother," he told Mr. Hartley Sedgwick, "has been infinitely helpful with my children." He knew a mad urge to claim Ben as his own. "I'd be so honored to have his brother and his betrothed as my guests."

At the word *betrothed*, a strange thing happened. Hartley rolled his eyes, Miss Crawford blushed and looked away, and Ben froze. Well, well. Phillip didn't know quite what to think, only that matters were not as straightforward as they seemed, and that this new intelligence pleased him out of all proportion.

Chapter Fourteen

Phillip was already in bed when he heard the knock on his door.

He knew before he had his hand on the latch that it was Ben. It couldn't be anyone else; the children were sleeping, a servant had already banked his fire, and houses, unlike ships, didn't generally have emergent situations. Even if there were an emergency, he would not be the person appealed to. This sense of irrelevance was not as disconcerting as Phillip might have liked.

He opened the door to find Ben in rolled-up shirtsleeves and a fierce expression.

"Did you decide to take me up on my offer and hit me?" Phillip asked. He had made that offer only half in jest. Ben didn't wear anger well. His cheerful, handsome face belonged in a smile.

"No," the vicar said, his jaw clenched.

"You'd better come in."

He stepped only far enough inside for Phillip to reach behind him and latch the door. "Why did you invite them?"

Phillip wasn't going to remind him that Barton Hall was his own house and he could invite whomever the hell he wanted. "Your brother and Miss Crawford? I thought it would please you to have their company," he said, because it was the truth.

"I cannot sit at the table with you and Alice. I can't."

"Ah. I see."

"And as for Hartley, he sees everything." He scrubbed his hand over his face. "I have to make a decision. And I damned well hate it." Ben seldom swore, and the coarse language, even more than his fierce expression, told Phillip of his distress.

"I know," Phillip said. There was nothing else he could say. He had already told the younger man of his own experiences, for what little they were worth, and there was nothing more than that he could offer. The decision had to be Ben's. Phillip reminded himself that it had nothing to do with him. He would be at sea long before Ben went through with the marriage.

"She's not well," Ben said. "For me to break the engagement would be shabby even if she weren't unwell. She's my closest and oldest friend, and she'll be left with precious little after her parents die."

"She's a beautiful woman," Phillip pointed out. "And lively."

"She can hardly walk. Even if she had occasion to meet a suitor, it's not every man who could see past that."

Phillip didn't know if this were true, but Ben believed it,

and that was the crux of the issue. "Can you set aside money for her use, if she's ever in need?"

"I put all my extra income—and this is not a wealthy parish, so don't think I'm some kind of philanthropist—into the poor box. But, yes, I do need to find a way to set some aside."

"Of course you give away all your money." Phillip would never stop being surprised by how decent this man was. "Of course you do."

Ben paid him no heed. "I feel like a cad and I'm not used to that."

Phillip smiled. Ben was used to being adored and appreciated. Phillip had learned that quickly—everyone in the village liked their jovial young vicar. And for good reason. "I don't envy you," Phillip said, and it was true. He tried to ignore the utterly irrelevant surge of hope that swept through him at the idea that Ben might not marry this girl. He tried to remind himself that it didn't matter, that it was ridiculous for him to be jealous of this young woman, that rolling around on the boathouse floor and groping against his desk had nothing in common with building a life and starting a family. But he couldn't banish either the hope or the jealousy from his mind, so instead he took Ben's hand in his own. "You really are a decent, good, kind man, and whatever decision you make will be for the best." The strangest thing was that Phillip actually believed the trite words as they left his mouth. The vicar, for all his youth, really was a good man, one of the best Phillip had ever known.

And Phillip had ruined it for him. Ben had been blithely

headed down a smooth path and Phillip sent him careening sideways. Well, that was done and there was nothing left but to ruin it some more.

"Come here," Phillip said, tugging him close.

Ben sagged against Phillip's body as if it were a relief to be close. And maybe it was. God knew that at the first brush of their bodies Phillip felt like he was taking a deep breath after swimming underwater for too long. It felt somehow easier to touch and hold Ben than it was not to touch him, which made no sense, because Phillip had never in his life touched anyone like this. He had never run his hands soothingly down anyone's back; he had never kissed anyone's temple; he had never whispered nonsense into anyone's ear as he was doing now. But it all felt right, like he was finally in his native habitat.

It was Ben who first turned the embrace into something more, turning his head so his lips pressed into Phillip's neck. Phillip held Ben's chin in his hand so he could see the man's face and get some idea of what he was thinking. The anger had fled and been replaced with want. Want, Phillip could work with.

Their lips met with more urgency than finesse, and Phillip didn't care because he had gone too many years with too few kisses, and he had gone his whole life without Ben, and now he had kisses and Ben and he had never felt better.

Ben was steering him backward. Towards the bed, Phillip gathered. He liked that, liked that Ben was taking what he wanted and that what he wanted was Phillip. They landed on the bed in a tangle of limbs, Ben a welcome heaviness on top of him. Phillip wore only his dressing gown, and not for long, because Ben shoved it aside and tossed it to the ground before pulling his own shirt off in one movement. Phillip watched with interest as he began to unfasten his breeches, sliding them down around his lean hips and exposing his already hard prick. God, he was lovely. He was golden and young and he seemed to glow with goodness and beauty. Phillip could have worshiped at his feet, but instead settled for pulling him down and rolling them over.

"I want," Ben rasped. "I want everything."

Phillip froze. "What does that mean?"

"I want to do anything you've ever liked."

"You don't know that you'd like . . . everything."

"If I don't like it, we won't do it again." He spoke as if it were so simple, and maybe it was. "And if it's terrible then it'll be terrible together. But I . . . I don't have the words. Don't make me blunder through. But I want you to touch me everywhere, and I want to do the same to you."

Phillip shuddered. "Yes," he managed. "I want that." *Want* was too weak a word. He *craved* anything Ben had to offer. He let Ben roll him over and watched in fascination as he knelt between Phillip's spread legs. Phillip was naked, utterly exposed, even more so when he took a shaky breath and bent his knees up. Phillip swore under his breath and fisted his hands in the sheets when Ben took hold of Phillip's cock, bracing himself so he wouldn't come undone at the touch of Ben's mouth.

He came undone anyway with first flick of Ben's pink tongue on the sensitive head of his erection. Spasms of lust rocketed through his body. He reached up to grab the bed frame, steadying himself. Ben's pale hair shaded his face, so with his free hand, Phillip brushed those strands away. Ben looked up at him and Phillip swore again. He supposed Ben's inexperience shouldn't triple his own interest in the proceedings, but his cock had perverse tastes and there was no reasoning with it. He groaned as Ben took the tip into his mouth and sucked.

"Do you like it?" Phillip asked. He needed to hear it.

Ben hummed in what Phillip assumed was assent.

"Show me how much you like it." Phillip didn't know what had gotten into him. This wasn't how things were done. He had gotten his cock sucked dozens of times, and his general posture was restrained appreciation. He had never wanted to seem too enthusiastic, lest the person on the other end of the transaction think . . . think what? How had Phillip managed to get so bloody stupid? All he wanted right now was for Ben to know how damned much he liked this, how much he needed it, how good and necessary this was. Because this was something they were sharing, something they were doing together. He wasn't receiving a favor; he wasn't having his lust conveniently slaked by a friend. This was some unholy combination of desire and friendship and something else, because apparently when you took workaday lust and combined it with affection and threw in garden-variety honesty, you got something new and totally different.

Ben, evidently in response to Phillip's request, gave an experimental suck on the head of Phillip's cock before taking him deeper.

"God, yes," Phillip groaned. "So good."

He heard and felt Ben's answering moan, which only made him harder still. And then he opened his legs a little wider and bent his knees a little more, deliberately giving Ben access to, well, whatever he might like. A frisson of something not quite shame, but adjacent to shame, coursed through his body. And, alarmingly, he liked that too. The idea that he was exposing himself like this, inviting Ben to touch him in a way he had never been touched, made his cock pulse. The idea that Ben made him want things he had never wanted, never allowed himself to want, was thrilling and terrifying all at once, and Phillip wondered exactly how much trouble he was in.

Ben had brought himself off imagining a man's cock in his mouth more times than he could count, but the actual sensation of Phillip, hard and thick, on his tongue and between his lips, was enough to make him almost delirious with pleasure. It took him a few minutes to work his way into anything like a rhythm, to learn how to make his hand and his mouth work in tandem. By the time he figured that out, Phillip's head had fallen back in pleasure, exposing the strong lines of his throat. Ben could have watched him like that all day— lips parted, hand gripping the bedpost as if it were keeping him afloat in stormy waters, hips rocking ever so slightly into Ben's mouth.

Once he felt confident that he was not going to choke, he took his hand away from the base of Phillip's erection and instead used it to cup Phillip's bollocks. He was rewarded with a groan of pleasure and the taste of salt on his tongue, so he kept doing it. Phillip's legs fell farther open, fully exposing his bollocks and even more private flesh beyond. Benedict wasn't certain if he was meant to do anything with this. He was not such an innocent as to be ignorant of the different ways men could come together but felt inanely shy about asking whether the captain had sodomy on his mind.

And yet. Conscious that he might irretrievably ruin the moment, but not wanting to hold back any offering of pleasure or sensation that Phillip might desire, he tentatively traced a finger lower. The hand that had been idly stroking Benedict's hair went still and Phillip's body went rigid, but not, Ben thought, with displeasure. With . . . anticipation perhaps? Ben played his tongue along the underside of Phillip's shaft while he brought his finger still lower, skimming along the crease of Phillip's arse.

And then a single word. "Yes." It was only a whisper on Phillip's mouth but it sounded like it cost a hell of a lot so Benedict kept touching him, not daring to push inside but circling Phillip's sensitive entrance while lavishing every care he could think of on Phillip's shaft. The caress of Phillip's hand on the shell of Ben's ear seemed impossibly gentle, somehow more intimate than what Ben was doing with his tongue and his fingers. And when Phillip mumbled a warning, Ben knew he didn't want to stop—he wanted to experience Phillip's pleasure as fully as he possibly could, so he swallowed and sucked until Phillip pulled him away, dragging him in for a kiss.

"Thank you," Phillip said, and something in the man's

slightly stilted tone told Ben that the veil of awkwardness was about to descend again. Of course it was. After anything that even bore a passing resemblance to vulnerability, Captain Phillip Dacre did his absolute bloody best to lock himself up right and tight. Well, too bad, because Ben wasn't having any of that.

"I'm still hard," he said, because it was true and because tending to his erection would at least defer the awkwardness. He palmed his erection and cast a deliberate, hungry glance at the captain's naked body. "What are you going to do about it?"

Phillip flashed him a rare, lazy smile. "You ought to bring that over here and find out."

Ben climbed up, intending to lie at Phillip's side, but the captain pulled him on top. "Like this," he said, wrapping his fingers around Ben's prick and forming a channel with his fist. "Into my hand," he murmured. It took Ben a moment to figure out what he was meant to do, then he started thrusting into Phillip's fist, pumping his hips fast and hard.

"Soon," he said, teeth gritted. He was already far gone, and after a few thrusts he came, knowing it was Phillip beneath him, receiving his thrusts, and wondering what that might mean.

They lay there, sweaty and sated, until their hearts returned to normal and Ben started to shiver. Ben probably ought to leave, but instead he pulled the covers over both of them. "Just for a few moments," he said, almost apologetically.

"I wish you could stay all night," Phillip said. That was

impossible, and they both knew it. They couldn't risk being discovered by the servants. That made it an easy offer to make.

"Do you really?" Ben asked. "I was beginning to think you wished me at the ends of the earth."

"So was I, but then I imagined you in your own bed, and that would put you inconveniently far from my cock."

Ben laughed softly. "Your cock has no say. It's fast asleep."

"It could be persuaded." They lay silently long enough for Ben to think that conversation was over. "You make me want things I shouldn't."

"Likely you mean that as a compliment but it isn't one. Just because I touched your—"

"You make me want to hold you all night and into the morning. You make me think I'll hate getting back on my ship. You make me wish I could stay here and give you what you deserve. That I could be what you deserve." That furrow had reappeared on Phillip's brow.

"Bugger deserve. To hell with it. Who are you to decide who deserves what? Some people are starving and others are eating peeled grapes and you can't mean to tell me that either group deserve a damned thing. You don't get to tell me what I deserve."

"I only meant that you deserve better than what I have to offer."

Now the same anger that had plagued Ben earlier this evening was seeping back into his mood. "*You* deserve better. You deserve better than a family you keep at arm's length and a lover you push away. You deserve better than that. And now I'm going to go back to my room." He dropped a kiss onto Phillip's worried brow, just to show him that his words were meant in a spirit of kindness, and left Phillip alone in his bed.

CHAPTER FIFTEEN

Alice greeted Ben with a loud, "*That* was your Captain Angry?" as soon as he entered the Crawfords' drawing room.

"Good to see you too, Alice," he answered. She was sitting in a Bath chair, which was an improvement over being propped up on the sofa like a rag doll. He was conscious that he had perhaps missed a few key stages in her recovery; he had only visited her once in the two weeks since Phillip's arrival. "And in a chair, rather than Hartley's death trap or the sofa. I congratulate you on finding a reasonable middle ground." Hartley was there as well, sipping tea and watching him with curiosity.

"Your captain behaved like a perfect gentleman," Alice continued. "I had been expecting a grizzled old man with elaborate mustaches."

"What do mustaches have to do with it?" Hartley asked.

"You should have heard your brother go on," Alice said, turning to Hartley. "He would have had us believe Captain Dacre was an ogre. And instead he seemed an amiable man.

Young, too, unless you consider five-and-thirty to be old. He was talking with you, Ben, while his children frolicked about like monkeys in the jungle, which doesn't sound like something a strict disciplinarian would do much of, does it, Hart?"

"No, Alice. I quite agree with you. I think our Ben has slandered his new friend." He looked shrewdly—too shrewdly—at Ben. Ben sighed. Hartley saw too much. That was the problem with having a brother so close in age to oneself. Hartley could read him like a book.

Ben thought back to how Phillip had been yesterday, his jaw unshaved, the bridge of his nose slightly sunburnt, a smile on his lips as he watched his family. How very unlike the stiff, cold man Ben had first thought him. Then he thought of Phillip—on him, under him, kissing him, and—no, he could not let his thoughts wander in that direction. Not in Alice's drawing room, not with Hartley's knife-sharp gaze on him.

"Captain Dacre is a prince among men and I viciously slandered him," Ben said lightly, as if he weren't dead serious. He was hiding the truth in plain sight, because this was the only way to end the conversation before he said something that confirmed whatever lewd suspicions Hartley was—quite justifiably—currently forming. "I thought you were going to wait until August to visit. What made you come home now?" he asked Hartley. Because he could read Hartley as well as Hartley could read him and he knew those lines around his brother's eyes hadn't been there the last time they had seen one another. "Is it Will?"

Something passed over Hartley's face. "No," he said, and they both knew it meant *not this time*. "He's much the same."

"Good," Ben said. "But then why—" He stopped short when he saw Hartley's gaze cut momentarily over towards the sofa where Alice sat. So whatever had brought Hartley home couldn't be mentioned in front of Alice. That was not a good sign. He doubted his brother was in a scrape, because Hartley was too concerned with what other people thought of him to get into trouble. Perhaps he needed money? No, it couldn't be that, because Ben and their father were the last people on earth to have cash at the ready. Whatever it was would have to wait until they were alone, he supposed.

Evidently they were being unsubtle about their intentions, because Alice rolled her eyes. "If you two boys need to be left alone, just chuck me outside. This infernal Bath chair won't fit through the garden door, but you can just pick me up and toss me out like the contents of a slop bin. I'd hate to stand between you and your very manly conversation."

Ben couldn't help but laugh. "Such a shrew. So unladylike."

"I know," Alice said. "Poor Hartley is going to go into fits. He's used to traveling in much more exalted circles and dancing attendance upon ladies infinitely more refined than I."

"I already knew you were a pair of rustics." Hartley sniffed.

"Yes, well, this rustic took three steps without assistance this morning, and I'm dreadfully proud of myself. Hartley brought me a set of paints from London," Alice said, turning to Ben. "I'm going to paint his portrait as some kind of Greek god. I was thinking Apollo—"

"Narcissus is more to the point," Ben interjected.

"This is all in shockingly bad taste," Hartley said languidly, buffing his fingernails on the lapel of his coat. "This is why I seldom leave London. My sensibilities are shocked by these lapses into vulgarity. Take me back to the inn, Benedict." And with that he rose to his feet, kissed Alice's hand, and swept Ben out of the room.

"Do you recall how Sir Humphrey left me that bit of property?" Hartley said when they were out of doors. "Well, Martin is contesting his father's will."

Ben knew nothing about legal matters, but thought one needed grounds to contest a will. "Can he just do that?"

"He's saying I had undue influence over his father."

"But that's nonsensical." Ben was conscious of Hartley's gaze intently on him. "He was your godfather and he was always very fond of you. People give money to their godchildren all the time."

"People give one another money for all sorts of reasons," Hartley said with a sigh.

"What aren't you saying?" Ben stopped walking and turned to face his brother. "And why couldn't you have told me that in a letter rather than coming all the way from London?"

"I just . . ." Hartley, usually so polished and confident, looked young and embarrassed. He shook his head. "Never mind. I want you to be careful in case Martin turns his sights on you. Be safe, Benedict. If you're going to marry Alice, now is the time. She is Easterbrook's cousin, after all."

"I don't know if I can do that."

"Of course you can. She needs to marry and you need a wife. Besides, you adore one another."

"Not like that," Ben whispered.

Hartley's eyes widened briefly. Ben knew he didn't need to fill in the details for Hartley, who would understand that this was the sort of knowledge that Ben would only learn the hard way—by falling for somebody else.

And he had fallen for Phillip. He had always thought the expression *falling in love* to be a mere idiom. He knew how to love—he loved his brothers, he loved Alice, he loved the Dacre children, and he loved many other people besides. God commanded him to love, and he did it with his heart and with his actions.

He hadn't realized that this other kind of love, the kind he felt for Phillip, had so much in common with falling off a cliff. He couldn't stop loving Phillip any more than he could stop gravity.

Phillip found Ben tramping up the hill in his shirtsleeves— did he ever wear a coat?—instead of returning to the hall.

"We missed you at luncheon," he said, conscious that he sounded peevish. Ben was under no obligation to attend luncheon, or any meal, or any other damned thing at Barton Hall. He was his own man with his own life, and Phillip would do well to remember that.

"I missed being there. But I had to call on some parishioners and make sure the church was ready for tomorrow."

Ah, that was right. Tomorrow was Sunday. "Where are you heading now, though?"

"I'm climbing to the top of the fell."

Phillip opened his eyes wide in surprise. "Why?"

Ben frowned. "Restless."

Phillip was all too familiar with the need to exorcise his demons by pacing the ship's deck or taking ill-advised swims. "Can you stand some company? I can keep quiet."

Ben appeared to take a moment to consider. "Come along. I'm only in a foul mood. It's not catching. I usually take pains to avoid people when I'm cranky but . . ." He shrugged as his voice trailed off.

Phillip felt perversely pleased that Ben had sought him out last night at the height of his ill temper and that he was comfortable sharing his mood today with Phillip. It felt companionable; it felt . . . it felt like something Phillip wasn't going to want to leave behind at the end of the summer.

The trees were heavy with leaves and the sun reflected off the lake. He had never properly appreciated how pretty this part of the world was. He had always measured out his time here in drips and drabs—a few weeks of leave here, a month between ships there. It wasn't enough to build a life, and maybe that had been his secret goal all along. Maybe he had been content to envision his family safe and sound, far away. Maybe that distance made it easier to assume all was well. It certainly made it easier to keep leaving.

This time he wasn't going to be able to leave with the same equanimity. His children weren't vaguely anonymous beings in the care of a loving mother. When he was back on the *Patroclus*, he'd wonder if Peggy was following the ship's travels on her globe. He'd wonder if Jamie had calculated the cubic footage of the new barn and whether Ned was going to go to university in a few years or stay here and tend to the estate. He'd wonder if they thought about him or if he had faded out of their memory.

Phillip determined that this time he'd write. He'd dictate letters and have his lieutenant or one of the younger officers write them out, and he'd figure out an excuse to ask someone to read the letters he hoped he would receive in return. It was always awkward, but he couldn't go another year or more with no contact with his own children.

That didn't solve the problem of Ben, though. He glanced over at the man. His freckles were out in force, and Phillip thought his hair had bleached from flax to nearly white over the past two weeks. His strong jaw was still clenched a bit more rigidly than usual, but it looked like most of his anger had burnt off during their walk.

Phillip didn't know how he would get by without seeing Ben every day, without his fearless honesty and unrestrained affection. Even if letters had been an option—and given that Phillip needed intermediaries to both write and receive letters, they most definitely were not—they wouldn't be enough. He needed Ben near him, with him. As if to underscore the point, he glanced over his shoulder and took Ben's hand. They were alone, safe.

Ben didn't hesitate before squeezing back. Of course he didn't. That was what Phillip valued about him, this frankness and openness.

"Come here," Phillip said, tugging Ben off the path and towards a copse of trees that would shelter them if anyone passed by. There was frank and open and there was utterly suicidal, and Phillip was—well, Phillip was none of those things. And he'd protect Ben.

He pushed Ben against a tree and kissed him. He meant the kiss to say the things he couldn't put into words. Affection, fondness, gratitude. Whatever the word was for when you knew you would miss somebody and hated thinking about it, even though the person was still right there before you, in the flesh. He meant the kiss to be gentle, tender, all the things he usually wasn't.

But Ben reversed their positions so it was Phillip with his back against the tree. The kiss turned insistent, almost rough, a clash of lips and tongues and teeth. Ben's hands pressed Phillip's shoulders, his body somehow seeming larger and more imposing against his own.

"Benedict," Phillip breathed. "I want you."

"When we get back," Ben murmured against Phillip's lips. "Whatever you like."

Phillip shuddered against Ben's chest. Did the man even know what he was saying? "We don't have to . . ."

"Please. I'm a grown man and I'm not likely to ever again meet someone I feel this way about. So, let's just agree to have everything together. While we can."

Those words shouldn't have sounded so melancholy.

CHAPTER SIXTEEN

They managed to get to the summit of the crag with their clothing on, because as much as Phillip wanted Ben, there were some things he was not willing to do, and fucking the vicar *en plein air* was one of them.

Phillip sat on a rock that formed a sort of bench overlooking the lake, and Ben sat beside him without waiting for an invitation. Their shoulders touched, and the familiarity of the contact warmed Phillip in a way he hadn't thought possible. Touching Ben, even being near him, felt like being joined with a half he hadn't known was missing. He felt newly complete, but couldn't quite enjoy it because that other half would shortly be wrenched away from him, and he didn't know how he was going to get on with his life knowing that there was a vital piece of him in Cumberland.

Ben wordlessly passed him a flask, and Phillip cautiously sniffed its contents. "Cider," Sedgwick explained.

Phillip took a long drink before recoiling at the taste. "You call that cider?"

"It might be a bit stronger than what you're used to." Phillip could hear the wicked smile in the other man's voice, and he smiled back. For a moment it felt like the sun that always seemed to shine on Ben was shining a bit on Phillip too.

"Right. Because in His Majesty's Navy we only drink weak tea." He took another, much shorter, pull from the flask before passing it back.

Ben drank. "It's a local specialty. They make it every fall and by the next summer it's a potent brew." Unsaid went the fact that Phillip would know this if he had spent more time here. "My father used to have it brought up from the inn in a dogcart. I grew up right over there." He gestured with his chin to the far side of the hill in the opposite direction from where they had come from. "My father still lives there."

Phillip already knew that, but he could tell that Ben had something on his mind. "Did you want to call on him?"

"I never want to call on him." Ben scrubbed a hand through his messy hair. "No, that's not fair. He doesn't mean any harm, but we don't see eye to eye about anything, really. He thinks that by being a clergyman, I'm serving my oppressors. He'd rather I live with a pair of lovers on borrowed funds while writing tracts about free love." Another long drink.

"A pair of lovers?" Phillip echoed.

"Or three. He doesn't believe in monogamy, which is all well and good. He believes in beauty and truth and while I'd like to think there's some overlap there with my faith, the fact is that he doesn't see the point in what I do. He thinks taking jam to invalids isn't something a grown man ought to devote his life to."

"You do much more than take jam to invalids. You're a very good vicar."

"What do you know of good vicars or poor ones?" There was more heat in Ben's voice than Phillip was accustomed to.

"I know that my children adore you." *And so do I*, he wanted to add. "And so does everyone else," he said instead. "They speak of you as if you hung the moon. That has to count for something."

Ben still looked out over the lake, across the water to the houses in the village. "Well, I hope so. I know this likely sounds half-baked to someone like you, but I think that by helping people—sometimes in small ways and sometimes in larger ways—I'm doing what's right. That . . . that I'm serving God. But it's hard to explain that to people who don't believe."

"I don't need to believe in God to see the value of what you're doing." Phillip didn't know how to talk about this in a way that didn't insult either Ben's beliefs or his own.

When the silence dragged out perilously long, Phillip feared he had bungled things. But then Ben finally turned to him and took hold of his hand. "You're a lovely man, aren't you?"

Phillip felt that he was being condescended to, and bristled despite himself. He made a dismissive noise, hoping to change the topic.

"I'll miss you when you're gone," Ben continued.

"I'll miss you too," Phillip said, his voice gruff.

"There's nothing to be done about it." Ben rose to his feet and dusted off his breeches.

"You really are in a foul temper."

"It happens so seldom I think I lack practice on how to best shake it off," the vicar said wryly, and flashed Phillip a smile only slightly dimmer than his usual one.

Phillip suddenly felt like he had stolen that smile, stolen this moment and this entire summer. He was only a temporary presence in Ben's life, and he didn't have any right to intimacy like this. Phillip meant nothing. He had once again become a convenient friend.

"Let's go back to the house where I can try to help with that mood of yours." He wanted to push this conversation away from the future, away from the things that divided them, and to the familiar ground of kisses and touches.

Maybe his effort worked, because Ben laughed. "You really are lovely." He pulled Phillip behind the rock, safe from view. And right there, on the summit of a mountain, he took hold of Phillip's lapels and kissed him. And the kiss felt stolen too.

Ben left Phillip at the place where the lane diverged, one path snaking over to Barton Hall and the other leading further down the hill to the village.

"We'll see you at dinner?" Phillip asked, and Ben could have wept at the frank hope in his voice.

Ben ought to spend the night at the vicarage instead of getting even more tangled up with Phillip. If he were even halfway prudent he'd head straight to the village, send for his valise, and not go back to Barton Hall until its master was away at sea. He ought to do whatever he could to protect his heart, to protect Phillip's heart, and try to save some remnants of the stable life he had worked so hard for.

"I'll be there," he said instead. He wasn't strong enough to say no. Or maybe he just knew that whatever he was feeling was worth more than mere prudence.

As if to fully commit to this path of guaranteed ruin, he reached out and took Phillip's hand. It was a handshake, nothing overly intimate, but when he looked in Phillip's eyes he thought the other man could see everything in his heart. Oh, blast it. They were both going to be miserable at the end of this, even without Easterbrook's machinations.

"I'll be there," he repeated, Phillip's hand rough and warm against his own.

Ben stood at that fork in the road for a few minutes, hoping to compose himself a bit before heading to the village. He was surprised to hear footsteps coming behind him, from the path he and Phillip had just traveled down. He turned to see his housekeeper, bearing what seemed to be several empty dishes.

"Mrs. Winston, what are you doing here?"

To his amazement, her cheeks turned crimson. "I had to get the empty pie tins from your father, didn't I?"

"There are—" he paused to count "—five tins. You've made my father five pies? If he's eaten five pies in the last week I'll expect to find him having some kind of fit the next time I see him."

"He didn't eat them alone, now, did he?" she retorted.

Ben had no idea why he was quarreling in the lane with

his housekeeper about his father's pie consumption or anything else. "You're kind to look after him," he said. "You don't need to—"

"I don't need to do a blessed thing I don't want to, Benedict Sedgwick, and you remember that."

"Quite," he said, holding his hands up in surrender. He thought it wise to let her proceed ahead of him quite some distance before starting towards the village himself.

His thoughts drifted to what Hartley had said, or rather what he hadn't said. Embarrassment and coyness were so far from Hartley's usual attitude that Ben had to believe he was holding back something of importance. For Martin to contest his father's will due to Hartley's supposed influence over Sir Humphrey, and for Hartley to be awkward about it . . . Ben kept turning it over in his mind, trying to make sense of it, but it was like a hand of patience that wouldn't work out because he couldn't make himself turn over one crucial card.

By the time the steeple of St. Aelred's came into view, he was more perplexed than ever. And that steeple needed repairs in the worst way, but Martin was holding back the money due to what seemed a childish resentment of Ben's family. After finishing his business in the village, Ben made up his mind to call at Lindley Priory right away and see if they could put their differences behind them. That, he felt certain, was the right thing to do. Perhaps he could even help Martin, who, after all, was young and possibly in need of guidance. He set off in the direction of Lindley Priory.

The priory had once been almost a second home to the Sedgwicks, Ben and his brothers coming and going at all hours. But the Lindley Priory that Ben saw now was only an echo of the house he once knew. The stableyard was empty of horses and grooms, the dog kennels were silent, the bowling green was overgrown and weedy, and Ben counted at least three boarded-up windows on an upper story of the house. All these details spoke of radically tightened purse strings.

"Oh, spare me, Sedgwick," Martin said when he found Ben waiting for him in the study. "You're here to lecture me on responsibility, but I don't have time for it, so can we just take it as read?" Martin looked rumpled and weary, as if he had slept in his clothes and been woken too soon. He didn't sit, so neither did Ben.

"I didn't come here to lecture you. I came to offer you help."

Martin rolled his eyes, reminding Ben of the child he had once been. "You're about the last person on earth whose help I want."

"I see that. But it wasn't my help I was offering. I thought Captain Dacre might be of some assistance. His estates are very profitable, even in his absence, and I thought perhaps—"

"He was here the other day, offering the exact same thing. At least make an effort to keep track of your do-gooders, will you?"

Ben felt a wash of pride in Phillip, that he had tried to help his neighbor. "Are you alone here?"

"Of course not." Martin turned away from Ben and made as if to fuss over something on the mantelpiece, but it was bare. "I still have a few servants."

"What I meant is that you don't have anyone to talk to.

I don't see how you have the money to contest your father's will if you're living like this." He gestured around him at the shabby room, the empty house. This was no way to live for a man of one-and-twenty.

The younger man spun to face Ben, his expression shifting from weary exasperation to frustrated anger. "That's a matter of principle."

"What principle, Martin?" Ben asked. "Your father left a small house to his godson. That's not unusual."

Martin huffed out an angry laugh. "My father left a house in Mayfair to his lover."

Ben stared, speechless. "That's not possible," he finally managed.

"The house—and your living, and Will's commission, and all your school fees—were payment for services rendered. I have letters," he said, looking nauseated on those last words.

"When? When did it start?"

"That winter we were snowed in at Fellside Grange. Right before you went to university."

Hartley would have been sixteen. "Oh my God." It was half a prayer. Had Hartley been coerced? He had been young and poor, and a proposition from wealthy Sir Humphrey would have been coercion indeed. "Oh my God." He was furious—with a dead man, but mainly with himself.

"I see you really didn't know. I'm almost sorry to have told you." He frowned, as if the vestiges of a stricken conscience were working on him.

"I'll have to resign."

"What? Why would you do a thing like that?"

"If you think I can eat bread my brother earned—like that—as a child—" He shook his head. "Consider this my official resignation."

"If you're going to have a moral crisis, do it somewhere else, thank you. I've been living with this revolting knowledge for ages, and I have no desire to discuss it."

Ben rose to his feet and left without saying goodbye. He needed to go to Hartley—except Hartley hadn't wanted to tell him his secret, which might mean he'd resent Ben's having found out. He wanted to ask his father if he had known, but he doubted whether Alton Sedgwick, who rarely even noticed a roof leaking onto his head, would have noticed something that had escaped even Ben's attention. Ben would never forgive himself for having failed to see what was going on that winter.

One thing that was certain was that he could no longer keep his living. Over the past several weeks he had watched his dreams fall apart one by one and float into the sky like dandelion fluff. He wanted an orderly life, a decent living, a family of his own. Now he was realizing he wouldn't have any of it.

He thought wistfully of his cozy vicarage.

He thought of Alice, and the life he already knew he couldn't have with her.

He thought of how if he weren't in Barton Kirkby during Phillip's rare visits, they wouldn't even have that small to-getherness to look forward to.

It was fine, he told himself. He hadn't counted on a last-ing friendship with the captain. He only knew that what he felt for the man was real and true. And *returned*. Whatever was between them, even if it was transient, was good and sweet and right. Life was filled with things that were both good and impermanent, he reminded himself. Flowers in bloom. Children in their infancy.

He'd just have to wring the joy and pleasure out of every moment he had with Phillip. That was all there was to it.

Usually Phillip lingered at the table for a few minutes after the children left, stupidly relishing every precious minute alone with the vicar. But tonight he didn't think he could bear it. He told the children that he'd love nothing more than to hear *Robinson Crusoe*, and followed them upstairs.

"Have you ever been shipwrecked?" Peg asked, as she settled herself in bed beside her twin.

"I do think he might have mentioned it," Ned said with a sidelong, amused glance at Phillip. At some point over the past fortnight, Ned had gone from being a surly, overgrown child to being very nearly an adult. It was as if now that he had his father and Ben around, two men he could trust, he could stop angrily protecting his younger siblings and start being himself. Phillip had found him poring over school-books that had been left behind by a fleeing tutor. He seemed to actually enjoy reading bedtime stories and tending to the home farm, but somebody would need to talk to him about his plans for the future.

"Were you ever a castaway, Papa?" Jamie asked. "Or a stowaway? Or really anything interesting at all?"

"No, I'm afraid not," Phillip said gravely. "I promise to let you know if that ever comes to pass."

He settled back in his chair and listened to Ned read aloud. After a few pages, he passed the book to Peggy. When she tired, Ned took over again, and they followed this pattern until Crusoe had several adventures of varying degrees of implausibility and Peggy started to yawn.

"Does Jamie not want a turn?" Phillip asked. The deathly silence that fell over the room reminded Phillip too much of his first days after his return to Barton Hall, and the contrast of that enmity with the present was so startling he almost didn't pick up on the significance of what was happening. Until then it hadn't occurred to Phillip that his own difficulty with reading might be something that ran in the blood. But when he saw Peggy and Ned exchange a wary look and Jamie look shame-faced at his hands, he understood. "Ah," he managed. "Not everybody cares for reading aloud." If Jamie couldn't read, then there was no wonder that everyone in this house seemed so dead set against sending him to school. Phillip thoroughly agreed. He would never wish for anyone, least of all his own child, to go through what he had endured. Even now, in his darkest moments, it was the voices of his schoolmasters that he heard in his mind.

"Did you want to take over?" Ned asked, holding the book out to Phillip.

"Ah. No." Phillip shook his head quickly. "I really can't. I don't enjoy reading any more than Jamie does." Was that enough? No, of course it wasn't. Yet again, Phillip did not have anything of value to offer. He'd have to speak to Jamie, but he didn't know what to say. He had never spoken of this matter to anyone; McCarthy had figured it out on his own and never made Phillip endure a conversation. Now, Phillip's own habitual secrecy and creeping sense of shame made it impossible to come up with the right words.

He heard the sound of a throat being cleared and saw the vicar leaning in the doorway. "I think it's time to leave Mr. Crusoe for the evening. Tomorrow is Sunday so I won't see you until supper. Behave," Ben said, mainly looking at Peggy. "Or, if you don't, at least be safe and let Ned or your father know where you are at all times."

"Yes, Mr. Sedgwick," the twins said. Phillip kissed Peg's forehead, patted Jamie's shoulder, and shook Ned's hand before shutting the nursery door behind him.

"I'm glad you'll be here when I'm back at sea," Phillip said, his voice ever so slightly gruff.

Ben looked at him with something like regret, and Phillip didn't know why. He didn't even want to know. "Let's go to bed," he whispered.

Chapter Seventeen

All hell broke loose before Ben returned from church.

First a pair of carriages arrived bearing Walsh, Walsh's sister, and a multitude of servants. When Phillip had invited Walsh to visit Barton Hall, he hadn't had any idea that the surgeon's family was the sort to travel with two postilions, a lady's maid, and a groom. Phillip couldn't even fathom where he was meant to put all these people.

"What the devil am I supposed to do about this?" Phillip asked the cook as they stood in the open doorway, surveying the chaos of horses, carriages, and servants. "Why don't I have a housekeeper?"

"You didn't need one when Mrs. Dacre was alive," Mrs. Morris said. "And then you did have one, for about a month, perhaps two governesses ago. She gave notice after the spider incident."

Now was not the time to inquire into the spider incident. If he didn't have a housekeeper, then Mrs. Morris could be his second-in-command. "On a ship, if the sailors were feeling put upon I'd order extra rations."

"It's the same idea. Your guests will leave a few shillings for the housemaids," Mrs. Morris said. "That's how it's done in the best houses. I'll make it clear to the rest of the staff that you'll give them an extra half day next week."

"Yes, of course." That was right. Phillip was so unaccustomed to the processes of civilized society he felt quite out of his depths. But perhaps running a household wasn't so terribly different from commanding a ship. "Right now we need extra hands on deck."

"The kitchen maid's sister is out of work and could come up to help with laundry."

"Do whatever you believe is needful," Phillip said. "In fact, consider yourself deputized."

The children had vanished into thin air, which likely meant they were in the stables, spying on the guests' horses, or perhaps taking advantage of Mrs. Morris's absence to steal sweets from the kitchen. Phillip had utter confidence that they were up to no good, but also that they'd come to no real harm. He had grown rather philosophical about misbehavior over the last few weeks. When he returned to the *Patroclus*, it might take him some time to get used to shipboard discipline, where any infraction needed to be treated seriously. *If* he returned, whispered some lunatic voice inside him.

"There you are," Walsh said, descending the stairs, just in time to stop that line of thought. "Daphne is getting changed but she'll be down in a moment." Daphne was Mrs. Howard,

Walsh's widowed sister, a woman of about thirty who had arrived in approximately an acre of gray silk. Phillip couldn't imagine what she was going to change into or why. Was he supposed to have arranged entertainment? Oh, hell, he most certainly was. Suddenly he remembered Sedgwick's brother and—damn it—Miss Crawford. They were lively and charming and he had said he would invite them for dinner. Well, he could send a footman to the village with a request for their company tonight.

When, still on board the *Patroclus*, he had invited Walsh to Barton Hall, he had thought he'd be desperate for a familiar face. Now, he was utterly stymied by the man's arrival. He had mere weeks left with his children, with Sedgwick, and he didn't want to waste a single half second of his time on anyone else.

"Let me show you the gardens," he said, because that seemed like a normal thing to say. He felt like he was playing the role of Affable Host in a stage play. Next, he'd be suggesting a game of charades.

Walsh looked at him curiously, as if he weren't quite sure whether Phillip was serious.

"The countryside agrees with you," Walsh said after admiring the shrubbery with due respect. "I haven't seen you look so well since, ah, that storm off the coast of Burma."

Walsh meant the storm where they had lost McCarthy, and Phillip was surprised to hear Walsh acknowledge it. Phillip had thought he had done a halfway decent job of concealing his grief.

"Perhaps the country does agree with me," Phillip said,

at a loss as to how else to answer. It stood to reason that he'd look healthier, happier, more whole after a fortnight such as the one he had just passed.

Oh, damn it. Damn Sedgwick and his easy charm and his general loveliness for ruining Phillip's peace of mind. Now Phillip would be unhappy at sea, and he certainly couldn't stay here at Barton Hall. His life was at sea. Wasn't it? And why the hell was he even doubting that?

This was insanity. Puppy love. Midsummer madness. He didn't even know what to call it, only that his head wasn't on straight.

And that it was Sedgwick's fault.

With so many perfectly worthy things to be concerned about—Hartley's past, Alice's future, his own vocation—Ben could somehow only manage to think about the one thing he couldn't do anything about. Ben was jealous. He envied Mr. Walsh's friendship with Phillip, their years of shared experience and the years they would spend together on board ship. He envied the doctor's sister, Mrs. Howard, who practically had a placard on her chest announcing that she was a wealthy widow in want of a home. He fairly seethed with envy when Phillip took her arm to lead her into the drawing room, and felt unreasonably surly that he couldn't do the same. He wanted to take Phillip by the arm, drag him into the nearest room with a door that locked, and make it perfectly clear that he, Ben, was the only one who was allowed to touch Phillip.

It didn't help one bit that the guests were all perfectly unobjectionable—polite to Ben, gracious to the children during the short time they had appeared in the drawing room, and brimming with amusing stories.

Nor did it help when Hartley and Alice arrived to join them for dinner. There was no hiding from Hartley's too-knowing gaze. And as for Alice, well, he felt like a rotter.

"You're walking," he said when he met them in the hall, stating the fantastically obvious. Her steps were uncertain and she leaned heavily on Hartley, but she was able to support herself.

"We couldn't fit the Bath chair in Hartley's curricle. Don't tell anyone but Hartley carried me down the stairs to the street. Mama said it was lewd, and I laughed so hard Hartley threatened to toss me out of the carriage."

"She has no conduct," Hartley said without rancor. "Rusticated chit."

"This rusticated chit took six steps. Well, Hartley did most of it, but I stayed vertical."

"You look lovely," he told her. And she did. Her honey gold hair was held up with pearl combs and she wore a gown of plain muslin that he recognized as her best frock. He took her hand. It was still cold and thin, and he wondered if this was only a temporary recovery. When she smiled weakly, he knew she harbored the same thought.

"What about me?" Hartley asked, breaking the mood. "Don't I look lovely?"

"You never let us forget it," Alice retorted.

"I spoke with Martin Easterbrook about his father's will,"

Ben said quietly after the introductions had been made and Alice was talking to Mrs. Howard.

"Ah." Only the briefest flicker of recognition passed across Hartley's face. "He has letters that he intends to produce in chancery."

"How bad are they?"

"Bad enough."

Ben squeezed Hartley's arm. "I'm so sorry. I didn't realize."

"You weren't meant to," Hartley said, raising an eyebrow.

Seated at the table, Ben tried to summon whatever remnants of good humor he had left, but he was almost relieved when a slightly frazzled-looking housemaid presented him with a folded square of paper. Thank heaven, somebody needed him elsewhere. A leak in the vicarage roof, anything at all would be preferable to enduring dinner with the brother he had failed, the woman he was about to fail, and Phillip. He supposed he and Phillip would soon be failing one another.

But then he unfolded the note and read it. It was in the village apothecary's scrawl. He got immediately to his feet, dropping the note onto the table. "I'm afraid I'll miss dinner. Mr. Farleigh has taken a turn for the worse." Everyone at the table murmured the appropriate words of concern. Phillip cast him a meaningful glance, but didn't follow, and Ben was left to his duties alone.

Dinner was going to be every bit as bad as could be expected. Without Ben, Phillip was left presiding over a table of people who seemed determined to be merry. Phillip felt about as merry as a marble bust.

"Hartley, tell the story of that time you had to rescue me from the tree," Miss Crawford said, a twinkle in her eyes.

"Do you mean the time you got chased into a tree by a lamb?"

"Be fair, Hart. It was a very frightening lamb."

Mr. Hartley Sedgwick then proceeded to regale the table with a tale that made both Miss Crawford and himself look amusingly hapless and Ben heroically competent. Mrs. Howard was wiping tears of laughter from her eyes and Walsh sat back contentedly in his chair, cradling his wineglass easily in his hand.

Everything would have been a good deal more manageable if Alice Crawford weren't so damned charming, if he could have pretended that he was the inadvertent means of impoverishing some kind of rural villainess. He ought to have known that any friend of Ben's would be a paragon.

Since there was no hostess, they all retired to the drawing room at the same time. Walsh materialized by Miss Crawford's side to help her from the table, and Hartley seemed occupied in brushing lint off his coat, leaving Phillip and Mrs. Howard to leave the dining room together.

Phillip had at first been slightly annoyed that Walsh was throwing Mrs. Howard at him. It could have been hideously awkward if Mrs. Howard hadn't taken it in stride. "Don't mind my brother," she whispered. "He can't help himself."

Oh, for heaven's sake. Was everyone determined to be gracious and charming when all Phillip wanted to do was scowl? As he walked past Ben's empty chair, he saw the note that had called Ben away from the table. He palmed it, not certain what to do. Once he had settled Mrs. Walsh in the drawing room, he unfolded it, hoping that the sender of the note wrote the kind of hand that managed to stay still. But he had no such luck: the note had been written hastily with what looked like an unsharpened pencil, so the writing wiggled and blurred its way across the page.

"If you'll excuse me," he said to his guests. He was being a terrible host, but he didn't care. "I ought to see to the children."

He found Ned once again reading aloud from *Robinson Crusoe*. When Jamie saw his father in the doorway, he shifted wordlessly to the side, making room in his bed for Phillip. Phillip squeezed in, and Jamie dropped his head sleepily to Phillip's shoulder. In the other bed, Peggy was already nodding off. When Ned reached what sounded like the end of a chapter, Phillip cleared his throat. "Mr. Sedgwick was called away urgently, and he left this note. Would you mind reading it for me? My eyes aren't up to the task. They, ah, never are."

Ned's eyes opened wide, but he took the paper Phillip handed him. "'Dear Mr. Sedgwick,'" he read. "'Mr. Farleigh has taken a turn. I doubt he will last the night. Mrs. Farleigh has asked for you.'" He put the note down. "It's signed Davis. He's the apothecary some of the tenants use." The boy's forehead creased with thought. "But the Farleighs don't have money for Mr. Davis."

"I called on him the other day and asked that he attend Mr. Farleigh and send the bill to me." He hadn't meant anyone to find out. He felt like he was getting too involved with people he'd soon be far away from.

"That was kind. Here's your note back," he said, passing the folded square to Phillip. "Do you need spectacles, Father?" He peered curiously at Phillip, and Phillip saw that Ned knew exactly what was wrong with his eyes.

"Alas, it's not something spectacles can solve," he said, glancing at Jamie. But Jamie was already asleep, his head pillowed on Phillip's shoulder. Peggy, too, had fallen asleep. Ned closed the book, whispered good night, and retired to his own bedroom next door. Phillip stayed in Jamie's bed for a while, listening to the sound of the children's breathing.

The night was clear and warm, still and moonless, as Ben carefully picked his way along the narrow lane. He arrived at the farm as the apothecary was leaving.

"I told Mrs. Farleigh I'd come back in the morning," the apothecary said. He had the weary look of a man who had been awake far too long and with little to show for it. "There's nothing I can do but give him laudanum." He sighed. This was not the first time he and Ben had met at the home of the ill or dying. "He's nearly eighty," he said, as if that made death more palatable. And it did, in a way; people several degrees away from death tended to find comfort in the idea that the departed had lived out his full allotment of time on earth. The nearest mourners never did. There was only scant comfort for them, and Ben knew it too well.

"And he's been suffering." This was Ben's part in the litany, the pretense that death was acceptable if it relieved pain. This ritual dispensed with, the two men nodded at one another, the apothecary left, and Ben went into the eerily still farmhouse. Tonight there wasn't even the stale scent of cooking or the crackle of an unseasonable fire. He found Mrs. Farleigh where he knew she would be, by her husband's bedside. He wordlessly sat beside her and waited.

There was nothing to do but sit. He offered to pray with her, but she shook her head, and they both knew there would be time enough for prayers in the following days. But he couldn't leave her alone. Eventually a neighbor or relation would arrive, and when Mr. Farleigh died, it would be the women who laid him out. It would be the women who had the work to do. All Ben had to do was bury this poor woman's husband.

All he had to do was watch as this woman had half her soul wrenched away. It didn't matter that he was old; it didn't matter that he had been sick; it didn't matter that she believed he'd be in a heaven more vivid and concrete than Ben could muster up any faith in. She was still going to lose him.

So he sat, giving her his presence while knowing it was inadequate, as so many necessary gestures were. He watched the dying man's chest rise and fall, his ragged breaths coming too irregularly. He remembered every other sickbed he had attended, every other person he had watched leave this earth, every mourner they had left behind, broken, incomplete, shattered.

He thought of Phillip, who had lost a wife but had also suffered a loss he couldn't even talk about because it didn't have a name. He thought about his father, who had also endured two losses—Ben's mother and then Will's mother. That second loss didn't have a name either. And maybe Ben had been quick to dismiss it as less than the loss of an actual wife. But Alton Sedgwick's grief had been real as he watched Will's mother grow weaker and paler until she could barely hold the blood-soaked handkerchief to her mouth. He ought to have done better by his father by recognizing that his grief may have affected his ability to care for his children. Shortly before dawn, the old man's breathing stopped entirely, and Mrs. Farleigh went perfectly still. Ben took her hand—another necessary but inadequate gesture—and recited the Psalm everyone always relied on at these times. Had anyone held Phillip's hand? Had anyone held his father's?

Would anyone hold his own when Phillip was taken from him? It was a senseless question, because he would never be with Phillip the way Mr. and Mrs. Farleigh had been together.

They only had the present. But they needed the present. *Necessary but inadequate*, his tired, overwrought mind recited back to him.

By first light, neighbors had arrived, and Ben left, promising to return in the evening.

CHAPTER EIGHTEEN

Phillip would have waited downstairs for Ben's return, if such behavior might have gone unremarked in a household that now seemed to teem with servants and guests. Instead, he left his bedroom door open, knowing he would hear Ben's footsteps when the man returned home. He didn't even dress for bed, wanting to be ready to go to Ben, if Ben needed him. But hours passed and clocks chimed and eventually Phillip dozed off in his chair. He woke at the sound of careful steps in the corridor and sprang to his feet.

In the scant morning light, he could see Ben poised by the door to his own bedchamber. His hand was on the latch, but he paused and looked over his shoulder at the snick of Phillip shutting his door behind him.

"You're back," Phillip whispered, when he was near enough to be heard. Ben had purple half-moons beneath his eyes and a ragged, worn-out look. "Is all well?"

"Mr. Farleigh died a few hours ago," Ben whispered, stepping into his room and waving Phillip in.

"I'm so sorry."

Ben made a gesture that struck Phillip as very . . . clerical. It was halfway between a shrug and a nod, and seemed to acknowledge Phillip's sympathy without making a fuss. Phillip realized Ben, for all his youth, for all his good humor and abundant cheer, was practiced in this situation.

When the door shut behind them, Phillip drew Ben close, trying to offer whatever small mote of comfort or understanding or even fellowship he could. Ben felt solid in his arms, strong and broad and hearty, but the way he sighed as he sank against Phillip's chest made Phillip feel like he was holding something unspeakably fragile.

It was Ben who reached behind Phillip and turned the key in the lock; it was Ben who changed the embrace to something warmer, kissing below Phillip's ear, sliding his hands to Phillip's hips.

"You must be tired. We don't need to," Phillip said, but it likely didn't sound terribly convincing because at the moment Ben had him pressed against the closed door, their bodies flush together and their mouths a hair's breadth apart.

"I lost track of where want crosses into need a while ago, Phillip. But this feels a lot like need. I need to be with you." He pushed his hips forward, as if Phillip needed this explained to him. "Together with you."

Phillip's blood heated. "That can be arranged," he said gruffly before cupping Ben's face in his hands and kissing him. Ben seemed to melt into his embrace, his strong body going almost boneless in Phillip's arms.

"We don't need to fuck," Phillip growled. The silence

stretched long enough for Phillip to worry that he had shocked Sedgwick with his language. "There are people who don't, you know. And that's enough."

Ben nodded. "I want to fuck."

Oh God. He somehow made the word sound sweet and filthy all at once, and it went straight to Phillip's groin. "I want that too," he whispered, and tipped Ben's chin up for a kiss. He wanted everything. He wanted closeness and honesty and safety and time, and out of those the first two were the only things he could even partly manage.

They fell onto the bed, clothes in a heap on the floor, Ben's weight a welcome presence on top of Phillip.

"Yes," Phillip said, arching helplessly up towards Sedgwick's body. At the sweep of Ben's tongue inside his mouth, Phillip let himself acknowledge exactly what he wanted. "I want you inside me," he said.

The other man went still, and Phillip feared he had miscalculated. "I thought we'd do it the other way around," Ben said, his voice hardly more than a whisper.

Phillip ran his hand up Ben's back. "So had I, at first." Now they were both whispering. "And I've never . . . I've never been the receiving party." Which seemed a laughably formal way to discuss getting buggered but Phillip found himself wishing for lovelier language than he knew.

"But you want to?"

Phillip's chest felt tight. "With you, yes." It shouldn't cost so much to admit it. Hell, it shouldn't feel like an admission at all. He had fucked men and they had liked it; he didn't think any less of them for it, but it seemed too open, too vulnerable, for Phillip himself to actually want. With Ben it didn't matter, though—he was already about as vulnerable as a person could get; mere physical vulnerability hardly seemed to signify.

"Well, I've never been either party, so it seems only right and proper that you ought to do it to me first. That way I at least know something of what I'm doing when we do it the other way around."

There would be another time. Phillip's mind latched on to that with disproportionate relief. "All right," he said. "I'll fuck you, then." He felt Ben's cock twitch against his belly. "You like when I talk like that?"

"I like everything about this." Ben kissed Phillip's neck, then his collarbone. "I like you. So much."

Phillip continued smoothing his hands up and down Ben's back, as if soothing him, but really he was the one who needed soothing. He felt that this would be irrevocable, that this next hour or so would either burn every bridge he hadn't yet destroyed, or build new ones to places he hadn't ever been.

He rolled them over and felt Ben's sigh of pleasure as Phillip settled over him. Phillip kissed each of Ben's palms in turn before holding his hands to the mattress and kissing him deeply on the mouth. He kissed down Ben's body, licking the scruffy underside of his jaw and sucking on the place where his shoulder met his neck.

Ben sighed, resting his hand on Phillip's head. Phillip flicked his tongue over one flat, tawny nipple and felt it pebble beneath his touch. Ben's hand tightened in his hair.

Phillip ran his lips along the taut muscles of Ben's chest and abdomen. He tried to make every touch, every kiss, every caress into an offering, and he knew it fell short. But he kept doing it anyway.

Ben was, frankly, slightly concerned. Even though he devoted an unconscionable amount of time over the past week to imagining Phillip inside him, the first touch of Phillip's callused fingers against the skin below his bollocks made him shiver in a way that wasn't entirely pleasurable. Even the warm wet heaven of Phillip's mouth on his cock wasn't enough to completely distract him from his misgivings.

When Phillip produced a jar of some kind of salve from his clothes press, Ben nearly changed his mind. But then Phillip sat on the edge of the bed and kissed Ben's knee. "There are a lot of other things we can do," he whispered.

Ben shook his head. He knew Phillip would be satisfied with more of what they had already done. But Ben wanted this. It was just him and Phillip. There was nothing about this act that could be scarier than actually falling in love with the knowledge that they would soon be parted—that, hell, everyone was parted, everyone lost one another at the end. "I want you," he said, smiling despite himself. When Phillip returned to stroking slick fingers over his entrance, Ben let himself relax into the touch. And when Phillip slid a finger inside him, Ben was able to accept it after only the barest moment of hesitation.

But then—"Oh, hell," he groaned when Phillip slid another finger inside and did something that made Ben feel like he had been lit up like fireworks.

"Yes," Phillip urged. "Yes. That's why I wanted you to fuck me. *That*," he said, as his fingertips twisted over that place again. "Oh God, look at you." Phillip's eyes were darting between Ben's face and where his fingers slid in and out of Ben's body. "Yes, just like that. Let me in."

That was what Ben wanted too. He tried to relax even further into the sensation. "I want more."

"Not yet. I don't want to hurt you." He slid another finger in and pulled at Ben's cock with his other hand. "You're beautiful."

And Ben felt beautiful, which had to be a silly thing to think about oneself especially with another man's hand halfway inside him, but with Phillip's gaze on him like that, how could he doubt it? "Now," he pleaded, lifting his hips in an effort to accept more of Phillip's fingers. The sensation was intense; it was too much and yet he wanted more of it. He wanted everything Phillip had to give.

Phillip made a noise that was awfully close to a growl and slicked himself up with the salve. When he brushed the thick head of his erection against Ben's body, Ben had another moment of near panic.

Then Phillip pulled away. "Roll over," he ordered in that commanding but gentle tone of voice Ben loved so much.

"Yes, Captain," he said as he turned over, and was rewarded with another growl. Phillip pulled Ben's hips up and used his knees to spread Ben's legs a bit further, and that slight show of command made Ben feel that he was safe, in good, experienced hands. Phillip's hands stroked down Ben's back, his lips skimming kisses along Ben's neck and shoulder. This time, when Phillip started to press in, Ben didn't flinch.

"You have to let me in," Phillip murmured, his voice rough. "Let me be in you."

At the sound of his voice, Ben would have done anything. He tried to relax his body enough to accept this new, strange, and not entirely pleasant sensation. One of Phillip's hands was on his hip, holding him steady, but the other came to caress the back of Ben's neck. And that felt lovely, too lovely, and when he felt soft lips brush against his shoulder, he thought maybe this odd experience might not be all bad. Even if it was uncomfortable, it was worth it, and it would be over soon enough and then maybe—

"Oh damn," he groaned. Phillip had hit that place inside him that felt like it was made of liquid pleasure. Ben could feel the sensation spiraling through his body, up his spine and down to his toes. It happened again, and all Ben wanted was more. The presence of Phillip's length inside his body was still foreign and strange but somehow the intrusiveness of it melded with the pleasure, and Ben found he craved both equally.

"Hush," Phillip murmured, his voice rough. "We have to be quiet."

They were being quiet, as quiet as two people could be, but Ben pressed his face into the mattress to muffle his sounds of pleasure, twisting his hands into his sheets. Phillip's body was strong and hard behind him, his fingers digging into Ben's hip as he thrust slowly in and out. Ben realized he was holding back.

"More," Ben whispered. "Please. *Phillip*."

Phillip groaned and shifted his stance, dropping a kiss onto Ben's shoulder before moving again. Ben gripped himself with a shaking, sweaty hand, stroking himself almost frantically. When Phillip's rhythm faltered and the fingers on Ben's hips were so tight it felt like Phillip was holding on to Ben for dear life, Ben let himself fall into a perfect wave of pleasure.

Mine, Phillip thought, looking at Ben sprawled on the bed, his skin lit by the pale early light falling weakly through the window. *Mine*.

Even as his mind formed the word, he knew it to be a fantasy. Ben wasn't anyone's, least of all Phillip's. If he could properly be said to belong to anyone, it was that girl he intended to marry.

"What are you thinking of?" Ben asked. "You have that line between your eyebrows." He traced a finger down Phillip's forehead.

"Nothing," Phillip said, automatically deflecting any attempt at sincerity. Ben looked at him steadily, and Phillip knew he wasn't going to be allowed to wriggle out of honesty. Ben never let him. When he had been inside Ben—a flush spread up his body, as if he hadn't just spent harder than he had in years, as if he weren't fast approaching forty years of age—he hadn't been able to pretend this was just a search for pleasure. At every moment he had been reminded that this was Ben, his Ben, beneath him. Those sounds were coming from Ben's mouth; the hand gripping his own was Ben's; the strong body that went pliant beneath him was Ben's.

"Well, I'm thinking about what we just did." Ben's mouth was still half-pressed into the pillow, so his words came out slightly muffled.

"Oh, are you now?" Phillip asked, pushing the hair off Ben's face.

"Fucking," he said, as if testing out the word. "Or, you know, the union of souls. Whichever way you want to put it."

"Is that what we did? Join our souls?" Phillip was slightly startled.

Ben propped himself up on his elbow so he was looking down at Phillip. "I think we've been doing that for weeks."

For a moment Phillip could hardly breathe. "Benedict. God. I don't want to let you down. You deserve so much better—"

Ben silenced him with a lazy kiss. "Don't you dare tell me I don't deserve this. Don't you dare."

CHAPTER NINETEEN

After last night's meditation on grief and this morning's time with Phillip, any doubts Ben had about his marriage had crystallized. He could no more utter the marriage vows to Alice than he could renounce his faith. Alice might hate him, the world might think him the worst kind of cad, he might be consigning himself to a lifetime of solitude and loneliness, but he didn't see that he had any ethical alternative.

He had expected to find Alice alone or with her mother, but instead he found Mr. Walsh and his sister sitting in the Crawfords' snug parlor. He had entirely forgotten that they had all dined together last night in his absence. Indeed, they were all so engaged in lively conversation that they didn't at first notice Ben standing on the threshold. He supposed they all had a jolly time and made fast friends while he had been sitting at a deathbed. He didn't like that thought, and he didn't like that he was petty enough to entertain it.

It was Alice who finally saw him. His expression must

have communicated some of his gloom, because the smile immediately dropped off her face. "Oh, poor Mrs. Farleigh," she said immediately. Mr. Walsh and Mrs. Howard made murmuring sounds that could have been condolences or could have been their excuse to leave, but in either event they rose and headed to the door.

"I'll run that errand for you in Keswick, Miss Crawford," Mr. Walsh said, looking over his shoulder on his way out the door.

"Oh!" Alice's face brightened, and Ben feared it would be the last time he would see that kind of joy on her features, certainly for a long while, possibly forever. "Thank you!"

"What's the matter, Ben?" she asked when they were alone. "It can't be Mrs. Farleigh, because, well, you've had people die before and you didn't look like that."

"It isn't." He sat on a chair across from the sofa where she lay—she was back to reclining, he saw. Perhaps her attempt to walk last night had been too much. He couldn't very well ask, couldn't express concern about her condition and then confess that he could not support her. He filled his lungs with air and let it out. "I need to cry off on our betrothal."

Her eyes went wide. "Are you all right, Ben?"

He shook his head. "I'd be better if I knew how to get you a bit of money," he confessed.

She appeared not to mark his words. "I can't figure out who it is."

"Pardon?"

"You must have met someone else, and you must be terribly in love with her, or I can't see you, ah, jilting me." She didn't seem angry with him, even though she ought to be. "But I know everyone you do, and even though I haven't gotten around much in the past few months, I hear all the gossip. And there just isn't any about you."

Thank God for that. "There isn't any other woman, Alice." He couldn't quite bring himself to lie to her. "It's a question of . . ." He tried to find something to say. "It's a question of ethics."

"Oh," she said slowly, something like realization dawning on her face. "Oh dear. I won't tell Papa. He did mention something about a sermon of yours being rather popish."

Ben opened his mouth in surprise and snapped it shut again. If she thought his misgivings stemmed from a belief that clergy ought not to marry, he wouldn't correct her. He certainly wasn't going to marry anyone else, so she'd never have any cause to be disabused of the notion.

"So, you see my predicament," he said carefully, not wanting to confirm or deny her suspicion.

"I suppose I do. Well. That does leave me rather up the creek, my friend, but I can't say I was delighted to be marrying someone who was only lukewarm about the prospect—"

He started to deny it but she cut him off.

"We've known one another practically all our lives, Ben. I do know when you're enthusiastic about something. And I know you love me. Just as I love you."

"I was looking forward to our marriage," he said feebly.

"So was I," she said. "But not, I think, in the way of the butcher's boy and the baker's daughter." He hadn't understood her meaning when she first invoked these two fictional lovers, but now he did. Now he knew all too well. "I was cross with you," she went on, "for not understanding that I want more than someone to put a roof over my head. I know that I'm crippled and rather poor, but I wish you didn't think it was impossible for me to find somebody who wants me. That's what I want, and I think it's what most of us want, and who are you to think I can't do better than charity?"

"I don't—"

"And I'm grateful to you, too, which only makes me feel ashamed of being angry." Her voice broke on her last words.

"Alice," he said, crouching on the ground before her sofa and taking her hand. "You're my dearest friend and I think you deserve everything that's good in the world. Everything. I know that after today I'm likely to lose your friendship, but before I leave I want you to know that."

"We're still friends, you idiot." She wiped her eyes. "I just wish everything were different."

Ben squeezed her hand. "So do I," he said. "So do I."

"Sit yourself down," Mrs. Winston chided as Ben whisked dust covers off the furniture in the vicarage study. After seeing Alice, all he wanted was to burrow in a hole like a wounded animal. He didn't want to return to Barton Hall, where he had found so much happiness, but had also diverted the course of his life. "That's my job you're at, and even if you didn't see fit to send notice that you meant to come back today, that doesn't make it any less my job to see that things are done the way they ought."

Ben attempted to fold one of the covers but Mrs. Winston snatched it from his hand. Dust covers seemed a bit excessive for so short an absence—had it only been a month ago that he left the vicarage for Barton Hall?—but Mrs. Winston liked things done properly. He didn't want to tell her quite yet that he only planned to be at the vicarage for as long as it took to arrange for a curate to take over his duties or for Sir Martin to appoint his replacement.

"Oh, you're going to be like that, are you?" she said, hands on her hips.

He attempted a sheepish smile, but it must have fallen flat because she raised her gray eyebrows so high they disappeared into her cap. "You'll be wanting tea," she said, and disappeared towards the back of the house.

He wadded up the dust covers and tossed them into a corner of the room for Mrs. Winston to *tsk* over later, then sat at his desk and buried his head in his hands. He tried to get past his anger and confusion and sort out what needed to be done. First he needed to write an official letter of resignation. Then he needed to write to Phillip.

He performed all the small acts of time wasting, tasks that were adjacent to writing but not actually putting pen to paper. He straightened his blotter, topped off the inkwell, cut himself a new nib. He smoothed out a creamy sheet of writing paper and dated it.

At the sound of tapping on the doorframe, he turned, fully expecting to see Mrs. Winston standing in the open doorway, bearing a tray of tea and demanding explanations for his sudden arrival. But it was Hartley, his hands in his pockets and a self-conscious air about him.

"I saw that the curtains had been opened," Hartley offered, still in the doorway. "And I thought I might come by."

"Of course. Sit, please."

Hartley shut the door behind him and sat in a chair that was covered in threadbare tapestry.

"I'm glad you came to see me."

Hartley raised his eyebrows in an expression of surprise. "Are you?" he asked with an air of insouciance.

Ben leaned towards his brother. "Yes, Hartley. Don't ever doubt it."

Hartley looked around the room. "I forgot how snug this little place is."

Ben glanced at the door, confirming that it was shut. "I'm resigning."

"What? Why the devil would you do a thing like that?"

Ben smoothed his hand across the still-blank paper before him. "I need to leave. I need a fresh start someplace new. Maybe I'll settle in a city and serve the poor." Surely that sounded plausible.

"Well, that's a fat lot of nonsense," Hartley said levelly. "You've never shown any interest in going farther than Keswick. What does Alice say? Does she fancy living in destitution among the urban poor?"

"I broke the engagement."

Hartley's jaw actually fell open. "Well," he said, recovering himself, "if we didn't have Easterbrook to worry about, I might be glad to hear it."

"But you've always liked Alice."

"Indeed I have, but as much as I hate to agree with our father about anything, it seems unwise to marry where there isn't love."

"I do love her!" Ben protested.

"You want to shag the captain, though."

Ben sucked in a breath. Damn it, he ought to have known that Hartley could have seen that. "That's ludicrous," he said, his voice thin.

"What's ludicrous is that you think I don't know." Hartley sighed. "Sometimes I wonder if my life would have gone in a different direction if I had an older brother who was less of a saint and more someone I could confide in. But that's neither here nor there. Listen, Ben, I don't much care who you fancy and who you don't. And I daresay the world is filled with happily married people—our parents among them— who fancy people other than whoever they're married to. But I can't see that it's a grand idea for you to marry a girl when you're keen to bed your employer."

"He's not my employer," Ben gritted out.

The room was silent for a moment as Hartley stared at him. "That's the part you object to?"

"Yes," Ben said finally.

"Ah."

Ben buried his head in his hands.

"And the captain?" Hartley asked.

"Can't talk about him," Ben said, his words muffled by his hands.

"Well, that's an affirmative. Lord. I go away for a few months and everything is quite upside down." He tapped his gloved fingers on the scarred wood of his chair. "I ought to go away more often."

Ben looked up. "Very funny, Hart."

"I'm not jesting. You seemed quite happy at Barton Hall. So did Captain Dacre, for that matter. Merry as grigs. Quite sickening. I congratulate you."

"I'm miserable now."

"Yes, well, it's my understanding that this is the general course for affairs of the heart. Not my field of expertise, but one does hear reports."

"So glad you're amused."

"I'm not. I do think resigning your position is a trifle dramatic, though." Suddenly his eyes flew wide open and his air of languor dropped away. "Oh, tell me this isn't because you think your living is ill-gotten gains. That I earned it on my back or whatever the vulgar saying is."

"Not entirely," Ben said, but he knew he was an unconvincing liar.

"Oh, Benedict. For what it's worth, I would have gone to bed with the Archbishop of Canterbury if it might have gotten you a better living than this."

"Hartley!" Ben wasn't sure whether to laugh or remonstrate.

"No, it's true. I have no morals. Or, if I do, bedding elderly gentlemen for gain isn't against them."

"You were a child."

"Sixteen. But I see your point," Hartley said thoughtfully. "I do indeed." He steepled his fingers and furrowed his brow. "Although I suppose it's just as well to resign. It must be unpleasant to affiliate yourself with an institution that holds your particular vice in such low regard."

"Don't call it a vice," Ben said fiercely. "Bother it all, Hartley. I hadn't really thought of it that way." He knew that his brother was invoking this line of argument to make him feel better about resigning, but that made it no less persuasive.

"If I were secretly a portrait artist, I wouldn't join up with one of those groups that believes graven images to be abominations. Perhaps because I wouldn't want other artists to think I despised them. Perhaps because I'd worry that after too long in their company I'd begin to despise myself."

Ben squeezed his eyes shut. He had tried so hard not to come to that conclusion. "There's good work to be done in the church."

"I daresay there is," Hartley said mildly. "There's good work to be done in a lot of places. Don't go live in a slum in Liverpool, Benedict. If you do resign, come stay with me in London. I have that whole blasted house that Sir Humphrey left me. And I'm quite alone."

If Ben hadn't been quite so wrapped up in his own misery, he might have remarked on the sadness in his brother's voice. But as it was, all he could think was that all his hopes were getting crushed, one by one.

Phillip had that nausea that comes with an ill-advised wager, a sense of having slid too many coins to the middle of a card table with too bad a hand to justify the gamble. What ought to have been a friendly game of cards had turned into something with far higher stakes, and it had happened right under his nose. He hadn't only wagered his heart, although that was bad enough. No, what was at stake was Phillip's entire sense of his place in the world. That morning, for one terrifying moment lying beside Ben, he had thought that perhaps he didn't need to return to his ship. Perhaps he could stay. Perhaps everything could be different. Perhaps he was different from who he had always thought he was.

It was madness.

"You haven't shaved," Walsh remarked. They were lingering at the breakfast table, Walsh reading the morning papers and Phillip staring out the window.

Phillip automatically touched his jaw. Walsh was right; he hadn't shaved in days.

"Never known you to go more than a day without shaving," Walsh said, not lifting his eyes from the paper.

That was also correct. Phillip had always maintained that shipboard discipline began with the captain, particularly with small things like polished buttons and neatly shaved jaws. He glanced down at his own wrinkled, soft, country clothes. It would be strange to put on his uniform again.

"I do apologize for my unfashionable ways," Phillip said facetiously.

Walsh made a dismissive sound. "It's just that there are

times one forgets to shave because one is happily distracted and there's nobody about to impress, and there are times one forgets to shave because one is too down in the doldrums to give a damn."

Was Walsh concerned about him? "It's not the latter."

They sat in silence a few moments.

"I'm hearing about men selling their commissions," Walsh remarked conversationally, turning the page of his newspaper. "Peacetime, and all that."

"Is that what you're considering?" He couldn't imagine life aboard the *Patroclus* without Walsh.

Walsh made a noncommittal sound and went back to his paper for a few moments before murmuring an excuse and leaving the room.

Phillip returned his gaze to the land he'd soon be leaving. During his weeks here, the trees had grown heavier and heavier with leaves, everything had become greener and riper and more emphatically lush. Even the air seemed thick with the sweet scent of summer blossoms and juicy fruit. This was not his first summer at Barton Hall. He was certain that over the years he had spent part of every month here at his house, on his land. But his experiences were fragmented: a week in February, then a month in summer, followed two years later by a few weeks in midwinter. He had never, not since his earliest childhood, spent an entire year here. Never had he watched a summer ripen and then tip gently into autumn.

He ought to know better than to want such a thing. But he did. He wanted to watch the trees lose their leaves. He wanted to watch his children and the changes each day wrought in them. He wanted to belong here, to belong to his children and to Ben.

He ought to know better, but he didn't, and that was alarming.

He pushed his plate away and went outside, where he found Jamie and Peggy in the garden, gathering a haphazard selection of flowers that would either be used to adorn the dining table, or perhaps to festoon the dog, themselves, or possibly a sheep, if the children's previous antics were any indication. "Your mother loved those dahlias," he said, and both children looked up at him in mild astonishment. "She had the gardener order them specially." Unbidden, a memory flashed in his mind. "She used to put dried tea leaves at the roots. The cook and housemaids didn't know what to think."

The children were looking at him expectantly, waiting to hear more about their mother. He had hardly spoken a word to them of Caroline since his return, assuming that their memories were more plentiful and recent than his own. But maybe that wasn't so, and maybe it didn't matter anyway. "When I met her, she lived in the city." She had lived in Bristol, where her father had been an importer and warehouser. "And she had never had a garden that was more than a patch of green behind her house." It had been a very grand house, and her mother had sufficient money to bring in hothouse flowers all twelve months of the year. "The first thing she did when moving here was to get to know the gardener."

"We ought to take some dahlias to her grave," said a wobbly voice, and Phillip turned to see that it was Ned, looking serious and sounding much older than his thirteen years.

"We've brought wildflowers," Peggy said.

"And rosemary," added Ned.

"But those weren't her favorite." Jamie's eyes were shiny with unshed tears.

"I'm sure she would have liked those." Phillip was in desperate danger of choking up, thinking of motherless children who would soon be as good as fatherless. And if he died, he wouldn't have a grave; he'd have the same watery ending that McCarthy did. Even if he were buried at Barton Hall, the children wouldn't know or care what flowers to put on it.

"Let's gather these dahlias and take them to her grave now, then," he suggested. But before they could leave, a footman appeared with a letter for Phillip.

"That's Mr. Sedgwick's writing," said Ned. "What can he be writing for when we'll only see him at supper?"

Phillip knew a moment of wild panic. What if something was wrong, and Ben needed him? How would he know?

Perhaps Ned had the same thought. "I think we need three more blooms to make this posy perfect," Ned told the twins. "I can read it, if you like," he said when he was alone with his father.

There was no real chance Ben would have committed anything to paper that couldn't be read publicly, but Phillip couldn't risk it. "That would be . . . thank you. But that won't be necessary." He already knew what the letter would say, because at that moment a servant was loading Ben's valise and box of books into a cart. Ben was leaving him. He had known all along that they'd be parted, that whatever he had to offer wasn't enough for Ben. It hadn't ever been enough, he didn't deserve—

"Father?" It was Ned. "You're in what Mr. Sedgwick calls a brown study. Melancholy," he added a moment later, when Phillip hadn't responded. "I can tell by the line on your forehead."

"What does Mr. Sedgwick know about melancholy? I've never met a less melancholic person in my life."

"I know," Ned said, and his face—so very like Caroline's—broke out into a smile. "But he's wise."

"He is, isn't he? Well, what wisdom has Mr. Sedgwick imparted to you about brown studies?"

"He says that sometimes our minds tell us all the ugliest things. That everything we do is useless, that everyone we know is better off without us." He hesitated. "After Mother died I had a number of brown studies."

"Yes," Phillip said. He put his hand on Ned's shoulder and the boy did not flinch away. "As did I."

"The important thing, Mr. Sedgwick says, is to remember that during brown studies our minds are not particularly honest. That if you want to know the truth, you need to wait."

Phillip took a deep breath and let it out slowly. "Your mother would be exceptionally proud of you," he said. "I know I am."

The twins returned with their posy and they all walked together to Caroline's grave. They weren't happy, but they were together, and maybe this was truer than the dark whisperings of his mind. He folded Ben's letter and put it safely in his coat pocket.

Chapter Twenty

It wasn't the first funeral Ben had officiated, nor even the first funeral for someone he had been fond of. He shouldn't have stumbled over phrases he had uttered dozens of times before. Perhaps the sense of unfamiliarity was because he knew this to be his last.

He looked out over his congregation. It was small on the best of weeks, but sadly diminished in the summer months when there was work to do and weather to enjoy. Ben had never faulted them; his God was in the hills and out on the lake as much as he was in the pews of St. Aelred's. But there were even fewer people present today than he could have expected. He wondered if word had gotten round of his broken engagement; perhaps people weren't eager to attend services that were presided over by a dishonorable man. It twisted his stomach to see a bare dozen people gathered together to mark the loss of a man who had been among them since his birth, and to suspect that it was Ben's own doing.

The church door cracked open, and two late arrivals slid

in. Ben lost his place in the reading when he saw that it was Phillip, and by his side, Ned, looking almost grown in his neatest suit of clothes.

Ben's eyes hadn't been quite thoroughly dry since the beginning of the service; the death of a man, the sorrow of a widow, the sparseness of the bodies gathered in somber rows, and his own plight accumulated to present quite enough to cry over. But at the sight of Phillip and Ned, he had to stop and collect himself. They weren't here for Mr. Farleigh, or for the religious ritual; they were here for Ben himself, and it was enough to make Ben almost weep with gratitude. He smoothed the front of his cassock and dragged his mind back to where it belonged.

After the burial, he lingered in the vestry longer than he needed to, hoping to avoid any straggling parishioners. He wasn't in the mood to answer questions about Alice or really to talk about anything at all. When he returned to the vicarage, he found that Mrs. Winston had left a covered dish in the kitchen, likely cold meats and bread. He could add Mrs. Winston to the list of people he'd miss in his new life, whatever that might be. He took off the lid to peek at the contents of the plate, when he heard the sound of polite throat clearing. The dish's lid fell to the floor with a crash. Spinning around, Ben found Phillip leaning against the hearth.

"You almost scared me half to death," Ben said, hand pressed against his chest. "How did you get in?"

"Your housekeeper said I was welcome to wait for you. She likely meant someplace grander than the kitchens, but I smelled cooking and wasn't going to be put off. I ate a full third of a cherry tart and I don't regret it. Jamie would likely be able to calculate the precise percentage, but you and I can approximate to one-third, I think. I stowed the remnants out of sight in the larder so I wouldn't be tempted to eat the rest." He was babbling. That was new and strange.

"There's some ham over there." Ben indicated the now-uncovered dish.

Phillip pushed off the stones of the hearth and stepped towards Ben. "I didn't come for food."

"No?" Ben's hands went automatically to Phillip's lapels, and he felt one of Phillip's hands settle on his hip.

"No," he murmured, already bending his head to Ben's. He tasted of cherries and smelled like a warm summer day. Ben knew he'd never enjoy either of those without thinking of Phillip, and winced at the future pain. "Ben," Phillip said, kissing the corner of Ben's eye. "I heard you broke off your engagement with Miss Crawford. Gossip travels fast."

"Did you hear that I resigned?"

"What? My God. Are you all right?"

"Yes," Ben lied. He almost always told the truth, but there wasn't even a truth to be told right now, standing in the arms of the man he loved, in the kitchen of a house he'd soon leave, the sounds of a summer day whispering outside the windows.

"Why the devil didn't you tell me any of this? I thought you knew you could talk to me about anything. Instead you left me that blasted note."

"The resignation is . . . hard to explain." He didn't want to tell Hartley's secrets. "As for Alice, I couldn't marry her after what happened with us."

"Why not?"

"I told you." Ben felt his face flush. Words that were easy to say while naked and sated with one's lover were rather harder to articulate fully dressed in the vicarage kitchen. "I couldn't say the marriage vows. Not after what we did."

"What we did." Phillip's voice was faint, incredulous even. He held Ben's chin so he couldn't look away.

"I don't know if I can explain."

"Try. For me?" Phillip whispered.

"Until we were together, I hadn't really understood what it meant to love a person, to worship someone with your body," Ben said. "That's what you have to swear to do in the marriage vows, and I can't make that promise."

"Is that what happened between us?" Phillip's voice wasn't skeptical, only curious, but Ben felt put on the spot, called to explain something he didn't quite understand.

"I'm fairly sure that's what I was doing, but I can only speak for myself. All I meant was that it meant something to me to be with you. And—" he took a deep breath "—I know I mean something to you, and I felt that when we were together."

The next thing he knew he was pushed up against the kitchen wall and being kissed within an inch of his life.

"How long do we have?" Ben asked, only lifting his mouth from Phillip's enough to speak.

"I'll be missed if I don't return for dinner," Phillip said before kissing the spot below Ben's ear.

Phillip needed to be leaving soon, then. Ben stepped back and straightened his collar, waited for his breathing to return to normal.

"Have you decided what you're going to do after you leave St. Aelred's? Would you consider staying at the hall as the children's tutor? I know it would be a step down in the world for you, and I'm not a rich man, but I could pay you a fair salary."

"I wish I could." He couldn't stay at Barton Hall as the recipient of Phillip's charity while Phillip was far away. He didn't hate himself enough to embrace that fate. "But it's out of the question."

Phillip knew he could spend the rest of his life memorizing the ways Ben responded to his touch, charting the way his strong frame went supple when Phillip pushed close. Now, pressed against the wall, he seemed to almost melt against Phillip's body.

"Come back to the hall with me," Phillip murmured into Ben's ear. "Even if it's just for dinner." He'd take whatever hours and minutes he could get.

"I can't," Ben said. "I need to write this week's sermon. It'll be my last."

"The children miss you." Phillip was not above this naked attempt at manipulation. He felt as much as heard Ben's answering laughter.

"They'd have to go without seeing me to actually miss me. Jamie was here at first light today, knocking on the kitchen door to beg sweet buns off Mrs. Winston."

"Did she give them any?" A fortnight ago, Phillip would have been outraged at the idea of his children roaming the village unattended and unauthorized. Now he was amused and rather touched that his children felt happy and welcomed everywhere they went.

"Of course she did. He acted like he had never been fed before in his life. And he took two back for Peggy."

"They'll miss you if you leave Kirkby Barton."

Ben was silent for a moment. "That's a low blow."

"I know." He would use every unsporting trick if it kept Ben near. "Stay at the hall."

"I can't be there without you. It would break my heart, Phillip."

"I'd like to know that you were there." Oh God, it would be such a relief to imagine all the people he cared about safe under one roof.

He felt Ben go rigid. "And would we know where you were?"

"No, but—"

"We wouldn't know if you were alive or dead. You'd come back every year or two, maybe even longer, and expect to take up exactly where you had left off."

Well, yes, that was exactly what he had in mind.

"That's not enough," Ben said. "It's not being a father or a . . . whatever this is between us. It's being a visitor."

Phillip wanted to protest that it was all he could manage, that he wasn't capable of more and didn't even know if he wanted to be. "I need to return to my ship," he said instead.

They stood together, Phillip's forearm braced on the wall behind Ben's head, their mouths almost touching. Ben tipped Phillip's chin so their lips were nearly touching, then leaned forward to close the gap. Their lips brushed together, achingly familiar.

"Come back to dinner with me," Phillip whispered. He was willing to beg for scraps at this point.

"Phillip." Ben sighed. He took Phillip's hand and pressed it against his chest. Phillip could feel Ben's heart pounding, knew he wasn't unaffected. "Don't you see that I can't? I love you, and it will kill a part of me to sit at your table as your guest, knowing we'll be parted in weeks."

Phillip took Ben's hand and kissed it. "I love you too. But I have to go. You know this."

"Do you really? I feel disingenuous invoking your children when I've already said that I want you here. But, Phillip, you're abandoning them. It was one thing for you to be at sea when your children had a mother. But for you to leave them now, effectively orphaned, for months and years at a time when you're all they have? That seems cruel."

Phillip stepped back, away from Ben. "I've spent most of my life at sea. That's what my life is."

"Would you even write? Ned told me you wrote maybe one letter a year."

He had a dozen excuses at the ready, any of which would serve to deflect Ben's question. But instead he tried honesty, tried for once not to put any distance between him and someone he loved. He tried to ignore the insidious whispers and listen to the truth, which was that Ben cared for him, and that he trusted Ben. "I have no more use for letters than Jamie does. I can only read a little and writing is quite impossible. I gather it's a family failing."

He watched as realization dawned in Ben's eyes. "I hadn't realized," he said weakly. "Phillip, I didn't know. I wouldn't have thrown it in your face just now if I had known."

"I know." He lifted Ben's hand to his lips and kissed it. "I'm very good at concealing it."

"You were so long at sea. You must have sent and received letters and kept records."

"My lieutenants read and write for me. I know how to get by on a ship. I'm a good captain and I know how to work around the one task I can't perform. Here, life is an endless parade of things I'm not equipped to manage."

"Oh, Phillip." Ben sighed. But then he drew himself up and put some distance between the two of them. "If that's your decision, fine. But you're leaving behind everyone who loves you."

Phillip gave him a tight smile. Yes, yes, that was exactly what he was doing, damn it. He was also leaving behind everyone he loved.

CHAPTER TWENTY-ONE

When the clock struck noon and the paper on his desk was still blank, Ben cast down his pen and gave up trying to write his sermon. The day was almost obnoxiously lovely and he wished he had someone to share it with. He could go to Barton Hall, he supposed, but he knew perfectly well how that would end: he'd stay for dinner, or the night, or indefinitely, and then he'd fritter away his time with no purpose, no income, nothing to separate him from those who had drifted in and out of his father's house.

He didn't dare call on the Crawfords, not until some more time had passed. If he knew Alice as well as he thought he did, she was likely insisting to all her visitors that she had broken the engagement herself. Mrs. Crawford, however, had no doubt told her tale of woe to enough talkative confidantes. He knew enough of village gossip to understand that it would blow over as soon as something more interesting happened; his broken engagement would only be mentioned in whispered asides. For heaven's sake, his father had lived openly with two women, and he had managed to ride out the scandal. Ben could weather a broken engagement.

But he wouldn't be here to weather it, and that was the crux of the issue. He couldn't envision a future in which he wasn't a part of Kirkby Barton. But he needed to find a way to earn a living, and there were no prospects in a village this small.

He opened the cupboard and took out his stoutest boots and oldest, most faded coat and went to the kitchen to tell Mrs. Winston that he meant to take a walk. But the kitchen was empty and cold, the fire banked, as if this was already not his home. So he stepped outside into blinding sunlight. He picked up a fallen branch to use as a walking stick and set off on the path around the lake he had taken so many times.

He had been born in the shadow of this crag and had only left sporadically for school and briefly for university. This was his home and he felt rooted to it. His brothers had all left, he was cordially distant from his father, Phillip was leaving, and he didn't know if he'd ever repair things with Alice, but he belonged here. Frustrated, he slapped his walking stick into the earth.

"Slow down for God's sake!"

Ben spun to see Hartley walking briskly to catch up with him.

"Damn it, Ben, but I nearly had to break into a run and I do not have on the boots for that. I'm sitting on the rock right here until I stop sweating. Revolting." Hartley fanned himself with his hand. "You've done a fine job avoiding me."

"I haven't been—"

"Don't lie. It doesn't suit you. Alice told me to fetch you for supper, and I, being more good than sensible, agreed. I might collapse."

"I doubt I'd be welcome at the Crawfords'," Ben said.

"Our Alice is cleverer than that. She and Mrs. Howard have planned a picnic, and I'm to deliver you."

Ben raised his eyebrows. "Where is this picnic?"

"Barton Hall," Hartley said, flicking dust off his breeches. "Before you come up with a transparently false excuse not to attend, let me remind you that Alice is your oldest friend and has gone to some trouble to arrange an outing so that she might see you without your having to endure her parents' disapproval."

"I take it Captain Dacre will be there," Ben said, narrowing his eyes.

"Naturally."

"Can't I just lick my wounds privately?" Ben grumbled. But he was already turning back down the path, heading towards Barton Hall.

Hartley had something up his sleeve; it was the only thing one could be certain of where his brother was concerned. But he couldn't abandon Alice, he couldn't resist Phillip, and he had nothing tempting him in the other direction except one last lonely walk around the lake.

Phillip emerged from the house to find Mrs. Howard directing the servants to put hampers of food on a flat spot near the lake. Miss Crawford was already sitting in a basket chair with an easel arranged before her while Walsh appeared to be holding her paints. Mr. Hartley Sedgwick was reading a book on one of the blankets that had been spread across the lawn.

"I'll burn it if I don't care for the way I look, Alice," Hartley said without looking up.

"You always like the way you look," she retorted, and Walsh laughed.

It was Mrs. Howard who caught sight of him. "There you are, Captain. Have you come to admire Miss Crawford's painting?"

"Mr. Walsh brought me a new easel and figured out how to set it up so I don't have to balance myself in the chair so awkwardly." Alice gestured to the easel, which seemed to be pitched forward so she could reach it while still reclining. Phillip knew the lady had been ill, and nobody spoke precisely about the nature of her illness, likely because nobody knew what it was, including Miss Crawford herself. But he had seen her have difficulty walking, and how tired she got after even so much as sitting at the dinner table. She did not, however, have the look of a woman whose hopes had been shattered by a broken engagement.

"Hartley, I changed my coat. I hope this meets your specifications." Phillip spun to see Ben, shrugging into what Phillip recognized as his second-best coat. "Oh, hullo, everybody's here already."

It had only been a day since he had last laid eyes on Ben, but seeing him now felt somehow like a relief.

"Mr. Sedgwick," he said, his voice thick and awkward. "Thank you for coming."

"Hartley very nearly abducted me," Ben said, but he was smiling broadly, as if he couldn't help but show how pleased he was to see Phillip.

"We're going to let rumor spread that we're quite cordial, Ben," Alice said. "So come sit by me. No, get me sandwiches first."

Ben flicked Phillip an amused glance before complying. Before long, the children arrived with a ball and the dog. The afternoon passed in a haze of sandwiches and easy conversation. Walsh stationed himself by Miss Crawford and Phillip noticed a handful of blushes pass between them, which he decided was very interesting indeed. Phillip seldom rose from the blanket, and couldn't remember the last time he had been so idle. He watched the sun make its progress across the sky. He watched his children laugh and play, and tried to store up the memory against future times when they'd be far from his sight. He watched Ben, and knew there was no way that his heart could be fuller or readier to break.

The sun had set and the party ready to break up when somebody first noticed that Jamie was gone.

CHAPTER TWENTY-TWO

It was Peggy who noticed her twin's absence, and it was Peggy who seemed the most distressed. If it hadn't been for the anxiety that was writ across her face, Ben would have assumed that Jamie had gone on one of his escapades.

"We always tell one another where we are going. Mr. Sedgwick tells us never to wander off alone without someone knowing exactly where we are. Jamie wouldn't have gone off without telling me," she insisted to the party at large.

"The dog is gone too," Ned whispered.

Scanning the small crowd, Ben sought out Phillip, who had the rigid posture of a man in shock. Ben crossed the lawn in three strides to reach him. "He's likely in one of the barns with a jar of greengage jam that he didn't feel like sharing with the rest of us," he said, trying to sound reassuring. "But we'll organize a search party."

Ben caught Hartley's eye. Years ago—it had to be more than ten years since—Will had disappeared on a November evening. It had been cold and pitch-black when Ben and Hartley had combed the hills, armed with torches and shouting Will's name. They had found him in the game-keeper's lodge at Lindley Priory. It had been terrifying at the time, and Ben's fear had only been increased by the lack of alarm displayed by any of the adults at Fellside Grange, who seemed to think it completely reasonable for an eight-year-old child to wander off for reasons of his own. *Children are meant to be free*, their father had always said.

That event had brought home to Ben the fact that if any-body was going to look after his younger brothers, it had to be him. He had scrimped and saved from the housekeeping money and pinched his father's pawnable belongings to make sure his brothers were safe and fed, at least.

Now he realized that it hadn't been his own doing, but rather Hartley's sacrifice, that had kept the family provided for. He tried to dislodge those thoughts from his head and come back to the present.

"I'm going to go look for him," Phillip said, his voice heavy with distress.

Ben put a steadying hand on his arm. "Yes. Of course. But we need to plan this out, otherwise we'll cross one an-other's paths." He turned to Hartley, because Hartley, for all his London clothes and polished manners, knew this coun-tryside as well as Ben did himself. "Can you search the hills between here and Lindley Priory? The dog once ran off to the wood between here and the Priory, and Martin didn't take kindly to the trespass."

Hartley nodded in understanding. "I can help," said Ned.

"Yes, you and Hartley go west. On your way, ask the

stable hands and, really, any strong person you see to come here and we'll tell them where to look."

"Wait, Ben," Alice said, "you go look by the crag. I'll stay here because I know the countryside well enough to know where to send people. Mrs. Howard has already gone to fetch lanterns."

It was scarcely past midsummer, so the light would last for several more hours, but lanterns were a good idea. That way the search could continue into the night if need be. God, he hoped it wouldn't be necessary. Mrs. Howard returned with the lanterns and a pair of manservants, and soon Ben had sent people in pairs to search the areas he thought Jamie most likely to have gone.

Ben's most pressing fear was that the boy might have fallen or gotten wedged between rocks. He glanced at Phillip and nodded, and they headed off together towards the crag. As they walked, Ben said a silent prayer—that Jamie was safe, that they'd have the skill to find him.

"Jamie knows these hills," he said to Phillip, "and he's a clever child. He's fine. I know in my heart that he's fine."

"I don't," Phillip said, and Ben squeezed his hand. "I mean, I know it's overwhelmingly likely that he's safe, but I don't *know* it, and I don't know how the hell I'm going to get onto that blasted ship and put myself months away from any reassurance that they're well. They could be dead and buried and I wouldn't even know. I don't know how I managed not to think about it."

"That was why it was easy for you to stay away," Ben said, the truth suddenly obvious. "You let yourself believe that since your children were out of sight, they must be fine and well."

"Stupid." Phillip's hand was closed tight around Ben's as they walked.

"And now you can't."

"People leave their families all the time."

"True. But maybe not if they don't have to." Ben's heart soared at the thought that Phillip might not leave, that he might stay with his children and put together some kind of family, even though Ben wouldn't be around to see it.

"Maybe not," Phillip echoed.

When they reached the summit of the crag they called Jamie's name but got no response. There was no sign of the child anywhere.

"Damn it," Phillip said, sitting on a rock and putting his head in his hands.

"One of the others surely found him. But let's go around to the other side of the hill and check over there."

Before they got far, they heard a dog barking. Ben, used to the barking of sheepdogs, hardly noticed, but Phillip went still.

"I think that's Jamie's dog," Phillip said.

"Let's see." Ben was mainly humoring Phillip, trying to play for time so that Jamie would be more likely to have reappeared or been found by the time they went back to the hall.

They heard the barking again. "This way," Ben said, taking Phillip by the hand again and leading him towards the sound. He didn't know if it was a trick of the echoing hills, but that bark did sound familiar.

It was Phillip who first noticed where they were.

"Ben. Isn't this your father's house?"

It was. And that was definitely Jamie's dog barking outside Alton Sedgwick's door.

At the sight of Jamie eating jam and bread at the table of a gray-bearded man who must be Ben's father, Phillip nearly collapsed from relief.

Ben all but pushed him into a chair and pressed a mug of cider into his hand.

"I'm furious," Phillip said, his fingers clenched white against the mug. "Don't ever do that again."

"I'm not going back," Jamie said, his chin tilted up.

"Why the devil not? I thought we were having a fine time this summer. I thought we were getting on well." He scrubbed his hand across his jaw and glanced at Ben, who was leaning against the wall beside his father.

"We were." Jamie's eyes were damp. "But you'll be leaving soon and sending me to school and I can't go." He swallowed hard. "I *can't*."

"No, you can't. You mustn't. I know that." Phillip reached across the table and took his son's hand. "I should have told you sooner. But why did you get the idea that I was sending you off to school? Why now?"

"Mrs. Howard was trying to convince me school would be fun."

Phillip groaned. "She was likely trying to do you a kindness. Her own children enjoy school terribly, she was telling me."

"But when you marry her, you'll want to send us all to school."

"Why the devil would I want to marry her?" Phillip asked.

"Everyone says you will."

"Who is everyone?"

"Cook. Mrs. Winston. Ned." He ticked the names off on his fingers.

"Well, I'm not marrying her or anyone else. And even if I were, you're not going to school. I'm hiring a tutor. And . . ." He took a breath, knowing that he shouldn't make hasty decisions while emotional, but if he was honest, this was a decision he had all but made days ago. "I'm not returning to my ship."

"What?" Ben and Jamie spoke as one.

"You heard me."

The old man was watching this entire exchange with evident interest and Phillip heartily wished he'd go away and let them have some privacy, even if this was his house. With the sense of things slotting into place, Phillip realized that his notion of familial privacy most definitely included Ben.

"But . . ." Jamie shook his head in confusion. "You're a sea captain. That's what you are."

Phillip had thought so too. "Over the past few weeks I've learned to be a good many things." He steadfastly did not look at Ben, but he knew Ben would understand that those words were partly meant for him. "Chief among those is being your father." He hoped Ben would hear the unspoken words, that Phillip had also learned to be something else, something to Ben. A lover, a friend. He didn't think there was a word, and he dearly wished for one, even if it was only whispered between them.

"Oh," Jamie said.

"I see." That was Ben, and if Phillip knew the man—and heaven help him, but Phillip thought he did—he really did see. He could see what was in Phillip's heart. Later on, Phillip would hope for a chance to tell him in words, in deeds, in any way he could.

"This is all very interesting," Alton Sedgwick said, stroking his beard. "Very interesting indeed."

"No it isn't, Father," Ben said firmly. "Commonplace domestic drama, absolutely not something I'm going to find in one of your poems next year."

"Do you read my poetry?" the older man asked.

"Of course I do, if only to see what slander you've committed. And I will not find anything titled 'The Reluctant Sailor' or something to that effect."

Alton Sedgwick shook his head disapprovingly. "That's a very poor title, Benedict."

"That's not the point. How did you come by Jamie in the first place?"

"I came here," Jamie said.

"Why?" Ben asked the question Phillip had been wondering.

"I didn't mean to. But then I ran into that man, and he asked where I was going, and I told him I didn't know. He told me to come here. Then I remembered you said your father always had sweets and never made you do lessons." Through the open windows, they heard the dog barking plaintively. "And that he was fond of animals," he added reprovingly.

"All true," Ben said faintly, looking like he had been hit in the head.

Before Phillip could ask who the man was who had directed Jamie to Fellside Grange, he found himself laughing. He couldn't help it. The situation was absurd. His son was safe. Phillip's own future was uncertain, Ben's even more so, but Phillip felt idiotically confident that they could find a way to at least be uncertain in reasonable proximity to one another.

The door to the outside swung open, letting in a soft warm breeze and a woman with a basket of greengages on one arm and Jamie's dog in the other.

"This poor rascal was half-frantic out there," she said, setting the dog on the ground. Then, noticing Ben and Phillip, her eyes opened wide. It took a moment for Phillip to place her, because he had only seen her wearing a large white cap and apron. Now, her salt-and-pepper hair was plaited over one shoulder and her clothing was decidedly disordered.

"Mrs. Winston?" Ben said, plainly astonished.

"*Somebody* has to look after your father," Mrs. Winston said, her hands on her hips.

"Looking after? Is that what we're calling it?"

"None of your business is what I'm calling it," she said.

"Diana," the older Mr. Sedgwick said. "They're all very testy today. This young scapegrace," he said, indicating Jamie, "ran off and gave everyone a fright."

"I step out for a quarter of an hour," Mrs. Winston lamented, shaking her head.

"This is good jam," Jamie said. "Are you going to make more with those plums?" He gestured at the basket on the housekeeper's arm.

"Yes, but not for the likes of you." But she put one of the greengages on the table before him.

"Quite right that it's none of my business," Ben said in measured tones. "Quite right. I wish you happy."

"Benedict," the older man said, "would you arrange for a license?"

"A license for what?"

"Marriage, of course."

For a moment the room fell silent except for the sound of the dog's wagging tail slapping the leg of the table.

Finally Ben spoke. "You and Mrs. Winston are getting married. The butcher's boy and the baker's daughter," Ben murmured cryptically.

"We fell in love," the older Mr. Sedgwick said with a shrug. "It happens."

Ben bit his lip. "It dashed well does. Well. I can't object. You're both certainly of age. If you come to the church tomorrow morning, we'll sort out the common license and perform the ceremony. No," he added, "let's say the day after tomorrow. Tomorrow I'm doing absolutely nothing."

Phillip thought it was high time to leave the lovebirds alone. "Thank you so much for taking care of my son, Mr. Sedgwick," he said, striving for solemnity. "I'll always be grateful." He grasped the older man's hand and shook it firmly. At this close distance, he could see the resemblance between father and son: the same warm brown eyes and firm jaw. Phillip was struck by a pang at the idea that he wouldn't get to see Ben's hair fade to this dusty gray, his face become creased with lines.

Bollocks on that. He was going to do whatever it took to create a future where he and Ben could stay here together and could make some kind of life side by side.

He took Jamie's hand, whistled for the dog, and looked directly at Ben when he said, "Gentlemen, let's go home."

CHAPTER TWENTY-THREE

Ben knew it was a mistake to go back to Barton Hall. He knew he'd catch another of Phillip's glances that seemed to say too much, that seemed to make promises that could never be kept. A part of Ben wanted to pretend, even just for a night, that the cold reality of their future didn't exist; he wanted to shut his eyes to grim facts and only see the joy and beauty of things that never could be. Perhaps this was how his father lived, cultivating an almost honest blindness to the things he did not want to acknowledge. For the first time, Ben sympathized.

On the way down the hill, Phillip spoke to Jamie about what he referred to as "the trouble with our eyes."

"Mr. Sedgwick and Ned are always saying I'm not stupid, but that's what they *would* say. You're not stupid, though," Jamie said, as if that settled the matter.

They talked about letters that did not behave as they ought, and instead crawled around the page, and in general both seemed quite delighted to have someone to talk to about their predicament. Ben tried to fall back, to give them some privacy, but each time he was beckoned closer, either by Phillip or Jamie or both.

Once, Phillip slid his hand through Ben's arm, and they walked that way for several minutes, side by side, along a path Ben had walked hundreds of times. The setting sun filtered through leaf-heavy treetops, casting glinting, dappled light over everything before them.

There was a general air of rejoicing at Jamie's safe return, and the prodigal son recounted the rather tame tale of his afternoon adventure. Peggy was quite put out, Ned exasperated, and Phillip rather too softhearted to send them all to bed at the proper hour. Even after Hartley had driven Alice back to the village, even after Mr. Walsh and Mrs. Howard had gone to bed, the children were treated with warm milk and anise biscuits in the nursery.

"Even odds Peggy turns up at your father's house within the fortnight demanding her own jar of jam," Phillip whispered.

They were sitting on the floor outside the nursery door, partly in an attempt to foil any attempted escapes, and partly because they had both more or less collapsed from exhaustion.

"Once rumor gets out that he has sweets and doesn't make one do lessons, I daresay he'll be overrun with urchins," Ben said dryly. "The only question is whether he'll even notice."

"I'd venture Mrs. Winston will." Phillip nudged Ben's shoulder with his own.

After his initial surprise, Ben decided that the most remarkable aspect of his father's connection with Mrs. Winston was the fact that he was bothering to marry her at all. But he knew that was unfair—his father had married his mother, and the only reason he hadn't married Will's mother was that it wouldn't have been possible. Now that Ben knew something of love that didn't align with other people's expectations, he felt less inclined to judge his father. "I wish them happy. Mrs. Winston is practical and won't let him spend all his money on brandy and calf-bound volumes of Greek poetry. And however negligent a father he was to me and my brothers, Mrs. Winston must be past the age where one has to worry about that."

Phillip moved his hand so it rested on top of Ben's. "You must have thought me a thoroughgoing bastard to leave my children the way I did."

Honestly, yes. He had, at first. But not anymore. "I think you're a fine father and a fine man. And I'm very glad you're not leaving."

Phillip laced his fingers through Ben's. "Will you stay? Here, with me? With us?"

"In what capacity? A tutor?" That wasn't what he wanted to do with his life. Ben couldn't sit idly in a comfortable house while there was work do be done, people to be helped.

"In any capacity you want."

"I can't do that. I can't live off your money and not have any vocation or purpose. Don't you see? That's almost exactly how I grew up. Only even my father has a purpose."

"You *have* a purpose. Money doesn't need to enter into it. I'm suggesting that you live here, or in one of the cottages nearby, because you very shortly will have no income and no house and I have a bit of extra space and the means to help. And I want to keep you near."

Ben wanted to say yes. It would be so easy to say yes. "It's not that simple."

"It's exactly that simple. My God, how often in life do you actually get what you want? Not bloody often. And don't even try to tell me that you don't want to stay with me. I can tell you do."

"I do. Of course I do," Ben said quickly. But over the last few weeks he had let go of everything he had set store by: vocation, marriage, family. The ability to stand on his own two feet was the only thing he had left. All these years he had thought he was earning his own living, but it turned out he only had that living because of Hartley. He couldn't erase that, but he could make sure that in the future he only took what he had earned. "But I can't."

"I want to be with you, and I don't care how. The details don't matter to me."

"They matter to me, Phillip. All I've ever wanted is something like a normal life. A house. A family. A way to put food on the table and clothes on my back."

"I'm offering you a house and a family. Don't you see?"

Ben didn't know how to go about explaining to Phillip, a man who had always had a place that was his, even if he chose to stay far away from it. "You're offering to let me be a permanent guest in your house. That's different."

"That's not—" Phillip broke off in a sigh.

"If I married Mrs. Howard, you wouldn't look down on her for moving into my house and eating my bread and cheese. If you had married Miss Crawford, you would have provided for her as a matter of course. Why can't you let me do the same for you? It's the only way I can think of for us to be together."

Ben buried his head in his hands. "I don't know."

"I love you, damn it, and why can't that be reason enough to let me do this for you?"

Ben turned his head to face Phillip, his cheek resting on his knee. "I love you. Of course I do." Phillip brushed a strand of hair off Ben's forehead.

They sat in silence. There had long since stopped being any sounds from the nursery. The children were out, and the summer sun was finally setting.

"What are you going to do, then?" Phillip asked.

"The bishop will have gotten my letter of resignation by now. So, I suppose I'll pack my trunk and . . . Well, I suppose I will have to stay here a while." He hadn't anywhere else to go. Drifting. Coasting. Hanging on the coattails of wealthier people who had taken a fancy to him. He was no better than his father, and all his work to secure his place in the world had come to naught.

"As long as you like. As long as you need."

They went to Phillip's room by unspoken agreement.

"I wake at first light," Ben said as he stripped off his shirt. "I'll be gone before the servants come." His skin was warm under Phillip's touch, as if he still carried the day's sunlight with him.

Phillip murmured something that was meant to be thanks. But he had a niggling sense of disquiet at having Ben skulk through the corridors. Surely Ben deserved better. He deserved love as honest and open as he was himself. Was that part of why Ben wouldn't stay? The fact that he'd be keeping a secret from the world? Was he ashamed?

But looking at Ben standing naked before him, tugging Phillip's shirt off as they tumbled into bed, it was hard to see any sense of shame. No, there wasn't a trace of it.

"Come here," Ben said, pulling Phillip on top of him.

They came together almost languidly, kissing and whispering and stroking. Phillip hadn't known lovemaking could be like this, hadn't known he wanted it to be. Their erections rubbing together, Ben's hands everywhere, Ben's mouth on his own—it was quiet and gentle, and when he came it was almost peaceful.

Later, they slept tangled together. Phillip, for whom the experience of sharing a bed was startlingly unfamiliar, woke so often he could have charted the moon's progress against the sky. Finally, the first light of dawn crept into the sky and Ben opened a sleepy eye.

"Hullo," Ben said, his voice muffled by the pillow. "I'll get up and rumple my sheets."

Like hell he'd lounge in bed while Ben got up. He didn't know how long he'd have before Ben left for good, and he'd be damned if he'd waste a single hour.

"I'll get up, too, and maybe you'll help me write a damned awkward letter to the admiralty?"

Ben raised his eyebrows. Even if Phillip could have managed the letter on his own, he wanted Ben to see with his own eyes that Phillip meant what he had said about not going back to sea.

When they reached the study, Phillip rang for tea. Ben stationed himself at the desk while Phillip perched on the edge, dictating a letter in which he gave up the only life he had ever known. They had the letter ready for the post before a housemaid appeared with a tray of tea.

"So that's that," Phillip said, after the maid had left with the letter. "We're both rather at loose ends." Phillip felt that he was standing at a dizzying height, looking at the world beneath him.

Ben smiled at him from behind his teacup.

It wasn't long before Ned appeared at the French doors, already dressed in his riding kit. "The ducks have laid fourteen eggs. Cook was right about the bone meal, dash it. I'm going for a ride but I'll be back by tea." He waved over his shoulder and strode away.

"I'll swear he was four inches shorter a fortnight ago," Phillip said. "And a good three years younger."

Was this what normal family life could be like? Drinking tea and making commonplace observations? Wondering whether fourteen eggs was a good outlay or a poor one? Catching glimpses of your beloved as he read the morning paper?

"I've been thinking about what I can do," Ben said, resting the paper on his knees. "I need to have a job, and as much as I love caring for your children, that isn't enough. It's what I'd do anyway, you see. But I thought that maybe you could help me arrange something."

"Yes," Phillip said immediately. "Of course."

"I was thinking there might be other children who aren't suited to a typical school and perhaps I could oversee their education."

"Are you talking about starting a school?"

Ben blushed. "That sounds preposterous, doesn't it?"

"Not at all."

"I don't have a head for business, but I think we'd need capital."

"I can help with that." Phillip rested his teacup on the table and leaned forward.

"And I think some of my father's set would be interested in throwing money at a school that seems modern, especially if it had the Sedgwick name attached to it."

"Where would you do this?" Barton Hall wasn't big enough for a school.

"I'm not certain. I haven't worked out any of the details."

"Will you let me help? The plain fact of the matter is that I need something to do with myself too. Smythe doesn't need me, and Ned is learning everything Smythe has to teach. But I'm—Ben, I don't have a lot of talents, but I'm good at telling people what to do and having them obey me. Let me do that in your service."

Ben looked at him with wide eyes. "Yes. Thank you." His voice cracked on the last word. "There's nothing I'd want more."

There was more Phillip wanted to hear from Ben, but this was a start, and for now that would be enough.

CHAPTER TWENTY-FOUR

Ben found Alice on the small terrace beside the Crawfords' house, Walsh kneeling on the ground beside her to adjust the angle of her easel. Alice spotted him first, greeting him with a wave of her paintbrush that caused a spray of green watercolor to land on Walsh.

"Oh, drat, sorry about that, Peter," she said, dabbing Walsh's collar with her handkerchief.

"It'll match the blue on my cuffs. Good morning, Sedgwick," he said cheerfully, getting to his feet and gathering his hat and coat.

"Don't leave on my account," Ben said. "I can come back later."

"Or you could both stay. For heaven's sake."

Ben watched with dawning comprehension as Walsh and Alice exchanged a long glance. Apart from the picnic, Walsh had been noticeably absent from Barton Hall these past few days, and Ben had wondered where he had gotten to. Now he gathered he had the answer. He sat on the low wall that edged the garden.

"I'll be back for supper." Walsh kissed Alice's hand, tipped his hat at Sedgwick, and strode out of the garden.

When he was out of earshot, Ben cleared his throat. "Peter, eh?"

Alice shot him a quelling glance. "Don't make too much of it." She made a great show of rinsing off a paintbrush and making herself busy. "Yet," she added, not meeting his eyes.

"You're fond of him?" he asked. "I'm asking as your friend, not as your former betrothed."

"I'm very fond of him. And he seems to be fond of me. Now, why am I being coy? He's dreadfully fond of me, which is so gratifying, Ben, I can't even tell you. But I'm just as fond of him, which seems impossible, but there you have it. In any event, he asked me if I'd mind his speaking to Father, and of course I said I didn't mind. And Father will likely faint with relief to have me off his hands, so I suppose I'll be getting married. Wish me happy!"

He kissed her cheek. "I wish you all the happiness." His voice was thick and his eyes were prickling with tears. "I hope you don't mind me telling you that I'm quite sickeningly jealous."

"Of Peter?"

"No, no, nothing like that. Of both of you."

She eyed him shrewdly, but not without compassion. "You, Benedict Sedgwick, are a mess."

"I can't argue with you there."

"Find a nice girl who you actually want to kiss behind hedgerows—"

"Dare I even ask what Walsh has been doing to you behind hedgerows?"

She waved a dismissive hand. "Find this nice girl, and then get over whatever ethical scruples are bothering you. You can't possibly believe that God wants you to spend your life alone."

"Some people are very happy on their own," Ben ventured.

"Of course they are. But you're not one of them."

He didn't know how to answer that, so he stayed silent and let her words seep into his mind.

"When you go back to Barton Hall, will you take this to your captain?" She handed him a sketch of Phillip, Peggy, and the dog on a picnic blanket. Phillip had an arm around Peggy, who was feeding tidbits of cold meat to the dog. On the surface it was a sweet domestic scene. But Phillip's gaze was directed at an object just off the edge of the paper. "I thought he might like to have it when he returns to his ship."

"That's very thoughtful. He's selling his commission, though, and staying on at Barton Hall." His mouth could barely form the words, and he could hardly tear his gaze from the drawing of Phillip's face, which had an expression of almost painful tenderness and devotion. It had been Ben himself that Phillip was looking at. Ben had been on the edge of that same blanket. If he hadn't already realized that Phillip's feelings for him were a mirror of Ben's own toward Phillip, he would have known it then. It struck him that if

Phillip was in want of money or a house, Ben would give him whatever he could, and gladly. And there would be no shame in Phillip accepting it, because that was what it meant to have a life together. It meant holding hands and jumping together into an unknown future.

Phillip was half asleep on the library sofa when he was roused by the sound of hoofbeats on the gravel drive. It couldn't have been Ned, because he would have ridden out from the stables, and Ben walked everywhere. At the sound of hasty, booted footsteps in the hall, Phillip got to his feet.

Sir Martin Easterbrook appeared in the doorway, glowering and carrying what looked like a bag of rags.

"I tried to stop him, Captain," said a flustered housemaid who was barely visible behind the visitor.

"Quite all right," Phillip said evenly. "Shut the door, Mary, please," he added, gathering from Easterbrook's stormy expression that there was about to be a scene. But then he noticed that the oddly-shaped bundle under the man's arm appeared to be wriggling.

"This," Easterbrook said, placing the bundle on the ground, "is the last time I return any of the inmates of this house." Out of the sack emerged the twins' dog.

"Oh," said Phillip. "That's . . . kind of you, Easterbrook." He tried to keep the astonishment out of his voice. "I'm in your debt."

"Damned right you are." Easterbrook made a noise of frustration. "Every blasted day this mongrel is sniffing around my kennels. I gather he must have been carrying on a romance with one of my hounds." A look of shame and regret passed over the young man's face. "But they're all sold off and this idiot hasn't caught on." The idiot in question was dancing happy circles around the baronet's feet.

"I didn't realize he was missing," Phillip said. "The twins had a bit of a late night so they're still asleep."

Easterbrook snorted. "I found one of them roaming the hills yesterday. Looked like he was off to take the king's shilling or join up with a traveling circus."

"You were the man who sent him to Alton Sedgwick," Phillip said.

"Figured even Fellside Grange is better than falling into a gorge," the baronet said, looking both annoyed and bashful.

"I'm very grateful you did that. Truly. Why don't you sit, Easterbrook?"

Easterbrook sat, and the dog promptly leapt into his lap. "Reminded me so much of that time Will Sedgwick ran off," he said, holding the dog at arm's length to dodge a kiss. "There was always a Sedgwick on the loose, making mischief and having adventures while I was stuck in the schoolroom."

"I believe the vicar mentioned something of the kind," Phillip said.

"The whole thing," Easterbrook said, gesturing around him vaguely, "reminds me of when we were children. Chaos. I don't like it. But I see that Ben Sedgwick is trying to make sense of it. Trying to make it less of a catastrophe. Anyway. I'll be going."

"No. Wait," Phillip said. "Don't leave yet."

"If this is about Hartley, save your breath. Tell your vicar that I'm not going to drag his brother to court to contest my father's will. I can't afford the fees, and I can't figure out how to do the thing without exposing my father for what he was, even though I have the letters to prove it. And that would quite ruin me, as well as getting Hartley put in the pillory, which would make me look a proper arse. Everyone would know I was ruined, to have kicked up such a fuss over so small a matter. My problems are greater than one London townhouse."

Phillip had no idea what Hartley Sedgwick, wills, or letters had to do with it, but he had met Hartley, and he could make an educated guess. "About that," Phillip mused. "I think there might be a way to keep you above water. Would you be open to letting Lindley Priory?"

"I'd be open to burning it to the ground, to be frank. But I sold most of the furniture and I don't know what kind of price I could get for an unfurnished house miles away from any civilization."

"Well, I'd be your tenant. My steward would take over the running of your land," he added, thinking aloud. That would mean he and Smythe would no longer have to undo the damage done by Easterbrook's bloodthirsty steward. "But you would still get the rents."

"I could leave," Easterbrook said, looking as Jamie did when faced with an entire jar of greengage jam. "I could go live someplace cheap on the Continent," he mused. In his distraction he forgot to keep the dog at bay, and was currently being accosted with kisses.

"I don't think this part of the world has many happy memories for you," Phillip said, feeling a kinship with this young man who had caused so much trouble.

Easterbrook's expression shuttered. "You're wrong there, Dacre. But no matter. I'll take you up on your offer."

"Write to—who's the solicitor in the village—Crawford. Ask him to come up now to draft an agreement."

Three hours later, Phillip—or rather an entity called The Sedgwick School for Wayward Children—was the tenant of Lindley Priory, and Easterbrook was riding south.

"This ought to cover your wages through Michaelmas," Ben said the next morning, pushing coins across the vicarage kitchen table where Mrs. Winston sliced damsons for a pie.

The housekeeper only spared the coins the briefest glance before turning back to her plums. "I don't need wages through Michaelmas but I'm getting married in about two hours, so I'll accept it as a wedding present." She deftly ran the knife through another plum and tossed the pit aside. "I heard Sir Martin is letting the Priory and going abroad. I had the news from Lottie Bannister whose young man is the gardener at the Priory. She said he left in the dead of night, giving orders for his solicitor to manage the lease without him. Apparently you made him leave."

"I did nothing of the sort! Captain Dacre arranged it."

"That's not what I've heard. Everybody thinks you're some kind of Robin Hood. You're in danger of having ballads written about you."

"I'm a man of the cloth," he protested.

"A daft one." She sprinkled sugar over the fruit. "Being as Sir Martin is running off to France or wherever, I doubt he'll find time to appoint a new vicar. There'll be nobody to give a sermon tomorrow."

Ben nodded. "I'll write to the bishop and see what's to be done."

"He won't get your letter in time," Mrs. Winston said. She was now thwacking and slapping a ball of pastry dough in a way that Ben found positively menacing. "You resigned, you weren't defrocked."

He shook his head. "I can't." The truth was that he didn't want to stand before his congregation. He had always been their affable, amiable, utterly conventional vicar. The last two weeks had exposed him—not only to the good people of Kirkby Barton but also to himself—as something more complicated than that. He didn't know yet how to live as that person, let alone how to be that person in the pulpit. Worse, he had begun to think Hartley had the right of it, and he couldn't stand in front of a congregation and align himself with people who thought he committed a crime every time he went to bed with the person he loved.

She made a frustrated sound. "It's not like you're going to steal from the poor box. You're an ordained clergyman and you ought to do what God requires of you."

"I have some doubts about precisely what God requires of me and how it lines up with what the Church of England requires," he said carefully, keeping his eyes on the dough rather than on Mrs. Winston's face.

She paused, her hands still on her rolling pin. "It's like that, is it? You've gone the way of your heathen father?"

"No," he said quickly, not pausing to wonder what kind of lively debates would take place in his father's household after this morning's marriage. "More like . . . Unitarianism."

She waved a floury hand and got back to rolling out her dough. The intricacies of the church didn't interest her. "I daresay you could do it once. Preach your heart out on whatever you want. Go out in a blaze of glory."

He stole a slice of plum. "That would cause quite a bit more of a stir than you're envisioning."

"Brotherly love."

He nearly choked on the plum. "Pardon?" he asked when he had regained his breath.

She turned her circle of dough neatly into the dish, a small bit of kitchen magic he never tired of watching. "You could preach about David and Jonathan."

He stared at her for a solid half minute as she poured the sugared fruit into the dish and covered it with another circle of pastry. Was it possible that she knew what she was suggesting? By the faint hint of pink on her weathered cheeks, he thought she might.

"Maybe it runs in the family."

"Pardon?" he asked faintly.

"Wildness. We all know what your father is, bless him. And you, breaking an engagement, whoever would have thought. Quite wild, the lot of you. It must be in the blood. Although," she added, turning her attention to crimping the pastry, "you were always a fine clergyman."

He still wasn't certain how much she knew, or whether she even disapproved.

"David and Jonathan," she repeated as she slid the pie into the oven. "That would be quite the thing." She nodded, wiped her hands on her apron, and nodded with the satisfaction of a job well done. "Now let's go to the church. I daresay your father's already waiting."

CHAPTER TWENTY-FIVE

Ben brought his few meager boxes of belongings to Barton Hall, but Phillip noticed that he hadn't unpacked them. Instead, the boxes stood against one wall of the room that was nominally his own. In practice, he had slept in Phillip's bed both nights since Jamie's misadventure, only stopping in his own room for fresh clothes and to give his bed sheets a plausible rumple.

When they made love, Phillip felt like Ben was trying to disappear inside his body. He delved inside Phillip with greedy, possessive fingers and sucked him until Phillip thought he'd be devoured. Even after Phillip was sated and oversensitive, Ben kept touching, as if there were a limited supply of touches in the world and he had to get his fill while he could.

Waking up beside Ben was achingly perfect, but it tore at Phillip's heart to think that it might not be enough. Their gentle touches and murmured words of love were everything to Phillip, but surely Ben deserved something finer and truer than a lifetime of creeping through hallways and keeping secrets from the world.

Then he remembered what Ned had told him. Perhaps these were the whisperings of his melancholy, and not truth.

"Ben," he murmured as they lay awake, waiting for those first fatal stripes of light to appear in the sky. "Will you be happy with me? Is this enough?"

Ben rolled to face him. "So much more than enough. It's just a different kind of enough than I had ever thought of, and it's taking my mind a little time to settle in."

Phillip understood that. He pulled Ben close, his fair head resting on Phillip's shoulder, and kissed the top of his head. His hair had bleached to the color of the palest wheat over the last weeks, and the bridge of his nose was covered in a welter of freckles. He also had a tenseness around his eyes that Phillip thought hadn't been there before.

"Will you come to church today?" Ben asked later as they were getting dressed.

"If you want me to, of course."

"It'll be the last time I do this. So, yes. I'd like it."

At the breakfast table, Phillip listened with some interest as Ben explained to the children that he would no longer be the vicar. "There are some aspects of church doctrine I don't agree with, and I don't think I can carry on as vicar."

"Blasphemy." Peggy's eyes sparkled with evident delight.

"Not quite that," Ben said, amused.

"The doctrine of the trinity?" Ned asked, more concerned than his sister.

"Not even as dramatic as that."

"Are you going to preach in a chapel and wear one of those odd caps the Methodists do?" Jamie asked, his mouth full of plum pie that Mrs. Winston had sent down from Fellside Grange. Evidently pie was now a breakfast food at Barton Hall.

"Certainly not."

That seemed to settle things as far as the children cared. They didn't ask what he did plan to do, apparently secure in the knowledge that he would stay indefinitely at the hall. Phillip wished he was as certain.

After breakfast, they all dressed in their finest, filled their pockets with boiled sweets to occupy their mouths, and set out for St. Aelred's.

The tiny church, which had been dismally empty the last time Phillip had entered it, was now hot and crowded. He gathered that whatever ill Ben had done his reputation by jilting Miss Crawford was undone by having sent Easterbrook packing, and Phillip was feeling quite satisfied with himself for having generated that particular tale himself. Mrs. Morris, his chief co-conspirator in spreading that piece of gossip, glanced over at him from her pew, nodding her head and tapping the side of her nose in acknowledgment.

The Crawfords were all together in their family pew along with a dark-haired man Phillip was startled to recognize as Walsh. He hadn't thought Walsh went in for churchgoing any more than Phillip did himself.

And yet Phillip was sitting in a hard-backed church pew anyway, because Ben needed him, and he would go wherever Ben required him. Perhaps Walsh had a similar motive; the very feminine pink parasol he held in his lap, the way Miss Crawford leaned towards him to whisper in his ear, and the expression of smug satisfaction on Mrs. Crawford's face all indicated that an offer might be in the making.

Yesterday, when Phillip told his friend that he wouldn't be returning to the *Patroclus*, Walsh hadn't evinced any surprise. "The admiralty won't be best pleased," he had said. "I'm afraid we'll both be in their black books." Phillip had been too caught up in his own thoughts to ask what Walsh had meant, but now he wondered if Walsh meant to marry Miss Crawford and resign his own post on the *Patroclus* as well. Very interesting indeed. He turned his attention back to the pulpit.

Ben made a very striking appearance in his cassock and surplice. He looked grave and a bit sad.

"This will be the last sermon I give at St. Aelred's," Ben said. "Probably the last sermon I give anywhere." A murmur went through the congregation. "It's fitting for me to use this, my last sermon, to talk about charity. Love. People more learned than I could explain the finer points of translation, but all of us here today know that we are commanded to love one another." He paused. "That's not what I'm going to talk about."

Phillip was not certain whether what followed was a good sermon, but the congregation followed with rapt attention and wide eyes as Ben spoke meanderingly of how the marriage of a friend was a fitting time for God to work a miracle. "Water into wine," he said musingly. "It would seem a petty use of God's power if it weren't a wedding present." Here his eyes strayed to Miss Crawford and Walsh. "And then there are the vows. There is that old, quaint promise to worship with one's body, another mingling of love and prayer." Phillip wasn't certain he knew what that meant, or if anyone else did, but what he did know was that Ben meant what he said.

Ben fell silent for long enough that the people in the pew behind Phillip started to rustle. Peggy turned around to glare, causing Ned to elbow her firmly in the side.

"And then there are David and Jonathan." Phillip had always been a lax student and couldn't immediately place the reference. "We're told that their souls were knit together. Jonathan gave David his robe and his sword, his bow and his belt. They loved one another and had a covenant. Not water to wine, but a different kind of miracle.

"Friendship and love," Ben went on. "Vows and covenants. It's the only kind of miracle most of us will experience, whatever shape it comes in."

Perhaps some of the other churchgoers were confused or disturbed, but Phillip would never know because he couldn't take his eyes off Ben. He knew Ben was saying this to him, and that it was important, and he didn't want to miss a word.

Ben spent longer than usual in the vestry, hanging up his surplice and cassock with more care than necessary, partly because it was the last time and partly because he didn't know what awaited him outside. He doubted most, if any, of his parishioners would have read between the lines to see his sermon as anything other than a meditation on the holiness of friendship and love. But Phillip had been there, and Phillip might have recognized it for what it was.

Ben had meant it as an offering, albeit a one-sided sort of one. He was trying to tell Phillip, in the only way he knew how, that he believed that the love between them was as good as any marriage that could be sanctified in a sacrament. He had officiated at too many weddings, believed too earnestly in the vows he witnessed, not to believe that those words had importance. Or, at least, they did to him. And he wanted, somehow, to tell that to Phillip. He told himself that he didn't need Phillip to reciprocate; Phillip loved him, and Phillip wanted a life with him, and that was all that Ben needed from Phillip.

He fussed over the cuffs of his street clothes, laced himself slowly into his boots, all while listening for the quiet that would signal that the church was empty and the churchyard had resumed its usual sleepy air. Leaving through a side door to avoid any straggling parishioners, the first thing he saw was Phillip leaning against the lych-gate.

"I sent the children home ahead of us," Phillip said, his expression too blank for Ben to guess his thoughts. "Go the long way with me?" he asked.

Ben nodded. The long way would circumvent the village. Probably the cleverest thing would be to let Phillip bring up the topic of the sermon, but Ben hardly made it twenty paces down the lane before he spoke.

"I meant every word of it," he said quietly.

"I know you did. You always do. It was the most reckless damned thing I've ever seen you do."

"It wasn't that obvious."

"Of course it wasn't. But it would have been if I had climbed over the pews and thrown myself into your arms, which I might very well have done."

Ben felt his pulse quicken and his heart pound madly against the walls of his chest. "Is that so?" he managed.

"It's damned well so." Phillip's voice was gruff. Ben didn't dare so much as glance at him. "But we can't talk about it now."

"Quite." Ben tipped his hat at a couple walking in the opposite direction.

"Because otherwise I'm going to shove you against the nearest wall and get us both sent to prison."

Once they were a safe distance into the wood, Phillip looked over his shoulder, then rounded on him and grabbed his arms. He made good on his promise by pressing him against the trunk of a thick oak tree and kissing him hard.

"Tell me again," Phillip growled.

"I love you."

"More. The rest of it. That night we first were together, you mentioned the marriage vows. I didn't understand then, but I do now. It means something to you. So tell me."

"I don't have any worldly goods to endow you with," Ben whispered.

"I'm not rich but I have enough for both of us to be comfortable. And you'll accept it? Will you, Ben? Not just as an investor in your school, but because what's mine is yours. You'll understand that it's nothing to do with freeloading or whatever it is your father did?"

Ben swallowed. "Yes. I understand."

"Now keep going. I want to hear the good part."

Ben laughed despite the tears in his eyes, and looked away.

"No, look at me when you say it."

"With my body, I thee worship."

"And I do too. Benedict, Benedict. The words may not mean the same to me as they do to you, but I'd swear it on anything you liked. I love you and never ever want you to doubt that. You're mine and I'm yours and . . ." He squeezed Ben's hands. "This is all new to me. I'm in a new world without a map or a chart, but you're my compass, Ben, and I know we'll find a way."

They kissed slowly in the shade of the oak tree, as if they had all the time in the world, because maybe they did. But the knowledge that there was a place where all of them belonged, a place where they could be safe and welcomed and together, made him feel like this was even more his rightful home than it ever had been.

"A month ago," Phillip whispered, "I was dreading going home, and now, well, I can't wait to spend the rest of my life here. With you."

Phillip brushed a kiss across his lips, and Ben could tell he was smiling. "Take me home, Phillip. Please."

Keep reading for a sneak peek at
Cat Sebastian's debut traditional
regency romance,

UNMASKED BY THE MARQUESS

Coming Spring 2018

Alistair ran his finger once more along the neatly penned column of sums his secretary had left on his desk. This was what respectability looked like: a ledger filled with black ink, maintained by a servant whose wages had been paid on time.

He would never tire of seeing the numbers do what he wanted them to do, what they *ought* to do out of sheer decency and moral fortitude. Here it was, plain numerical proof that the marquessate had—finally—more money coming in than it had going out. Not long ago this very library was besieged by a steady stream of his late father's creditors and mistresses and assorted other disgraceful hangers-on, all demanding a piece of the badly picked-over pie. But now Alistair de Lacey, eighth Marquess of Pembroke, could add financial solvency to the list of qualities that made him the model of propriety.

This pleasant train of thought was interrupted by the sound of an apologetic cough coming from the doorway.

"Hopkins?" Alistair asked, looking up.

"A person has called, my lord." The butler fairly radiated distress. "I took the liberty of showing her into the morning room."

Her? It couldn't be any of his aunts, because those formidable ladies would have barged right into the library. Alistair felt his heart sink. "Dare I ask?"

"Mrs. Allenby, my lord," Hopkins intoned, as if every syllable pained him to utter.

Well might he look pained. Mrs. Allenby, indeed. She was the most notorious of his late father's mistresses and if there was one thing Alistair had learned in the years since his father's death, it was that the arrival of any of these doxies inevitably presaged an entry in red ink in the ledger that sat before him.

And now she was sitting in the morning room? The same morning room his mother had once used to receive callers? Good Lord, no. Not that he could think of a more suitable place for that woman to be brought.

"Send her up here, if you will, Hopkins."

A moment later, a woman mortifyingly close to his own age swept into the library. "Heavens, Pembroke, but you're shut up in a veritable tomb," she said, as if it could possibly be any of her business. "You'll ruin your eyes trying to read in the dark." And then she actually had the presumption to draw back one of the curtains, letting a broad shaft of sunlight into the room.

Alistair was momentarily blinded by the unexpected brightness. Motes of dust danced in the light, making him uncomfortably aware that his servants were not doing an adequate job with the cleaning, and also that perhaps the room had been a trifle dark after all.

"How can I help you, ma'am?" he asked in frigid tones. "Do take a seat," he offered, but only after she had already dropped gracefully into one of the chairs near the fire.

The years had been reprehensibly kind to Portia Allenby, and Alistair felt suddenly conscious that the same could not be said for himself. She had no gray in her jet-black hair, she had no need for spectacles. The subdued half morning she had adopted after his father's death made her look less like a harlot whom the late marquess had acquired as part of a drunken spree across the continent some eighteen years ago, and more like a decent widow.

"I'll not waste your time, Pembroke. I'm here about Amelia."

"Amelia," Alistair repeated slowly, as if trying that word out for the first time.

"My eldest daughter," she clarified, patiently playing along with Alistair's feigned ignorance. *Your sister*, she didn't need to add.

"And which one is she?" Alistair drummed his fingers on the desk. "The ginger one with the freckles?" All the Allenby girls were ginger and freckled, having had the great misfortune to take after the late marquess rather than their beautiful mother.

Mrs. Allenby ignored his rudeness. "She's eighteen. I'd like for her to make a proper come out."

So she wanted money. No surprise there. "My dear lady," he said frostily, "you cannot possibly need for money. My father saw to it that you and your children were amply provided for." In fact, he had spent the last months of his life seeing to little else, selling and mortgaging everything not nailed down in order to keep this woman and the children he had sired on her in suitably grand style.

"You're quite right, Pembroke, I don't need a farthing." She smoothed the dove-gray silk of her gown across her lap, whether out of self-consciousness or in order to emphasize how well-lined her coffers were, Alistair could not guess. "What I hoped was that you could arrange for Amelia to be invited to a dinner or two." She smiled, as if Alistair ought to be relieved to hear this request. "Even a tea or a luncheon would go a long way."

Alistair was momentarily speechless. He removed his spectacles and carefully polished them on his handkerchief. "Surely I have mistaken you. I have no doubt that among your numerous acquaintances you could find someone willing to invite your daughter to festivities of any kind." The woman ran a monthly salon, for God's sake. She was firmly, infuriatingly located right on the fringes of decent society. Every poet and radical, not to mention every gently-born person with a penchant for libertinism, visited her drawing room. Alistair had to positively go out of his way to avoid her.

"You're quite right," she replied blithely, as if insensible to the insult. "The problem is that she's had too many of those invitations. She's in a fair way to becoming a bluestocking, not to put too fine a point on it. I hope that a few evenings spent in, ah, more exalted company will give her mind a different turn."

Had she just suggested that her own associates were too serious-minded for a young girl? It was almost laughable. But not as laughable as the idea that Alistair ought to lend his countenance to the debut of any daughter of the notorious Mrs. Allenby, regardless of whose by-blow the child was. "My dear lady, you cannot expect—"

"Goodness, Pembroke. I'm not asking for her to be presented at court, or for vouchers to Almack's. I was hoping you could prevail on one of Ned's sisters to invite her to dinner." If she were aware of what it did to Alistair to hear his father referred to thusly, she did not show it. "The old Duke of Devonshire acknowledged his mistress's child, you know. It can't reflect poorly on you or your aunts to throw my children a few crumbs."

So now, after bringing his father to the brink of disgrace and ruin, she was an expert on what would or would not reflect poorly on a man, was she? The mind simply boggled.

"Of course, I wouldn't expect to attend with her," she continued.

He reared back in his chair. "Good God, I should think not."

Only then did she evidently grasp that she was not about to prevail. "I only meant that I would engage a suitable chaperone. But I see that I've bothered you for no reason." She rose to her feet with an audible swish of costly silks. "I wish you well, Pembroke."

Alistair was only warming to the topic, though. "If I were to acknowledge all my father's bastards I'd have to start a charitable foundation. There would be opera dancers and housemaids lined up down the street."

At this she turned back to face him. "You do your father an injustice. He was not a man of temperate desires, but he and I shared a life together from the moment we met until he died."

"I feel certain both your husband and my mother were touched to discover that the two of you had such an aptitude for domestic felicity, despite all appearances to the contrary." Mr. Allenby had been discarded as surely as Alistair's mother had been.

Was that pity that crossed the woman's face? "As I said, I'm truly sorry to have bothered you today." She sighed. "Gilbert is a regular visitor at my house. I mention that not to provoke you but only to suggest that if you're determined not to acknowledge the connection, you ought to bring your brother under bridle."

She dropped a small curtsy that didn't seem even slightly ironic, and left Alistair alone in his library. He felt uncomfortable, vaguely guilty, but he knew perfectly well that he had behaved properly. His father had devoted his life to squandering money and tarnishing his name by any means available to him: cards, horses, women, bad investments. And he had left the mess to be cleaned up by his son. Alistair, at least, would leave the family name and finances intact for future generations.

He paced to the windows and began pulling back the rest of the curtains. It annoyed him to admit that Mrs. Allenby had been right about anything, but the room really was too dark. He had been working too hard, too long, but now even with all the curtains opened the room was still gloomy. The late-winter sun had sunk behind the row of houses on the opposite side of Grosvenor Square, casting only a thin, pallid light into the room. He went to the hearth to poke the fire back to life.

His plan had been to double check the books and then go out for a ride, but the hour for that had come and gone. He could dress and take an early dinner at his club, perhaps. Even though the Season had not quite started, there were enough people in town to make the outing worthwhile. It was never a bad idea for Alistair to show his face and remind the world that this Marquess of Pembroke, at least, did not spend his evenings in orgies of dissipation.

There came another apologetic cough from the doorway.

"Another caller, my lord," Hopkins said. "A young gentleman."

Alistair suppressed a groan. This was the outside of enough. "Send him up." He inwardly prayed that the caller wasn't an associate of Gilbert's, some shabby wastrel Alistair's younger brother had lost money to at the gambling tables. He glanced at the card Hopkins had given him. *Robert Selby.* The fact that the name rang no bells for him did nothing to put his mind at ease.

But the man Hopkins ushered into the library didn't seem like the sort of fellow who frequented gambling halls. He looked to be hardly twenty, with sandy hair that hung a trifle too long to be à la mode and clothes that were respectably, but not fashionably, cut.

"I'm ever so grateful, my lord." The young man took a half step closer, but seemed to check his progress when he noticed

Alistair's expression. "I know what an imposition it must be. But the matter is so dashed awkward I hardly wanted to put it to you in a letter."

It got worse and worse. Matters too awkward to be put in letters inevitably veered toward begging or blackmail. Alistair folded his arms and leaned against the chimney piece. "Go on," he ordered.

"It's my sister, you see. Your father was her godfather."

Alistair jerked to attention. "My father was your sister's godfather?" He was incredulous. There could hardly have been any creature on this planet less suited to be an infant's godparent than the late Lord Pembroke. "He went to the church?" Really, the image of his father leaning over the baptismal font and promising to be mindful of the baby's soul was something Alistair would make a point of recalling the next time his spirits were low.

"I daresay he did, my lord," Selby continued brightly, as if he had no idea of the late marquess's character. "I was too young to remember the event, I'm afraid."

"And what can you possibly require of me, Mr. Selby?" Alistair did not even entertain the possibility that Selby was here for the pleasure of his company. "Not an hour ago I refused to help a person with a far greater claim on the estate than you have."

The fellow had the grace to blush, at least. "My sister and I have no claim on you at all. It's only that I'm in quite a fix and I don't know who else to turn to. She's of an age where I need to find her a husband, but . . ." His voice trailed off, and he regarded Alistair levelly, as if deciding whether he could be confided in. Presumptuous. "Well, frankly, she's too pretty and too trusting to take to Bath or Brighton. She'd marry someone totally unsuitable. I had thought to bring her to London where she would have a chance to meet worthier people."

Alistair retrieved his spectacles from his coat pocket and carefully put them on. This Selby fellow didn't seem delusional, but he was speaking like a madman. "That's a terrible plan."

"Well, now I know that, my lord." He smiled broadly, exposing too many teeth and creating an excess of crinkles around his eyes. Alistair suddenly wished that there was enough light to get a better look at this lad. "We've been here a few weeks and it's all too clear that the connections I made at Cambridge aren't enough to help Louisa. She needs better than that." He shot Alistair another grin, as if they were in on the same joke.

Alistair opened his mouth to coolly explain that he could not help Mr. Selby's sister, no matter how good her looks or how bad her circumstances. But he found that he couldn't quite give voice to any of his usual crisp denials. "Have you no relations?"

"None that suit the purpose, my lord," Selby said frankly. This Mr. Selby had charming manners, even when he met with disappointment. Alistair would give him that much—it would have been a relief to see Gilbert develop such pleasant ways instead of his usual fits of sullenness. "Our parents died some years ago," Selby continued. "We brought an elderly aunt with us, but we grew up in quite a remote part of Northumberland and if we have any relations in London, we've never heard of them."

Northumberland? Now what the devil could Alistair's father have been doing in Northumberland? Quite possibly he had gotten drunk at a hunt party in Melton Mowbray and simply lost his way home, leaving a string of debauched housemaids and misbegotten children in his wake.

That made something else occur to Alistair. "There's no suggestion that your sister is my father's natural child?"

"My—good heavens, no." Selby seemed astonished, possibly offended by the slight to his mother's honor. "Certainly not."

Thank God for that, at least. Alistair leaned back against the smooth stone of the chimney piece, regarding his visitor from behind half-closed lids. Even though there was nothing about Selby that seemed overtly grasping, here he was, grasping nonetheless. There was no reason for this man, charming manners and winning smile, to be in Alistair's library unless it was to demand something.

"If you want my advice, take her to Bath." He pushed away from the wall and took a few steps towards his visitor. Selby was a few inches shorter than Alistair and much slighter of build. Alistair didn't need to use his size to intimidate—that was what rank and power were for—but this wasn't about intimidation. It was about proximity. He wanted a closer look at this man, so he would take it.

Selby had tawny skin spotted with freckles, as if he were accustomed to spending a good deal of time outside. His lips were a brownish pink, and quirked up in a questioning sort of smile, as if he knew what exactly Alistair were about.

Perhaps he did. Interesting, because Alistair hardly knew himself.

Alistair dropped his voice. "Better yet, go home. London is a dangerous place for a girl without connections." He dropped his voice lower still, and leaned in so he was speaking almost directly into Selby's ear. "Or for a young man without scruples." The fellow smelled like lemon drops, as if he had a packet of sweets tucked into one of his pockets.

For a moment they stood there, inches apart. Selby was ultimately the one to step back. "I knew it was a long shot, but I had to try." He flashed Alistair another winning smile, more dangerous for being at close range, before bowing handsomely and showing himself out.

Alistair was left alone in a room that had grown darker still.

"What did he say?" Louisa asked as soon as Charity returned to the shabby-genteel house they had hired for the Season.

"It's a non-starter, Lou," she replied, flinging herself onto a settee. She propped her boots up onto the table before her. One of the many, many advantages of posing as a man was the freedom afforded by men's clothing.

"He turned you away, then?" Louisa asked, looking up from the tea she was pouring them.

"Oh, worse than that. He asked if his father had gotten your mother with child, then advised me that if I allowed you to stay in London you'd end up prostituting yourself."

Louisa colored, and Charity realized she had spoken too freely. Louisa had, after all, been raised a lady. "Oh, he didn't say that last thing quite outright, but he dropped a strong hint." She hooked an arm behind her head and settled comfortably back in her seat. "Besides, what does it matter if he thinks we're beneath reproach? He's never even heard of us before today. His opinion doesn't matter a jot."

"Maybe he's right, though, and I shouldn't stay in London." Instead of looking at Charity, she was nervously lining up the teacups so their cracks and chips were out of sight.

"Nonsense. As soon as these nobs get a look at you, you'll take off like a rocket."

Louisa regarded her dubiously. But it really was absurd, how very pretty Robbie's little sister had turned out to be. Her hair fell in perfect flaxen ringlets and her skin was flawless. Other than her blond hair she looked nothing like Robbie, thank God, because that would have been too hard for Charity to live with.

Charity shook her head in a futile attempt to dismiss that unwanted thought, and then blew an errant strand of hair off her forehead. "I only have to figure out how to make them notice you in the first place, and if that prig of a marquess isn't willing to help, then we'll find another way."

"Was he really that bad?"

Charity put her hand over her heart, as if taking an oath. "I tell you, if he had a quizzing glass he would have examined me under it. He seemed so dreadfully bored and put upon, I nearly felt bad for him. But then I remembered all his money and got quite over it."

That made Louisa laugh, and Charity was glad of it, because it wouldn't do for the girl to worry. Charity was worried enough for both of them. Louisa did need a husband, and she needed one soon, because Charity wasn't sure how much longer she was going to be able to keep up this charade. Dressing like a man didn't bother her—quite the contrary. But pretending to be Robbie when the real Robbie was cold in his grave? That was too much. It was a daily reminder of what she had lost, of what she would never have.

Louisa put down her teacup and clasped her hands together. "I'd be glad to go to Bath for a few months. Remember that the Smythe girls found husbands there."

Charity remembered all too well. One of them had married a country clergyman and the other had gotten engaged to an army officer on half pay. She'd be damned if Louisa threw herself away like that. Hell, if she had gone through with this farce for Louisa to wind up marrying a curate she'd be furious.

She had to forcibly remind herself that her feelings were immaterial. This was her chance to see Louisa settled in the way Robbie would have wanted. It was only because of the Selbys that Charity was here in the first place, clean and fed and educated, rather than . . . Well, none of that bore thinking of. She was grateful to the family, and this was her chance to take care of the last of them.

"Listen, Charity. When I think of the expense of this London trip—"

"You mustn't call me that," Charity whispered. "Servants might hear." And if Charity knew anything about servants, which she most certainly did, it would only be a matter of time before one overheard. And then their ship would be quite sunk.

"Oh!" Louisa cried, clapping a hand over her mouth. "I keep forgetting. But it's so strange to call you Robbie."

Of course it was. Not everyone was as hardened to deceit as Charity had become. She had been assuming this role for years, from the point when the real Robert Selby had decided that he did not want to go to Cambridge and would send Charity in his stead. She, at least, was used to answering to his name. But since Robbie had died two years ago, she increasingly felt that she no longer had his permission to use his name. The deceit was weighing heavier on her with each passing day.

All the more reason to get Louisa set up splendidly. Then Robert Selby could fade gracefully out of existence, leaving his Northumberland estate free for the proper heir to eventually inherit, while Charity would . . . Her imagination failed her.

She would figure that out some other time. First, she'd take care of Louisa.

"If all else fails, we'll go to Bath or a seaside resort. I promise." And she flashed her pretend sister her most confident smile.

A LETTER FROM THE EDITOR

Dear Reader,

I hope you liked the latest romance from Avon Impulse! If you're looking for another steamy, fun, emotional read, be sure to check out some of our upcoming titles.

First up we have a delightful new story from superstar Eloisa James! MIDSUMMER DELIGHTS is a short but sweet dip to the world of her beloved Essex Sisters. Don't miss this short story collection featuring a brand-new novella about a proper debutante who, after two failed seasons, has decided causing a scandal is way more exciting. Eloisa always delivers a witty, charming read and this collection is no different!

We also have a brand-new title from Mia Sosa for all you contemporary romance fans! PRETENDING HE'S MINE is delicious, trope-y goodness about an uptight Hollywood film agent who can't seem to keep his mind—or his hands—off his best friend's sassy, free-spirited little sister. Mia delivers another funny, sexy, inclusive romantic comedy in her *Love on Cue* series and you don't want to miss it!

For historical romance fans, we also have a brand new Victorian romance from Charis Michaels! ANY GROOM WILL DO, the first in the Brides of Belgravia series, features a spunky, independent lady who puts out an ad for a husband, hoping they will wed and go their separate ways . . . except a marriage of convenience becomes anything but when love gets in the way!

You can purchase any of these titles by clicking the links above or by visiting our website, www.AvonRomance.com. Thank you for loving romance as much as we do . . . enjoy!

Sincerely,

Nicole Fischer

Editorial Director

Avon Impulse

ABOUT THE AUTHOR

CAT SEBASTIAN lives in a swampy part of the South with her husband, three kids, and two dogs. Before her kids were born, she practiced law and taught high school and college writing. When she isn't reading or writing, she's doing crossword puzzles, bird watching, and wondering where she put her coffee cup.

Discover great authors, exclusive offers, and more at hc.com.